Mercy

KC DECKER

ISBN: 978-1-7329645-2-5

Do not be ashamed of the wars

your soul has fought

to save itself.

Isra Al-Thibeh

Prologue

They say your value doesn't decrease based on someone's inability to see your worth, but what if that sentiment was just dried up words? A phrase, delivered before falling to the ground to be stepped on and forgotten about? The truth is, sometimes, someone's *perception* of you has the power to change the entire trajectory of your life.

Perception is critical. That concept has altered my life in ways I can't even quantify, much less understand. In my case, my parent's perception of me reduced my value to nothing. My very name whispered on a breeze, tasted like brimstone in their mouths.

Suffice it to say, my take on my own situation is quite different than the fanatical religious zealots that brought me into this world, only to discard me at the whim of a ripe old man with too many wives. That's right, my parents abandoned me as a child because our sect leader convinced them I was evil. Can you begin to understand how that perception of me may have altered my life?

Ironically, my name is Mercy, though my parents showed me none. If you buy the nonsense they're selling, you'd think my very birth foretold of a dark prophesy. You'd believe my tiny infant breaths had cursed the righteous and that my childhood cries bespoke of madness.

While that telling is all very dramatic and compelling, it's not the whole story. The truth is, I was almost ten years old before the religious cult began to insist I'd been kissed by the devil. At the time, I bought into their snake handling and all the thrashing around on the floor because I was an impressionable kid, and having been born into such rituals, I emphatically drank the Kool-Aid.

Even back then, I knew something was wrong with me, though my childhood mind didn't have the shakiest grasp of understanding the cause. I simply took the sect leader's word for it—right along with the blast of spittle from his mouth.

It's easy to believe you harbor demons inside if you wake up screaming in terror and hosed down with sweat four nights a week. I was too young to understand the nightmares, so my entire childhood was bloated with the sanctimonious crap fed to the believers regarding their origin. I knew something ugly lived in me, but their poisonous ideology was just as deadly as the snake venom used to flush out my sickness.

It's only after years and years of reflection that I no longer believe in their staunch conclusions, and now, I certainly question the ritualized manner in which they landed upon them. In a lot of ways, the aforementioned years were akin to jumping from the frying pan into the fire, but again, perception is everything.

Nowadays, how people perceive me is clouded by a different set of convictions and a whole new doctrine. It's a different batch of Kool-Aid, but I still have no choice about whether to swallow it or not. Not while I'm here and labeled a *ward of the state*.

I've worn all types of labels over the years—non-believer, deranged, orphan…It's all in my file if you care to understand me better. But the label that seems to have implanted the deepest and garnered the most attention is the one I wear like a Scarlet Letter. It precedes me when I enter a room and is whispered about like a schoolyard crush.

Paranoid Schizophrenic.

Chapter 1

The countdown has begun. The hands of fate will soon shift my circumstances once again. You see, I'm nearly twenty-one years old. That particular age may serve as a different milestone for more traditional young adults, but not for me. The legal drinking age and the dizzy haze of alcohol hold absolutely no draw for me. I take enough meds here to keep my ears ringing and maintain a constant high, so at this point, cracking open a beer is pretty much child's play. Amateur hour at best.

I've spent half my life bobbing for air as part of the system, and that cycle has only differed in the length of time spent underwater. I've had countless foster families over the years and been welcomed into a variety of living environments. Then, *boom,* an episode lands me right back here.

Being juggled by interim parents is difficult and often a bit of a calculated risk—not just for them, mind you, I've had to weigh the risks myself. Does one remain guarded? Or embrace them fully, knowing the tide can shift at any moment?

Of all my placements, the worst foster families for me have not been the borderline abusive or the neglectful ones. No, the worst placements have been the loving ones—especially the families with their own biological kids.

You may find that hard to believe, but it's as true as the psychosis behind these locked unit doors. The loving families have always been the hardest for me. They are the ones who have damaged me the most. They've left the deepest scars—and wounds of the heart don't ever fully heal. First, they fester. Then, they lie dormant until you cease to acknowledge their existence. Only then do they grow bold and begin to manifest themselves in ways you never see coming.

Wounds of the heart are vicious, destructive beasts, and unless you can figure out how to excise them from the root, they will continue to feed from their host. They are the worst kind of parasite because they are the ones we unknowingly nurture.

In order to fully comprehend my bitter sentiment, you would have to understand the blowback from my abandonment. My parents discarded me just shy of my eleventh birthday, and every foster parent since has followed suit.

Some foster parents treated me like Cinderella. Some forced me to rub bunion-riddled feet on a nightly basis. I've eaten nothing but canned goods for weeks at a time. I've been backhanded, tickled inappropriately, screamed at, and ignored. But nothing comes close to the savagery of being loved and then sent back.

After the first couple of placements, I got the lay of the land. Rule number one, don't get too comfortable. I would say after the first six months of getting bounced around, I had a steady grasp of how things would play out. In fact, I learned rather quickly that I almost didn't even need to unpack if there were biological kids involved.

Like I said, the families with their own homegrown kids were the worst. The fear of my psychosis somehow damaging their perfect, God-given children was always far more compelling than the bouts of love and kindness they ever pointed in my direction. Which brings me to lesson two, fear is always stronger than compassion.

The grooves worn into my soul from the cyclic nature of being passed back and forth between foster parents and the state psych ward are devastatingly deep. Some would say unrecoverable.

Anyway, I dealt with that implosion of self-worth for damn-near a decade before my eighteenth birthday threatened to dump me out onto the streets to figure shit out on my own. That thought gnawed through my stomach like an ulcer the whole of my seventeenth year before anyone started whispering about the Fostering Connections to Success and Increasing Adoptions Act.

That little bit of legislation allows me to remain in the system under federal funds until I turn twenty-one. The only stipulations being that I complete 80 hours a month either, attending high school, getting a GED, enrolled in a college, university, or vocational school, or by participating in a job training program.

Those parameters, although well-meaning and I'm sure, quite necessary, always caused me to snicker a little bit behind my hand. To me, 80 hours a month is a lazy show of intent. Someone like me, who's always searching for ways to validate themselves, tends to be a much higher achiever. I had my high school diploma by the time I was sixteen and a bachelor's degree in graphic design three years later. Since then, I have bided my federally funded time stacking up post-graduate certifications and doing freelance work because, the truth is, I have nothing else to do.

I think it's safe to say I work very hard at proving to everyone that despite my mental illness and repeated abandonments, I am a high functioning, capable, *worthy* person. I may not have acquired a whole lot of love outside of these walls, but I do get important doses of it in here.

The psych ward.

Day to day life in a locked unit is a little redundant and overly structured, but it's not too bad. Usually, the day starts with 7:00 am morning checks. I say *usually* because this morning was a little different. It started with a shriek that all but dumped everyone from their beds at twenty after six.

It was Veronica. She is a sweet girl, but she comes up with some extravagant tactics to remove herself from approaching mealtimes. She has been here long enough to have picked up some tricks from the schizophrenics too. Though she has a whole host of legitimate issues, suffering from delusional psychosis is not one of them.

So, when her screaming at monsters and clawing at the wall had the desired *and entirely pre-meditated* effect of bringing the code team in to restrain and sedate her, she effectively opted out of breakfast this morning.

Veronica is as messed up as a bag of hangers. Not because she is receiving psychiatric care—because we are all here for a reason, but because her OCD requires her to count everything that has to do with eating. How many bites, how many times she chews on each side of her mouth, how many breaths between bites, how many blinks between bites, how many heartbeats between bites, how many times she licks her lips or swallows. She counts **ev-er-y** thing. Apparently, her ritualistic eating habits ease her anxiety and prevent bad things from happening to her.

I know how to talk to a schizophrenic in the throes of psychosis, but I have no idea how to talk to someone with obsessive-compulsive disorder. A psychotic episode requires a certain amount of finesse, and it's always important to validate the person's feelings while at the same time letting them know you don't see or hear whatever it is that they are experiencing. With Veronica's OCD, I can't bring myself to validate her feelings because I don't understand how the rituals prevent something bad from happening.

Zombies, beetles, spiders, demons, voices, cackling laughter— everything sensory I can validate because it is very real to the person in crisis. But I can't get my head around Veronica's illness. I like her a lot, and she is one of my best friends, so I say all the same stuff to her as I do to the hallucinating schizophrenics, "I don't see that *(or understand how counting every damn thing helps)* but I can tell it really bothers you, so I understand it must be very difficult." It's a canned response at this point, but I suppose I owe everyone the same level of support.

Logic doesn't work on this floor anyway. It's pointless to reason with the delusional because if someone sees rats pouring in through the window, it's futile to explain that we are on the 5th floor of a unit without functional windows and that there couldn't possibly be rats coming in through them. Rationale has no place here; it just doesn't work. Not for OCD and not for schizophrenia.

In most cases, though, we schizophrenics are self-actualized enough to know we may see and hear things that others don't. In fact, not a day goes by that someone doesn't ask me if something is real. I personally never ask. If something is real to me, it's real enough. I don't need anyone else's input. I may not see the laughing mannequin, or the coyote eating a bloody rabbit in the corner, or the clown skipping down the hall, but I see plenty of my own shit.

So, turns out, I'm pretty screwed up too. I said Veronica is as messed up as a bag of hangers, but she really isn't that bad. At least she is nowhere near as bad as the new chick that *sings* everything. Tracy's singing voice has a way of crawling up your spine like a cat in the curtains. I would never have guessed that listening to a melodically delivered conversation would be quite so aggravating, but sure enough, it is. In summary, we have all kinds here.

Anyway, long story short, Veronica will miss breakfast today.

***

It's Monday, so after breakfast and morning meds, they require me to meet with my psychiatrist, Dr. Sigmund. Just so you know, the irony of his name is not lost on me, it's just that I ran out of Freudian jokes five years ago.

After a few years in and out of his care, I started calling him Dr. Siggy. And now? Now, I just call him Sig. It's not out of disrespect though, it's because he is more like a father to me than a psychiatrist. I quit with the formalities ages ago and have grown rather used to his long-suffering glances.

Sig has been with me almost since the beginning. I was only at St. Vincent's Children's Home for a couple of years before my age demanded I spend the time between foster families in the Juvenile Behavioral Unit. The JBU is where Sig became my psychiatrist until the ripe old age of eighteen—or, more specifically until they moved me to the Adult Behavioral Unit.

After I left, it wasn't more than four months before Sig left the JBU in favor of this wing of the state hospital, though. I like to think he preferred working in the adult unit because he could monitor my care, but he may have just been fed up with the adolescent wing.

I, for one, broke him in pretty good over there because I was twelve when they moved me from St. Vincent's. He was well versed and prepared for all types of neurology and psychiatric based care, but I spent the duration of our first session balled up on the floor with crippling menstrual cramps that he couldn't navigate through or make sense of. Sadly, the pain wasn't even what had me in hysterics. It was that I had just gotten my first period and had not one single clue what to do about it.

Unable to avoid my situation, Sig made a run at consoling me and tried his uncomfortable best to explain that *I was a woman now*, but I didn't give a damn about that. At the time, I could not see past the fact that Neil and Benji had laughed at the blood on the back of my sweatpants and that my uterus was trying to shift itself inside out.

Anyway, from 12 to nearly 21 years old, he has been pretty consistent in my life. I often missed him during my foster home placements, but he was always here when they sent me back.

Chapter 2

Sometimes I knock on Sig's door, other times, not so much. I figure we have been at this song and dance for nine years. He should be expecting me on Monday mornings by now.

When I walk in and plop down on the requisite leather couch, his back is to me, and he is studying his bookshelf. He likes to pretend he reads all those books, but I think he's just an old man that can't let stuff go. I'm sure the field of psychiatry has evolved in the forty years he's practiced, but his bookshelf hasn't.

"Mercy, good morning," he says as he turns around. He does a pretty good job of masking his annoyance, but the candy jar from his desk is now poured out on my lap so I can dig out all the cinnamon ones.

"Morning, Sig. What's on the agenda today? I haven't had a med change in a while. Maybe it's time to shuffle things around—you know, keep the nurses on their toes."

"Why would we do that? You're on a therapeutic dose, and you haven't had any hallucinations in months."

"But my mouth is really dry."

"Mercy," he says with fatherly disappointment, as he takes a seat behind his desk, "That's not a good reason to take you off the Seroquel."

"Fine. If my dry mouth is of no consequence, what else should we talk about?"

I watch him shift around uncomfortably in his seat until my mind starts to wander, and I all but diagnose him with hemorrhoids. After many minutes of sifting through the crappy butterscotch candy and patiently awaiting his psychiatric preaching, Sig opens his mouth to say something. Before he even makes a sound, he clamps his mouth shut. This very uncharacteristic gesture gets my attention quick.

I still have several months until I turn 21, so it can't be about my ward of the court status. My gaze lands on him and stays there. I'm no longer feeling calm, but I'm humoring him just the same. The crease in his forehead makes him look ancient. Worn out, even. I hope his loss for words isn't because he is about to divulge something horrible about his health.

"Well, spit it out, we only have an hour," I say with false bravado. If he is dying, I'll lose my mind.

"Mercy—"

He stops, regroups, and tries again, "I...I—"

"I need to talk to you—" he finally says, his tone grave yet solemnly determined. He's choked up. I think his chin might be quivering, but that could also be a visual side effect of my meds.

"About something serious," he continues.

I sweep my lapful of candy to the floor as I sit forward on the edge of the couch. He's the only person that has stuck around. The only constant in my life. Where is this conversation going?

"The Board of Directors has asked me to resign."

He drops that bit of knowledge like a bomb, and at first, I'm relieved he didn't just use the word cancer, but then the fallout rains down, and I realize what he is saying.

He's leaving me.

I've been around catatonics before, but this is the first time I have understood what they might be experiencing. I haven't moved. Haven't even blinked, but the world around me is somehow swirling about at a breakneck speed. I hear everything he says as though it's shouted in my face, but nonetheless, it sounds like it's coming from underwater. Now my limbs have swollen to the point they can't bend, and my vision blurs enough that I can't make out Sig's face anymore. Suddenly, he is an inch from my nose, but I can't see him. The only thing I'm aware of is a horrible screeching sound in my head. Or, maybe the sound is coming from my mouth.

***

"Why am I talking sooo slooow? And why are my hands floating?" I ask out loud. It's the first coherent thought I've had in an age. This must be a side effect of my new meds. Instead of answering me, Colleen, one of the nurses, asks her own question.

"How do you feel, Sugar?"

"Like my moooutth has rusted shuuut. What's wroong with me?" I ask. I'm puzzled by my current status and feel like my body is full of foam.

"Not a darn thing is wrong with you, Mercy. You are perfect, just the way God intended. You've been asleep for a bit, that's all. I imagine you are probably thirsty, right?"

I nod and then sit up to take the offered cup of water. As I chug, I present my arm for the blood pressure cuff that's already headed my way. They do that a lot here. They are always checking people's vitals as if our problems lived outside of our heads.

"Go back to sleep, Mercy. I'll see you at breakfast in the morning," Nurse Colleen says. It takes her a minute to get to her feet because of her sore knees, but at least she isn't wondering if it's the middle of the night right now.

I look over at my roommate, Lyla. She is lost to a benzodiazepine slumber and most likely has not so much as rolled over since committing herself to the act of sleeping.

What the heck day is it?

Chapter 3

The next morning is fairly tranquil, and for once, I feel rested. It's not until I'm hovering over my oatmeal that I remember that Sig is leaving me. When the realization hits, I scoot my chair back and dry heave into my lap for a few shaky minutes.

I feel Lyla's hand rubbing my back, and ironically, it's her physical contact that garners the attention of the staff, instead of my questionable mental state.

"**Lyla!**" it's delivered like the crack of a whip, and I feel Lyla's instantaneous reaction. If I could get a deep breath, I would have an issue with them speaking to her like that. She tried to kill herself a short while ago, she needs to be nurtured and fortified—not scolded for trying to comfort someone.

Finally, I sit up, but mostly so my diaphragm is no longer restricted to a compressed little bundle. As breakfast wears on, I'm able to nod when I think people are talking to me, but I'm mostly in my own head. It's an inhospitable place, full of dread and anxiety, but it's familiar.

After breakfast, of course, is group therapy. You can't walk five feet in this place without tripping over some kind of group. We have community group, process group, coping skills group, wellness and nutrition group, goals and reflections group, communications group, behavioral therapy group, and a zillion expressive therapy groups. Those are my favorites because they involve some type of art or music or writing, and they are much less soul-baring.

If you want to look, the schedule is posted on the unit, but I never care enough to check. Mainly because at this point, I could send all the counselors, therapists, and social workers home, and I could run each session by myself. I've heard the same song for years upon years. Always among different faces, but the tune is the same. I've absorbed it and wrung it out so many times I'm hardly aware of how saturated I still am.

However, there *are* some people here that could stand to attend the same group, not just multiple times, but exclusively. I'm talking about the psycho-educational groups that teach a skill, say, anger management, for example. In fact, a decent amount of the men here could benefit from a lifetime membership to that haggard circle of chairs.

Besides the psycho-educational therapy, the other group that adds a distinct value to this floor is the dialectical behavioral therapy group. Distress tolerance and emotion regulation are both hot topics in a mental health unit. That group is particularly useful for the folks with mood disorders and suicide ideation—of which, there are many in here. Some are even learning to shift negative behavioral patterns like cutting or abusing drugs, so the groups are important. They are just tedious as hell for me, having memorized the information years ago.

I've been in and out of this hospital for so many years, I feel like I've run the gamut as far as my group participation goes. For years, I dove in and absorbed every single word. I participated enough that other people must have thought I just liked the sound of my own voice. I gave my mental health *everything* I had.

Over the years, I became cynical and then downright jaded. I used to think if I could just get better, someone would keep me. Christmas mornings would be more than empty words and sterile hallways. Family outings would be commonplace. Goodnight hugs and sweet endearments would become my new routine.

I begged and prayed to a God I didn't understand for nearly a decade to make me normal. To take away the horror between my ears and grant me some type of peace. My pleading was met with blank stares and deaf ears. So, pretty soon, my prayers faded to nothing more than a tickle behind my eyelids and a dampness on my state-issued pillow.

Following each return to the unit, each searing disappointment, I let go of a little more hope. Every time they sent me back, I returned without another piece of myself. Then, once I was all hollowed out, I understood that no one would save me. All my silly hopes of rescue were futile and dusty. I knew God wasn't going to intercede on my behalf, and there was no one left to save me.

It was after that particular realization that my participation in life was affected. And, more specifically, my participation in group. As long as I was physically present and potentially still absorbing the discussions and information, the staff had been directed by Sig to go easy on my fragile state.

In time, my engagement dulled to what it is now—which is limited to nodding my head, maintaining brief eye contact, and rattling off a few sentences of profound insight at the beginning of group, before flying under the radar for the remainder of it.

I have been cautious where I lay my pearls, so to speak, and for the most part, I've maintained a comfortable emotional distance with the ever-evolving list of patients. My group of friends is small but mighty— and they're only allowed to the table recently because it's finally safe for me to make friends. In the past, with no end in sight, forget it. Having friends was like a gut wound, you know how it ends long before you actually bleed out. There has been some repetition over the years, but most people get the help they need and then can assimilate back into their outside lives using the tools they learned here.

Psych wards, overall, are healing places. The dark and seedy institutions depicted in books are not an accurate representation of real life. The demented people chained to beds and rocking back and forth while digging at their scabs, in reality, are people like me. People who eat oatmeal and then go to group counseling before working on an art project.

Some of us have fits of terrifying psychosis and were thought by our parents to be possessed by the devil. Some count everything and rely on ritualistic behavior to temper their anxiety. Some sing every-God-forsaken-thing that comes out of their mouths. However, the lion's share of patients are here for major depressive disorder, and a fair amount of them landed here after a suicide attempt.

Sorry to disappoint, but the various illnesses here are well managed with medication and therapy, so even here at the state hospital, the fictional drama you may be expecting is rather rare. No straitjackets. No lobotomies. No crazy science experiments. The melodrama is mostly limited to new intakes.

I may have to modify that last statement because the only open chair in group this morning is next to Simon, and he is a little out there. He suffers from paranoid schizophrenia just like me, but whereas I have hallucinations and see and hear things that aren't there, he has paranoid *delusions* which result in some pretty wacky beliefs.

I sit down next to Simon but don't look him in the eyes when I acknowledge him. To do so would start one of those dramatic episodes that I just stated were rare.

You see, Simon believes aliens monitor his every move. Worse yet, he thinks they track him and can read his thoughts through his pupils. So, naturally, he assumes anyone who happens to look him in the eyes is here to keep tabs on him. To prevent this bothersome tracking, he wears blacked-out glasses that are seven times too big for his petite, almost feminine face.

Unfortunately, a patient or two have found it humorous to pretend they really were sent by aliens and claimed to be reading his thoughts and tracking his whereabouts, placing his intolerance of people hovering somewhere between DEFCON levels 3 and 4. Nowadays, with trust in his fellow man effectively broken, we are all just along for the ride.

"Good morning, everyone. Welcome to process group. As many of you already know, this is where we talk about and work through challenges, as well as learn to process change. Who would like to start?" Jana is leading group today. She is really great—but damn, does she need a haircut. Her hair is so long she can almost sit on it. She is a decent social worker, but I find her hair to be wildly distracting.

I don't know why, but every single person in the room looks over at me—*even Simon*, with his vulnerable pupils. Actually, it's possible they all saw my breakfast breakdown, served with a side of apple juice. Well, move along, folks. The show's over.

I open my mouth to deny having any challenges for the group to work through, but nothing comes out. Mostly because of the universal expressions of pity and the solemnly nodding head of too-long hair.

I freeze, with nothing to say. Usually, this is where I smile and nod to encourage someone else to share. So much for staying off the radar.

Michael, who is on my left, leans in and whispers under his breath, "Last night at reflection group, we all discussed Dr. Sig leaving and how we can support you." Michael is one of the patients I say hello to, but little else. He's a short-timer and will be gone soon, so there is little point in investing in him.

All I can do right now is stare at my hands in my lap. I've always preferred to swallow my pain deep down, and never acknowledge it because that limits how much it can hurt me. I prefer not to revel in it. Plus, if I never dignify the anguish, is it really there?

"Someone needs to just fucking say it. Dr. Sigmund got shit-canned for being an ineffectual doctor and mismanaging his patients and their meds." This, from another short-timer. I'd like to slam his head in a car door a few times and see if it has an impact on his volume button. He is always talking loudly and acting aggressively. If you ask me, he should make another run through AA and anger management classes because until he gets a handle on his addiction to alcohol, he will forever be angry when he's not drinking.

For a few seconds, you can almost hear crickets chirping because the room is so still. Everyone with an ounce of compassion is afraid to speak, so Jana, group leader that she is, takes the helm.

"Okay, let's start with that. But I'm going to need everyone here to conduct themselves with some basic human respect, and if you can find it in yourself, perhaps a tiny bit of empathy. Being able to put yourself in someone else's shoes to try and understand how they might be feeling is an important life skill. Some of you may have no feelings one way or another about Dr. Sigmund stepping down, but others are experiencing some incredibly strong feelings of loss. Now, let's talk about some strategies we can use when we experience these types of feelings."

***

After process group is over and everyone has scattered like mice, Jana comes over and sits in the vacated chair to my right. There is a familiar ringing in my ears that I have grown used to, but at the moment it's more intrusive than usual.

"Mercy, I'm so proud of how you conducted yourself in group, you are an inspiration to so many of us." Then she breaks a hard and fast rule about touching, and she takes my hand gently between both of hers. It feels shockingly foreign, human touch. If the racket in my head weren't so distracting, I might have flinched at the contact.

"I need you to know something, Mercy. You are a *warrior*, and I have no doubt that you will get through this, but we are all here to help you, okay? Whatever it takes." Her smile is kind, but I have a hard time looking her in the eyes because behind that gaze is a mountain of pity.

"Thank you, Jana. You don't have to worry about me, I will be fine." *I always am*, is the part I don't say out loud. I take a deep, cleansing breath and purposely make eye contact with her. I have to fight looking away by imagining that I can track her thoughts through her pupils. Simon might be on to something because if I can focus on her thoughts, then I don't need to concern myself with my own.

"Sig is waiting for you in his office." She waits a few seconds before continuing, possibly to gauge my reaction to the news. "I want you to use some of the strategies we just talked about, okay?"

"Jana, I've got this. *I'm fine*." Hell, if I was *half* as fragile as everyone thinks I am, I never would have made it this far. I would have, long ago, shriveled up and blown away on the nearest breeze.

I stop outside Sig's door, which strikes me as unusual. Something's different, and it's not just the pitch of the incessant ringing. I push the door open, and what I see stops my heart.

Everything is gone. Well, everything except a dusty bookshelf, an empty desk, and a leather couch. The same couch I've sat on weekly since I moved from St. Vincent's. It's not old and familiar, though. It's haughty and self-righteous. Instead of welcoming me, it repels.

Sig is standing behind what was once his desk. Everything has happened in the blink of an eye. I sat in here *yesterday* and received the news that he is leaving. What happened to giving a few weeks notice? To staying onboard until they find a suitable replacement? Why is everything **gone** already?

I want to shout all these questions at him, but when I slam the door shut behind me, it breaks his rigid composure. Then, he holds his arms out to me. I refuse to walk into his offered embrace. I refuse to make this abandonment easy for him. His eyes are damp, and he struggles to control his face, but I will not allow him to hug me. I reserve that kind of gesture for someone who cares about me. Sig? Yeah, Sig can go straight to hell.

"Don't forget to take your candy dish with you when you go." I spin around and leave his treachery behind me. There's lots of it back there, so he has plenty of company.

He doesn't even call out to me when I'm gone. No one ever has a hard time letting go of me. I'm not sure I would know what to do with it if they did. It started with my parents, and the cycle will never end. I am doomed to repeat this horror no matter what brilliant strategies I employ.

I hold myself together until I try to go into my room and am refused entrance. It's bad enough that everyone looks at me like I'm about to trip a land mine, but this is too much.

"Mercy, honey, listen to me," Margret, one of the day nurses says, as I back her into my vacant room. She knows she is playing with fire, but she deals with worse than me on a daily basis, so she is undeterred.

"You are needed in the day room. They are painting. You love to paint."

"Not today, Margret. I just need some space for a little bit." I'm able to keep my voice under control, but beneath the surface is something violent. Something that scares me.

"I know you are upset. But let's grab on to something, no matter how small, that makes you happy, and run with it. You can put all your feelings down on the canvas instead of keeping them bottled up inside."

"Not today, Margret," I repeat. I'm clenching my teeth, so it comes out like a growl. I need to be careful, or the code team will be in here administering something that burns in my vein. I don't want oblivion right now because I'll still wake up in the same hell. I need my anger. It's fuel. It's the armor that protects my pathetic vulnerability. With it, I'm powerful, and no one can break me.

They are treating me like someone on suicide watch. This is bullshit. I've put in my time. I've earned the right to have a few minutes to myself. The thing is, painting wouldn't be so bad if everyone would leave me alone, but they won't. They will talk, talk, talk. They will insist I express my feelings and work through them. Well, if I expressed myself right now, my rage would bring the walls down around us. I don't even want to see Lyla, and she is one of the best things I have left.

"I'll tell you what," Margaret says conspiratorially as she glances out into the hallway. "You and I are gonna take ten minutes to try and process some crap—however you need to, and then you are going to go to expressive therapy group and paint. Deal?" I shrug. There is no use arguing with her.

"However I need to?" I reiterate.

"Within reason, and of course, in a safe and productive manner."

"If you have to crowd me right now, can you at least be quiet?" I ask. It's the most I can hope for right at this moment.

"Yes, Mercy, if that's what you need from me right now, then I will absolutely be quiet."

I drop down onto my bed, but instead of curling up into a tight little ball and losing my shit, I sit facing her. She has adopted the same posture as she sits on Lyla's bed, hands resting on her thighs, meeting my gaze. She isn't challenging me; she is proving a point.

Ten minutes will never be enough time for me to process my crap, so we simply sit—and stare at each other. I'm not sure how much time goes by before I feel a tear land on the back of my wrist. I'm not even thinking about anything, I'm just sitting here. Then another one. It's warm, and I know it's salty against my skin.

It doesn't register when she moves, but all of a sudden, Margret is holding me. I sob like I've just cracked apart, and life is gushing out of every fracture.

I guess she made her point. She's here for me.

Chapter 4

The incident with Margret, the nurse, was cathartic and helpful in the same way that putting a band-aid on a severed femoral artery would be. After that, they asked me to *take a snapshot of my feelings* and transfer it to the canvas. Which I did. Too bad I'm still bleeding out.

After lunch, we have rec time, which is the only instance in which I hate combining the men and women. Meals and group therapy are fine for uniting the wings, but rec time becomes insufferable. Mainly because of the ceaseless *tap, tap, tap, tap, tap, tap* of the God-damned ping pong ball.

Lyla, Veronica, Matty, and I like to sit by the windows and read. It's a perfectly good way to escape—were it not for the hollow ball sailing back and forth like it's its job.

During our reading time, Veronica doesn't need to count everything, and Matty and Lyla get a reprieve from their depression. They are both here following suicide attempts, so luckily, and *selfishly* for me, their stays are longer than all the short-timers.

The four of us have talked about living together when I leave the system at the ripe old age of twenty-one. My aging out is the only thing I have to look forward to, so we talk about it a lot. That, and staying together because we have become a family in here.

Acquaintance "friends" have come and gone from my life, but knowing I have a future outside of this building relatively soon was the only reason I allowed these three into my orbit. I have true friends now, friends that I get to keep.

I have my suspicions about the origin of Matty's depression, but I don't think he has fully come to terms with it himself, so I will accompany him on his journey at his own pace. It's a shame that the outside world has so much to say about an individual's personal path. If everyone was allowed to be themselves and were welcomed into society with equal merit, places like these would echo instead of hum.

Before the Sig debacle, the only anxiety I ever deal with anymore is the thought of Lyla or Matty succumbing to their depression. The fact that they are both here after trying to take their own lives is a galactic size helping of unease and a fist around my heart. I can take nearly anything that comes my way but not losing one of the only true friends I've ever had.

"May I sit and read with you guys?" The singing voice interrupts my thoughts, but not my reading because my book is still face down on my lap. It's, of course, Tracy. Nothing ever comes out of her mouth that's not delivered like a song. She even *cusses* melodically.

"Of course, have a seat," Matty says with a hundred-watt smile aimed right at her. He is nice to everyone, even the ones who don't deserve it. I'm not saying she doesn't deserve it, just that I prefer to take her in small doses.

"Have you guys met the new psychiatrist yet?" she sings, and her voice annoys me as much as her question. Lyla must feel me gearing up because she places a decisive hand on my thigh. It's like she is trying to telepathically communicate that Tracy is new, and she doesn't know the situation with Sig.

"What, Sig's been gone for fifteen minutes, and we are all supposed to have had sessions with the new shrink?" I spit out. I'm not usually this much of an asshole, that must be why Veronica and Matty both look at me like Santa sat down on my lap.

"No, silly. I didn't have a session with him. I just saw him moving some boxes in. He's not bad on the eyes, so I introduced myself."

26

I've had enough of her voice and the ping pong racket, so I decide to stand up and go check out the usurper. I've already decided not to let him into my head, this is more to help me close the door on Sig. It will do me some good to see the fresh air in his stuffy old office.

Just to establish seniority here, I don't knock on Sig's door—it's already open anyway. I hate myself for looking for the candy dish, it's gone, and so is Sig. You know who's not gone? This fool. Thinks he can put all his shit on the bookshelves and settle right in.

"Mercy, hello. I'm Dr. Sutton." Why exactly does this joker know my name? And why is he extending his hand—we don't touch here.

"So you are."

"I'm glad you came by."

"Aren't you a little young for this gig?"

"What makes you say that?"

"The vernix on your skin."

"Mercy—" he drops his head. I don't know if it's in disappointment or if he found my comment *funny.*

"They will eat you alive here," I say, I'm not sure if it's a warning or an insult. Probably both.

"I disagree. Like yourself, I'm a high achiever." His smile and his comment deflect my snark. He is definitely not backing down.

"Don't pretend you know me. You only know what's in my file— and that's all you are going to get."

"Oh, good! Now that that's out of the way, can we sit? My tiny newborn legs can no longer support my weight."

"You sit. I'm not staying." I turn to leave, but he stops me dead in my tracks.

"Sig left you a letter." My pause lasts longer than I am entirely comfortable with, but my feet feel like cinderblocks, and I can't force them to lift.

"Well, isn't that cute? You can go ahead and put it in the g-file."

"The g-file?"

"Yeah, hotshot. The g-file. As in…*the garbage*." Now my feet do work. In fact, they work double-time and carry me swiftly back to my crew as though I teleported there.

"Very handsome, right?" Tracy sing-songs, and it raises my hackles.

"I wouldn't say *handsome*. I'd say, young," I answer, with only a fraction of my former voice. I feel like someone opened my faucet, and my entire being gushed out of it. I am disgusted about the thought of another doctor being here. But the really shitty part is that everyone will love him just because of how he looks. He could be completely inept as a psychiatrist, and no one would even notice.

"What does he look like?" Lyla asks as she hugs her knees to her chest. "God knows there is no one else to look at in here."

"I don't know. He's tall," I offer. That's all they're going to get from me. They can form their own opinions about him.

"I hope he *is* hot; I need some new material for my alone time," Veronica says as she strains her neck to look toward the nurse's station, hoping for a glimpse of him. "Look at them, all huddled together. What a bunch of gossiping hens they are."

Out of nowhere, right as I'm about to point out that we look like a similar bunch of hens, Matty puts his arm around my shoulders and speaks into my ear so only I can hear what he says.

"I know you miss him. Do you want to talk about it?" He's brave, touching me like this, but he knows the staff are all busy fanning their loins. I lean my head into him, comforted by his presence.

"I don't think so. Not yet, anyway," I answer. The truth is, I will never want to talk about it. If I talk about it—I can't very well ignore it, can I?

"Okay, then, will you French braid my hair?" he asks as he's already retrieving his arm and moving to the floor in front of me. I have an intense urge to kiss the top of his head. What he wants in life is so simple, so automatic for most people. And so forbidden to him.

"Of course I'll braid your hair. One or two?"

Chapter 5

I've waited all day for a moment of peace to myself, so I can think about the fact that Sig left me a letter. Now, as I lie here in my bed, I can't decide if I want to cry or scream into my pillow. After nighttime meds, Lyla is usually quick to fall asleep and hard to wake up, so either choice is a viable option. Tonight, however, my girl wants to talk.

"Have you ever had a crush on someone here?" she asks. She's whispering because we have to look like we are asleep when the RNs do their checks.

"No. Wait—have you?" I ask, somewhat horrified. I've all but decided I'm asexual. I don't look at *anyone* with any type of sexual interest or attraction, ever. I'm almost twenty-one, and I can count on one hand how many times I've masturbated. Even those few times, it was only to figure out what all the fuss was about. I brought myself to orgasm once, but it took so damn long that it's not been worth the hassle since.

"Sure, here and there. I'm asking about you though, don't you want to date when you get out of here?"

"God, no!" The thought is revolting. I don't want some dude pawing at me all the time. Touching was not allowed at St. Vincent's, it was never very common in any of my foster homes, and it's treated like the Black Plague here. The thought of someone's hairy, nude body rubbing against my nakedness and sweating all over me is enough to turn my stomach.

"I think you would like sex," she states, confident in her assessment.

"Lyla?"

"What?"

"When do your meds kick in?"

***

At breakfast, I know my eyes are red and swollen, but my friends have the grace not to mention it. I pour the cup of GrapeNuts into my yogurt, knowing full well that I have no intention of eating any of it. Veronica is here counting away, and for once, the distraction is soothing.

I know having nothing in my stomach except coffee and meds is asking for trouble, but it's almost like I welcome the nausea. Maybe I'm punishing myself for driving yet another parental figure away. Usually, they leave me after a psychotic episode. Not Sig, though. He was the one who picked up the pieces of my discarded being. He was never scared of my psychosis.

After the nurse checks my vitals, she informs me that I need to go to Dr. Sutton's office. I don't know if she is worried because it's been a pretty quiet morning for me or if this is something standard with a new doctor. Either way, I don't care. I'll go through the motions because I have to, but as far as I'm concerned, Dr. Sutton can go pound sand.

For the first time in my life, I knock on Sig's door and don't know what to expect. The fact that I wait until Dr. Sutton opens the door is evidence of that fact.

"Hi, Mercy."

"Why am I here? It's not Monday."

"Honestly? Because it might take us until Monday for me to complete my evaluation. Don't worry though, I brought snacks, and I have a little fridge over there with bottles of water," he says with a charming smile that has already worked its magic on the entire staff and seeped through both wings of the unit.

"Why would it take that long? Oh—never mind, you are new to all of this, you will probably need to Google your way through it," I say. He snorts out a laugh as if I was being funny instead of mean. Clearly, he doesn't know me at all. Too bad he can't get to know me by reading my file. Nice try though, Doc.

"Nope, I'm ready. But I figured I would need to account for the hard time you will give me, right?"

"You might need a bedpan then, doc. I've got the bladder of a camel."

"Duly noted. Shall we initiate the standoff?" he asks. His smirk is pinched at the side as though he finds all of this amusing, but is trying not to laugh outright.

"Whenever you're ready, Chief."

"This is so exciting, should we sit—or remain standing?" He rapidly rubs his hands in front of him as if the anticipation was truly genuine. I didn't expect him to employ charm or wit in our session, so I don't know how to combat it.

"You do you, doc. I'm gonna sit." Actually, I do one better, I lie down on Sig's couch. Nothing feels the same, though. I wish it wasn't 9:00 am, I'd take a nap.

"First, I'd like to go over your medications. Does that work if we start there?" he asks as he takes a seat behind Sig's desk. Why is he asking innocuous questions? He can see what meds I'm on by glancing down at my chart. I'll give him credit for not starting with the fanatical religious zealots that were my parents. No use fighting him on a question about meds.

"Go for it."

33

"You are currently taking 400 mg of Seroquel?"

"Yes."

"Any side effects?"

"Not anymore."

"Are you still having hallucinations?"

"Sometimes."

"Are they auditory or visual? Or both?"

"Both."

"Any tactile hallucinations?"

"Yes."

"Are you aware that others may not see or hear them when you are experiencing them?"

"Other people seeing them or hearing them doesn't impact me at all." I keep my gaze directly on his. He is going to push, and I'm going to push right back. I'm not going to let him define me by my diagnosis or pretend he has the slightest clue what I've gone through.

"I'm trying to understand if you know they are hallucinations in the moment, or if you think they are real."

"Sutton, they are more real than you or I."

"Can you tell me about them?"

"I don't think you could handle them."

"You don't think I've heard worse?" he asks as he stops writing, lays his pen down, and meets my gaze again.

"No."

"How about you tell me about the tactile ones. Do you always feel the same thing?"

"No."

"Do you feel like something is crawling on you? Or, like someone is grabbing you?"

"Like I'm being pinned down."

"Are you ab—"

"And carved apart with rusty nails." He wants to go there? Fine, we'll go there.

"Does it se—"

"And then sprinkled with acid."

"Okay, and th—"

"And then something is shoved in my mouth."

"Mercy?"

"And my insides swell up and burst."

"I'm going to be honest with you—even though I get the distinct impression you are not giving me the same courtesy."

"I told you you couldn't handle it," I say pointedly.

"Dr. Sigmund's notes never mention the nature of your hallucinations, only that you have them. He also notes that you were always sedated following an episode. Is that true?"

"Not if I was in a foster home."

"Did he ever talk to you about the specifics of what you were seeing, hearing, and feeling?"

"I was a kid when I started seeing him."

"You were a kid when he put you on *antipsychotics*. That is a big deal, Mercy. I'm trying to make sense of his notes. Clearly, he went the pharmacological route, but it's not appropriate to simply medicate and sedate psychosis. There are a lot of elements involved. I'm not seeing any of that in your file."

"And you think he should have re-hashed all that trauma instead of medicating the hallucinations away?"

"Don't you think that's relevant information?"

"No. He was protecting me."

"Are you telling me the truth about your hallucinations?"

"Yes."

"Can you tell me more?"

"What do you want to know?"

"What do you hear?"

"Shouting."

"Can you make out what's being said? Are the voices encouraging you to hurt yourself or others?"

"No, I can't make out what's being said, and no the voices don't encourage me to hurt anyone."

"Do they encourage you to hurt yourself?"

"No."

"Have you ever *wanted* to hurt yourself?"

"Yes, but not anymore."

"Have you ever wished you weren't alive?"

"All the time when I was younger."

"Were you ever treated for depression or anxiety?"

"No. I was depressed because of my circumstances, not my brain chemistry."

Dr. Sutton drops his head, probably in defeat. I knew he couldn't handle my shit. I've hallucinated since I can remember. My schizophrenia is the reason my parents threw me away, and the reason all my foster families sent me back. My psychosis isn't something Sutton can waltz in here and fix with a smile and the twinkle in his eye. I have a lifetime of terrifying, debilitating hallucinations under my belt. A new shrink won't fix that.

"Mercy, I want you to be successful when you leave here. You have a tremendous light to offer the world."

"*Okay.*"

"I know you were very close to Dr. Sigmund, and I am not trying to step in and fill the role he played in your life. I know I could never replace him in that regard. But if you can work with me, and learn to trust me, I think I can help you." He looks sincere and no longer amused. Apparently, his youth affords him something that tends to grow cold over the years. Optimism.

"I'll work with you because I have to, but I don't like talking about my illness. I've learned to live with it, and I don't want to harp on such things. That's why Sig didn't make me blather on about it."

"Mercy, we don't need to talk about the schizophrenia beyond me determining if you are on the right course of treatment. Okay?... You know what I want to talk about?"

"The Yankees?"

He gives a smile that succeeds in disarming me a little more. First, he's witty about anticipating a standoff—I didn't expect that approach *at all*. And then he goes and admits that he isn't trying to fill Sig's shoes. On top of that, he told me I have a light to offer the world.

Nobody has ever acknowledged that light before. In fact, it may be burning a little brighter right now. And not because of the way his hair is styled just right. Not because of his insanely blue eyes either.

"No, Mercy, not the Yankees. I want to talk about the sadness behind your eyes. I want to explore how much garbage you have been carrying around with you, and see how much of it you can leave behind when you go."

Chapter 6

Sutton's words have been working their way under my skin for the last few days. A big part of me wanted to laugh in his face when he talked about me leaving some garbage behind. My whole life is garbage, if I don't take it with me, what do I have left? Another part of me was angry he called me out about my sadness. I challenge anyone to go through what I've gone through and not have a little residual sadness.

However, the part of me that wanted to crumble into a sniveling puddle of tears has been the one echoing in my head. That part's the one with the loudest voice outside of my psychosis.

What would that be like to walk away from some of the pain of my past? Try to forget all the people who promised to love me only to discard me. Try to forget that I have the devil inside me. The devil that screams in my face and cauterizes my body with hellfire. Try to forget that childhood is supposed to be carefree and not so stinking heavy to carry around.

"What do you think about that, Mercy?"

"I'm sorry, what?"

"That Dr. Sutton was all psychoanalyzing Tracy—Wait, did you hear *anything* we were talking about?" Lyla asks with raised eyebrows and a quirk to her smile.

"Uhhhh, maybe some of it?" I answer. It's a lie, but whatever.

"Sutton said Tracy sings as a way to escape and comfort herself because of sexual abuse," Matty explains.

"No, he did not!" Lyla jumps in, scandalized. She is looking at Tracy, trying to gauge how much damage Matty just did, while also holding the heart in her chest with one hand.

"I was paraphrasing," Matty says with a shrug.

"He didn't say *anything* about sexual abuse, Matty. You better stop, that's how rumors get started." Only now does Lyla allow her eyes to pan the group.

*"He **did** say I sing to retreat into my mind, and more importantly, to comfort myself. Do you think he might be right?"* Tracy asks me.

"I don't know—*are you comforted?*" I ask, more aggressively than I meant to. Why does everyone think Sutton is such a genius? They all act like he's going to swoop in and save the world. As if he has the magic key that unlocks everyone's issues.

Plus, Matty and I already suspect Tracy was traumatized as a child and emotionally regressed to that stage of her development. Her tiny childlike voice speaks to that, never mind her singing—we haven't delved into what the heck that's all about yet. Our armchair psychology designations stop short when it comes to the singing.

"Sometimes, it soothes me to sing myself to sleep."

"Okay then, it's soothing. Problem solved," I scoff.

"Damn, Mercy. Why are you so crabby anyway?" Matty asks. I don't answer because I don't know. I think it has something to do with Sutton, though.

***

Midway through late afternoon yoga, which is actually one of the forced activities that I enjoy—I shouldn't say *forced*, they don't actually force us to do the activities, but they hover over you if you don't, so, let's say it's aggressively encouraged. Anyway, I like centering myself, and it's one time that I don't mind being in my head. And Sutton ruins it.

"Mercy? I'd like to see you in my office, please."

"Great, I'll be right with you," I say as I shift poses, with absolutely no intention of being swept away mid-class. After a few minutes go by with Sutton still standing there, arms crossed over his chest like some kind of haughty mercenary, the yoga instructor/social worker pipes in.

"Go ahead, Mercy."

"No, that's okay. I'm good." I have a feeling resistance is futile, but I'm not going without fighting it a little bit.

"That's not how this works, Mercy. I'll see you next time," the instructor says, as though I'm trying her yogi patience.

Great, it's not even Monday, and here I go—off to my headshrinker. I don't like how he stood there with so much damn authority. He was basking in the fact that everyone was conscious of his stupid Armani presence.

Sig never wore jeans to work, he was a professional. *This guy*, who is supposed to outrank us all in the maturity department, is wearing trendy brown ankle boots—all loosely laced, and a V-neck t-shirt! If his hipster style doesn't scream *millennial adulting*, I don't know what does. The whole staff has taken note of his ill-fitting shirt, too, except instead of thinking he shrunk it in the dryer, which is probably what happened, they are all twitterpated about how it accentuates his chest and arm muscles.

He closes the door behind himself, having gallantly waved me in first, but I'm the first to speak.

"How do you expect me to take you seriously in that get-up?" I ask with a snotty raise to my eyebrows.

"Mercy, let's be honest here," he says as he takes out two water bottles from his over-indulgent office refrigerator, "You are not going to take me seriously no matter what I wear. Should I have gone with the hoodie, though?"

"Don't you have any Vans?"

"Good call. Tomorrow, Vans and a hoodie."

"Sig wore a tie every single day of his life."

"I don't aspire to be like Sig," he says assertively before continuing, "Do you know that only about six patients here even address me as *Doctor Sutton*? You wouldn't know anything about that, would you?"

"What do you expect? It looks like you just put down the Xbox remote."

"Maybe I did."

"I wasn't joking!"

"Well, as long as my game is paused, can we get started?" He's not asking, by the way, so I don't bother answering, I just sit on the couch and accept my fate. Sutton twists off the top of one of the water bottles and then hands it to me before going behind his desk and opening a drawer.

The next thing he does surprises me. He closes the drawer, comes back around the desk, and sits down on the opposite end of the couch. Then he hands me a bag of cinnamon candies. I don't know what to do because Sig always sat behind his desk, **and** I had to dig through all the nasty butterscotch and peppermint candy to fish out the cinnamon ones.

"You can buy them separately, you know," he says with a disarming smile. I really don't want to take the bag, but my brain is conditioned to want these little things while I'm in here. Me and Pavlov's fricking dog.

"So, is it okay if we back way up?"

"To my parents abandoning me at St. Vincent's, you mean?"

"Before that."

I don't want to answer him because not only is it hard to admit that I wasn't worth keeping, but I also have to acknowledge that my parents thought I was possessed by the devil. I sigh and pop a cinnamon candy in my mouth. Here goes nothing.

"I've been having hallucinations since I can remember. Because of that, my parents believed the devil was inside of me. They...they were afraid of me." The statement is hard to get out, and horrific to dignify with words.

"Would you say you'd had those hallucinations for years before going to St. Vincent's?"

"Oh, yeah. For many years before that."

"I'm just—" he shifts himself on the couch so his arm drapes over the back of it, and he can face me better. The change in position doesn't help him look any more professional, but I guess I'll have to let that go. "It's just that... that early of onset is highly unusual."

"I guess I'm just lucky."

"Have the hallucinations always been like the ones you told me about?"

"Yes."

"So, your parents thought you were possessed because you were a child who was scared of the horrifying hallucinations you were experiencing? Did I get that right?"

"Yes."

"I'm sorry you were saddled with such imbeciles as parents," he says, as though we were old friends at happy hour instead of in a psychiatric session.

"Me too."

"Did they ever take you to a doctor? I don't have any records before St. Vincent's."

"No."

"They did not take you to a doctor to rule out any other diagnoses?" he asks incredulously.

"No."

"It couldn't possibly have been a folate deficiency or a systemic illness. It **must** have been a case of *demonic possession*. I'm disappointed they ever drew breath." He runs his fingers through his hair, also highly unprofessional, then his gaze lands on mine. "And here?"

"And here, what?"

"Did anyone run a single test on you to rule out the countless other things that could have been affecting your childhood mind? Or did everyone just jump to the six-year-old having paranoid schizophrenia?" Sutton is angry right now, also kinda unprofessional, but I like his righteous stance on my dubious upbringing.

"In their defense, it doesn't sound all that plausible that a folate deficiency would be screaming in my face and burning my skin."

"Mercy, I am ordering a full battery of tests. And yes, it could be as simple as a folate deficiency. It could also indicate thyroid disfunction, a brain lesion, anemia, renal impairment, an electrolyte imbalance…I could go on all day—"

"No, it's fine. But to be honest, I have no doubt about my diagnosis—I've seen a lot of it in here."

"You might be right, but I wouldn't be doing my job if I didn't at least start at the beginning."

"Suit yourself."

"One more official question, then I'd like to move on to something else."

"Officially, seven." When I answer his unasked question, he raises his brows and cocks his head a fraction as though confused. "Foster homes."

"Although that adds to the degradation of my faith in humanity, that's not what I was going to ask you." Now *I'm* cocking my head in puzzlement.

"I was going to ask if you are ready for Dr. Sigmu—for Sig's letter. I'll hang on to it forever if you want me to, but I think you are ready for it. You don't have to read it, but at least hang on to it. If you pitch the letter now, you take away your choice down the line. And I promise you, someday you'll wish you had read it."

I think about what he said for a few laborious minutes, then decide to take it. I'm not going to read it, maybe ever, but I don't want Sutton to ever talk to me about Sig's abandonment ever again. I need to remove this from his arsenal.

"Okay," I say, dismissively. I think he was expecting some pushback, but there is no reason he needs to be a part of this equation. And *that* should do it for official business. I wonder if he will let me keep the rest of these cinnamon candies? I've sucked my way through a few already.

"What are your plans when you leave here?"

"You mean, when I'm released from the system?" I question. He laughs and then nods. His strength is that he's unassuming, and it keeps catching me off guard. I find myself discussing things with him that I never intended to—like this.

"I'm going to live with my friends, get a dog, and continue doing freelance graphic design work." He smiles at me again. What's this guy so happy about? Maybe he is surprised one of my degrees is in graphic design—but someone needs to utilize the Photoshop program on the old, Humpty Dumpty, antiquated laptop computer that was donated specifically for my educational needs.

"What kind of dog?"

"A haggard one. One that nobody wants. It'll be like my spirit animal."

"I admire you, Mercy. You have been chewed up and spit out, but each time you come back fighting, and you still want to contribute kindness to the world."

My reply gets jammed in my throat. It's probably not worth explaining that it's not the world I have a problem with, it's people. There are a few people that I want to keep forever, Lyla, Matty, and Veronica for sure, and maybe to a lesser extent, Tracy. She's growing on me, or my tolerance for her singing is growing, one of the two. The rest of the people in the world can vanish to Stephen King's Langoliers, and I'd be happy.

"What about inane stuff like cooking and laundry and bank accounts with automatic bill pay?"

"I'm pretty sure I can cook. I watch a lot of cooking shows. Laundry doesn't require a Harvard scholar—I'm sure I'll pick it up. And I've had a bank account for years—gotta establish good credit, you know?"

"You're amazing, you know that? What about a driver's license?"

"Yeah, that will take me a minute because I don't know how to drive...or own a car."

"These are all things I can help you with. Let me make some phone calls, and together we will make sure you are ready to conquer the world when you leave here."

Despite the fact that my face might crack and turn to dust, should I ever display even a note of joy, I smile. Sutton might be growing on me too. Like a warm glow in my belly. Plus, he wants to help launch my ass out of here.

***

Sig's letter is burning an envelope-sized brand into my hip, where I have it shoved into the elastic of my sweatpants. I am not sure if I want to read it because the sooner I forget about Sig, the better off I will be.

I know as soon as I rip it open, I can no longer deny and ignore what happened. The thing above all else that I want to avoid is his pity. I cannot handle pity when it's directed at me, it only fuels my rage. I would, a thousand times over, choose the powerful emotion of anger than the weak emotion of feeling pitied.

I decide to read it, but the first indication of anything other than the most sincere, heartfelt apology he can deliver on paper, and I will shred the letter. Screw him. However, I can *promise* you that I will not be reading or shredding it in front of the staff and other patients.

I stop at the nurse's station and plead for some Ibuprofen and five minutes to rest in the dark of my room—you know, to get a handle on the debilitating, *non-existent* migraine that's currently rocking my world.

Funny enough, if I ask for twenty minutes, they'll give me five. If I ask for five, they'll give me twenty.

They are going to check on me every two seconds, but this isn't my first rodeo. I will have a damp washcloth ready to cover my crying eyes, and I'll have my hand primed and ready for a thumbs-up when they pop in my room.

I swallow 400 mg of Ibuprofen, hand the paper med-cup back to the nurse, then turn on my heal. I will only have a few minutes to read the damn letter, then the rest of the time I've carved out for myself will be to process whatever I've read.

I don't have time to hesitate, so I cut my hemming and hawing short and rip it open. Strangely enough, this is the first letter I have ever received. I used to eagerly wait every time they passed out mail, hoping a foster parent would have second thoughts and alert me to their imminent rescue, but I haven't been that kid with those lofty ideas for a long time.

Mercy, my girl:

Please know that this is not my doing and that, for once, I have no control over the situation. I am not allowed to visit nor contact any of my former patients. This stipulation has been adequately stressed and profusely reiterated. In time, I hope you will come to understand my position.

Do not worry for me, as I know you endlessly do. I will spend my retirement at my cabin, whittling my days away fishing under the sun and relaxing beneath the lazy stars.

I wish you well, Little One, because it's time you learn to show yourself something that no one ever has before. Your namesake, Dear, learn to show yourself some mercy.

You are the light of my life, and I will miss you forever.

Fondly,

Dr. Chester Sigmund

'Sig'

I have enough sense to shove the letter under my mattress before my spine dissolves, and I crumple to the floor. Violent, heaving sobs rattle my body, and I am desperate for the nothingness soon to be delivered by the code team.

I have seen patients in a hysterical state before—often, in fact. Usually upon admittance and always when the truth of their situation dawns on them. It's partly due to their loss of control over the situation and partly due to the intense hopelessness that wraps you in its grip and holds on for as long as it can.

Me? I want to disappear. Fate, that fickle bitch, seems to extract joy from my suffering. Above all else, the unfairness of it all is what has me gasping for air. I've never been the light of anyone's life—not ever. Now, the one person who sees me as such has been ripped away from me forever.

"Mercy! Girl, what's wrong?" Colleen swoops in and holds me like the angel she is. We are both on the floor with her Haitian arms wrapped tightly around me—they are the only thing holding me together right now.

"*Mercy, Mercy*, everything is going to be okay—I promise you that. Just tell Mama what's wrong."

"It hurts so bad!" I have lost control of my wailing, my tears, my snot, my *self.*

"Yes, baby, I know it hurts." She has no idea, but she's in the trenches with me, and I love her for that. She glances up at the dozen eyes on the threshold of my room, all filled with horror.

"Someone go get Dr. Sutton," her voice is as controlled as ever, and her calm demeanor is all the more terrifying to the spectators. Matty breaks through the feeble barricade and tries to scoop me from Colleen's arms. His eyes are wide with panic, and I'm irrationally struck by the fact that he is wearing eyeliner.

"Give her to me!" he demands. "Colleen! They are going to take her! Give her to me!"

"It's okay, Matty. She will be fine."

"Colleen! They're coming!" Matty screams, it cuts through my wailing and precedes the code team by mere seconds. Then he is swept away with the others, but I can still hear his strained objections from down the hall.

"Shhhh, shhhhh," Colleen coos as she rocks me in her arms while they ready the sedative.

"Stop! I will handle this, do NOT put that in her arm!" Sutton's sharp and commanding voice seems like it's all that's left in the room. It might be, because even my empty shell wants to evaporate into the ether. Nothing remains in here but his voice.

Sutton dismisses the code team, even amongst the keening that radiates from somewhere inside of my head. Then he and Colleen help me onto my bed, where I clamp my body together and try to dissolve into the sheets. They speak, but I can't make out what they say. Soon, Colleen is gone as well.

Sutton sits on the bed behind my coiled body. He leaves the light off, and because evening is stealing in, the environment is darkened. The room and my soul, fading to black.

He doesn't say anything. Not at first. He just gently rubs my back and brushes the sticky hair away from my face. Touching me will get him fired, but he doesn't seem to care.

When my anguish finally turns to mild shaking punctuated by tiny gasps of air, I peel my swollen eyes open. I focus on the texture of the wall and try to dismiss the fact that Sutton is still rubbing my back. It's quiet, though there is ruckus beyond my closed door. Evening reflection group is probably starting to take shape by now.

"This is part of it, you know," Sutton murmurs as he again swipes his fingers across my cheek. I don't respond, I have nothing left to give—least of all, my voice.

"Acknowledging the grief is an important step. It doesn't make you weak. On the contrary, having the strength to finally face all this requires incredible strength. I've never seen you so strong—so formidable." His words bring another round of hot tears to my eyes. I am a lot of things, but formidable is not one of them.

"You are courageous in allowing yourself to feel all this. It's the first step to tackling it and claiming your future without the shackles of your past. Mercy, every single one of your feelings is relevant and deserves to be *felt*," he murmurs.

"It hurts so bad." In a shocking display of vulnerability, I again give voice to the truest words I've ever spoken.

"Mercy, it's supposed to hurt. You've been through a lot, so let it hurt. *Feel* things instead of denying them as though you're not entitled to have those emotions. It will hurt like hell, and it will continue to hurt like hell—until, one day, it doesn't hurt quite as bad, and the next day, it hurts a little less, and the next day even less."

"It hurts too much."

"Mercy, one day you will see what I see, and you will know how special you are—how resilient. But we can't get you *there* if you are stuck here. And I mean that figuratively, not literally. You are stuck *here*," he whispers as he gently taps my forehead.

"If I'm so special, why doesn't anyone want me?"

"You have no idea," his words sound full of ache and confusion before they trail off.

"I've always scared people away. It's me. I'm the common denominator. I'm broken." My voice is a squeak, and it's barely audible.

"Your *experiences* have tried to break you," he clarifies. "But guess what? You are far from broken. Don't you see? There is nothing wrong with you. The schizophrenia is a challenge, nothing more, and it can be managed. As far as all the people who you think rejected you, guess what? They were ill-equipped to deal with a child's psychosis, but they did not reject *you*. If they rejected you, they never would have brought you into their home. All those families wanted you so bad, they decided to overlook your special needs. They wanted *you*—they couldn't handle the psychosis."

"I am the psychosis."

"No, Mercy. You are not. You are a million things, and only one of those things is schizophrenic."

"Why do you talk to me like that? Like I matter to you?" I ask as I sit up and face him. I want to look him in the eyes when he answers me.

He immediately swipes a lock of hair behind my ear. His penetrating blue eyes are almost too much for me because our faces are only about a foot apart. I think I want him to hold me. Not like a lover, but as someone who comforts me and makes me feel like I'm going to be okay. The fact that I don't like to be touched except by a select few also unsettles me a bit. Is it because he is good looking and says sweet things to me? Or am I just starving for human touch?

I lean in, partly to break the intense eye contact and partly because I do want to feel human touch—from him. He reads the situation correctly and wraps his arms around me. If one of the nurses sees this, he will be gone in an instant.

"I talk to you like that because you *do* matter, and someone should have told you those things a long time ago." His answer is soothing, so I bring my arms up to return the hug. His back is muscular, and he smells good. Clean, like a burst of fresh air.

Touching him and inhaling his essence feels like a basic instinct to size him up. It's something primal. Like I'm choosing a mate who can ensure strong offspring. Someone who can protect me and make me feel important.

"And because as hard as I try, I can't stop thinking about you," he finishes.

Chapter 7

Later that night, my heart beats an anxious rhythm that threatens to pound right out of my chest. I can feel the sweat trickling into my eyes, and the saltiness burns and blurs my vision. I know I'm strapped down—or at least held down. I cry out when they shove the stick between my teeth because it cuts into the tender skin inside my lip before they force me to bite down on the rough bark.

The panic is here. Sometimes it takes a little time to build up, but not tonight. My breaths are so short and shallow that there is no chance of oxygenating my blood, and my hands and feet go numb.

My thoughts become particularly pervasive when they rip off my clothing. It's only a dirty smock, but I prize my underwear above all else because I'm often not allowed to wear them. My breasts have begun to bud as well, so the indecent display is more shameful than the filth they shout in my face.

Once I'm naked, a surge of adrenaline courses through me, and I fight like a wild animal to get free. I scream through the branch clamped between my teeth, but my voice is raw and ineffectual. It will be gone soon; the human larynx is not meant to sustain such strain. I'm going to die. This time, they will kill me.

I'm cold from the sweat that pours off of me, but my face is hot with fear. I can no longer make out the words they scream around me. It's bad. The chaos, the fear—all of it. There is raw hatred here. Hatred, contempt, and death—it's all around me.

I stop screaming when clammy hands take hold of my leg, followed by more hands. When they pull my legs apart, the scream overtakes me, and the fight inside my body tries once again to take over. Then the burning comes, and my scream is enough to pierce time.

"Mercy! Oh, my God! Mercy! It's me, stop!" The voice is Lyla's. Why is she here?

"Everybody out!" Someone yells. I'm shivering on the floor, flopping like a fish out of water, gills expanding, yet drowning nonetheless. I'm terrified, and my throat is raw and scratched open. The night nurse drags the blanket from my bed and tries to wrap me in it.

I rasp out an objection and scurry as far away from her as possible. Lyla is crying, but she is allowed to stay in the room. Sutton gave the night staff explicit instructions, but everyone seems hesitant to shoo away the code team.

My desperate screams have evolved into raspy sobs. I know I am in my room, but the fear has followed me home. A distinct marker of schizophrenia is when the hallucinations reflect a profound fear, along with losing the ability to tell what's real or not. And right now, I'm having a hard time distinguishing what is a danger to me, and what is not.

I *do* know that if anyone tries to touch me, I will lose it so completely the staff will have no choice but to sedate me. In Sig's day, I would already have found my sweet oblivion.

My senses come into focus a little at a time. Right now I can feel that I am soaked, and I can hear Lyla crying. The only other sound in the room is a distant chattering. It sounds like someone's teeth chattering together.

After thirty or so minutes, Lyla moves from her bed and takes a seat near me on the floor. When I don't react badly, she reaches out her hand and lays it on the ground, palm up, next to me. Without too much hesitating, I place my hand in hers, and she tightens her grip.

Taking that opportunity to speak, the nurse informs me that I'm cold and shivering and should take the blanket from her. That's as far as she gets because this is the moment Sutton storms into the room.

He invades my space without sparing a second thought and summarily dismisses the night nurse. He gently tips my chin up so he can look into my eyes, and then takes quick stock of everything else. This is when he notices Lyla holding my hand. I know she is afraid to keep holding it, but also afraid to let go.

"You are a good friend, Lyla," Sutton says with tenderness. I can feel her blush with his acknowledgment, but I also know she thinks about him sexually, so his proximity probably plays a role in that blush.

"Mercy, I need to see you in my office. Would you like Lyla to come with us?" he offers. I like that he isn't reprimanding her for touching me. It's like he understands that some rules should be broken.

"Lyla can go back to sleep. She's probably fighting the Benzos," I mumble. She gives my hand a squeeze and then climbs back into her bed. I think partially because she is tired and partially because she is only wearing a tank top and panties—like me, but I have no desire to go back to sleep, or to remain in this room, for that matter.

"Can you stand up?" he asks as he rises to his feet and extends his palm to assist me. I take his offered hand and get to my feet. I'm still freezing cold. I also know the worn-out cotton of my shirt has adhered itself to my body, but it is kind of dark in here, so maybe he won't notice the obscene display.

"Let's get you some dry clothes first," he says as his eyes drift down my body and then make their way back to my eyes. He definitely noticed my nipples and maybe my stomach, where the shirt clings a little higher than it should.

"Lyla, can you help her? I'm going to get my office unlocked and the lights turned on, then I'll be back to get her."

"Of course, Dr. Sutton. Thanks for coming in tonight," she says shyly. When he leaves, she wastes no time before saying, "If all I had to do to get him to look at *me* like that, is hallucinate, I would totally do it—at least a few times."

"Lyla?"

"Yeah, hon?"

"Too soon."

"Right, sorry."

***

I don't feel so bad about my rangy hair and dumpy clothes because when we get to his office, I notice Sutton is wearing faded, torn jeans and a plain white t-shirt. He is the one with the MD, so if he isn't worried about how he is dressed, I don't care that I'm wearing old scrub pants and a dry tank top—the skimpier-than-normal shirt was on Lyla's insistence.

"I want to start by telling you that I am not surprised you had a nightmare. Anxiety manifests itself in all kinds of ways, and after yesterday, and the letter—well, I'm just not surprised." He takes a throw blanket out of his closet and hands it to me before sitting down on his end of the couch.

"Sutton? Are you *special* or something?"

"My mom thinks so."

"I'm serious, you must be a little slow. Why else would you minimize something like that?"

"I haven't minimized anything. Anxiety is no joke. Neither are panic attacks."

"Do you actually think that was something as trite as a nightmare?" I ask, disgusted with him.

"Mercy, what are we talking about here?"

"The same damn thing we've been talking about all along! That was no *nightmare*, Sutton!" I say the word nightmare like it tastes dirty in my mouth. He raises his hand in a defensive position.

"Hold it, I'm trying to understand things. Are you telling me that you were awake in bed when you hallucinated or that you were asleep when all that happened?"

"I don't know."

"Have the hallucinations ever happened at night like that before?"

"Yes! Of course."

"Wait. Do they happen during the day, too?"

"Mostly at night."

"Mercy—"

"You don't understand. I can *feel* them burning me. They physically hold me down."

"I'm not suggesting they do not feel 100% real, but are you ever awake when they happen?"

"I've had hundreds of them. I'm sure some were during the d—"

"Holy shit! Mercy, have you *ever* hallucinated in the light of day?"

"I don't think so."

"**Oh, my God!**" his hands rake through his hair, and he looks at his lap like it holds the answers to my psychosis. To be honest, I'm starting to wonder again if he is cut out for this job.

It takes him a few minutes and a couple of stops and starts before he can form words again.

"Mercy. We need to back up. I need you to tell me everything you can remember about your childhood."

Chapter 8

Were it not for his broke college kid outfit and tousled hair, I might actually think he looks sort of professional now. He has adopted the look of stern concentration and added some hipster glasses to his studious note taking. At this point in our impromptu session, his brows are now permanently knitted together.

"Were your parents kind to you?"

"Being kind is an awfully subjective term when it comes to my parents."

"When you were little, did they hold you and kiss you? Did they tuck you in at night?"

"Yeah, I suppose."

"Did they love each other? Or were they constantly fighting?"

"I don't remember them ever fighting."

"What was their economic status? Did they have jobs? Did you live in affluence? Poverty? A house? A shack? Tell me everything you can remember."

I wrap the blanket around me tighter, it smells like Sutton, and I don't know how to feel about that. I also don't like to think about my past. That door closed a long time ago, and I prefer to keep it that way.

"I remember my mom used to make clothes. She made them all pretty much the same because uniqueness was not really a priority. Us girls weren't allowed to go to school, but she taught me to read anyway. I was proud of that until my dad found out and slapped my mom. It was the only time I ever saw him raise a hand to her, but he hit her so hard, she fell down."

"Did he ever raise a hand to you?"

"No."

"How about his voice?"

"No, he was a gentle, quiet man."

"Why couldn't girls go to school?"

"It's a little hard to explain now that I have some perspective, but women were very subservient to men. Men were the chosen ones and were treated with reverence, sometimes even awe."

"What do you mean when you say *awe*?"

"Just that…it sounds stupid to say out loud. Sutton, I need you to understand that my childhood is incredibly shameful for me. So much so that I've never told anyone about it. Not a word." I can't even look at him. I feel dirty and nothing but disgust for myself. Once I tell him everything, there is no going back. Once I speak it, it will have to be true, and he will know my shame.

Sutton drops his notepad to the floor and scoots across the couch. Now he is very close to me, and there is no way I can tell him the things that happened.

"*Mercy*," now he takes my hand, and I have little doubt he can feel it shaking. "Let's be clear about something. You were a *child*, and none of what you tell me has any reflection on you. Nothing at all. You should not be carrying this shame. Do not take ownership of something you had nothing to do with."

"I did, though. I shared all their views. I was a Believer."

"No, Mercy. You were an impressionable kid."

"*I was a Believer.*" Now my chin is shaking.

"You trusted your parents. How can anyone find fault in that?"

"*I was a Believer*," it comes out as a whisper.

"From what you've told me so far, it sounds like you were raised in a cult, and I have little doubt that it plays a massive role in your *psychosis*."

"It didn't feel like a cult. Not at the time."

"What can you remember about the leader?"

"He had a lot of wives. He was a prophet, so he spoke directly to God. He said God would protect the true Believers when he cleansed the world of its wickedness."

"Everyone believed him and trusted him without question?"

"Oh, yes. He could drink poison. it was clear he was protected by God."

"Now that you are away from his influence, can you understand that he was lying about drinking poison?"

"He wasn't lying."

"No?"

"No." I can feel my throat hitch, and I only realize he is still holding my hand when he firms up his grip. I feel a little stronger with him holding on to me. It sort of feels like he is there too, standing in the dirt, watching everything happen.

"He gave it to a goat first." There is a faraway look in my eyes, and I can see the disturbing scene perfectly in my mind's eye. "Nothing happened at first, but after a while, the goat crumpled to its knees—only his front legs. Everyone said he was praying." I can still see it.

"*Can you see him suffering?*" I whisper before I realize what I've asked makes no sense because we are sitting in Sutton's office.

"*Yes*," he whispers back.

"It wasn't just the goat." Inexplicably, I burst into tears that I didn't feel coming. He wraps his arms around me, and I dissolve into someone I don't recognize. It's like I've opened a gas valve, and any second, the whole place will ignite.

When I finally collect myself, I want to tell him the rest. I sit back, and he swipes the tears under my eyes with his thumbs—but he doesn't let go of my face.

"What else did he give the poison to?"

"The boy babies."

"Jesus Christ!"

"And my brother."

***

It took Sutton a long time to respond to my words, and when he finally did, it was with a litany of expletives. Now, he is pacing his office and can't complete a full sentence.

He comes back over and takes a knee in front of me. Both of his palms are flat against the leather of the couch on either side of my legs.

"Mercy, when was the last time you thought about your brother?"

"Not since I watched his mouth foam up, and he coughed and choked on his last breath." Now, I've admitted to being a monster, and Sutton won't want to help me anymore. He is disgusted with me; he has to be.

"Mercy, that is your brain protecting you. That was a horrific experience."

I laugh sardonically, "No, it's not my brain. It's because he wasn't a true child of God. He wasn't a Believer, so we weren't permitted to think about him."

"How old was he when he died?"

"I don't know, he couldn't walk yet."

Sutton's eyes well up before he blinks the moisture away. He knows what a horrible person I am, and I feel worse about my secret being out than I do about my choking baby brother. My parents were right. I have the devil in me.

"Mercy? It's 4:30 in the morning, is there any part of you that could go back to sleep right now?"

"Not a chance."

"Then, I want you to do something for me." He stands up and walks over to his discarded notebook, tears out the pages he wrote on, and then hands me the blank pad of paper.

"What was your brother's name?"

"Elijah,"

"I would like you to write a letter to Elijah. No one else is going to read it, not even me. You can say anything you want to him; it can be as long or as short as you want, and you can take as long as you need to— even weeks. I want you to tell him everything you would say to him if you could, use all the paper you need. Does that seem like something you can do for me?"

I try to think of an objection, but I'm whittled to the bone and can't come up with one. "I think so."

"I'm going to make some coffee, I'll be back in five minutes. Oh, and Mercy?"

"What?"

"The cinnamon candies are in the top drawer."

He walks out, leaving the door open as I stare at the notebook in my lap. What would I say to Elijah now? I hardly knew him. I put the pen to the paper and write the first thing that comes to mind.

I'm sorry I couldn't protect you. I will carry you in my heart forever.

Love,

Te-Te

I tear out the paper and fold it in half just as Sutton walks back into the room. "I didn't know if you like cream or sugar, so I brought both."

"Thanks, I'll take both." I feel a little lighter. Two sentences of words lighter. Sutton looks at the folded paper in my lap and smiles.

"Did you already get started?"

"And finished," I say as I gratefully accept the mug of coffee.

"Why don't you hang on to it for a few days, just in case you think of something you'd like to add." I shrug as he continues, "I'd like to meet with you Monday through Friday if that's okay with you."

"Why? To solidify your disgust with me?" I ask the question sincerely, but the truth is, if he still wants to help me after everything he heard tonight, he might be more cut out for this job than I thought.

"No, Mercy. It's so I can confirm what I already know, that you are the least broken person I have ever met."

Chapter 9

After group, where there was a slight incident with Simon and his alien-monitored pupils to keep things exciting, my eyeballs started to feel powdery. I never did go back to sleep after meeting with Sutton. I had languished in bed, thinking about what he said.

He'd said I wasn't broken and then gone on to clarify that all my feelings and reactions were exactly what he would expect. I'd never felt so normal. Those words ring in my ears even now.

He also told me not to eat or drink anything for breakfast except the water to swallow my pills because someone from the lab was going to come take blood and urine samples for further testing. Poor Sutton, still looking for a folate deficiency.

I've also thought a lot about my letter to Elijah and haven't come up with anything to add. He would be about fifteen now, and that thought sticks with me like a rock in my shoe.

I think the part that bothers me right now is that I don't know if he knew how much I loved him. He used to call me Te-Te because he couldn't say Mercy, and he always said it with such excitement on his angelic little face. I remember Elijah in the baby swing. I used to play with him and pretend he knocked me over every time he swung forward in the swing. His laughter was everything to me then. It only changed for me when I could hear it in the night after he was gone.

It's rec time now, so of course, the ping pong ball has been sailing back and forth for the better part of forty-five minutes. My friends seem a little quiet, so I decide to address both last night, and my regret about Elijah not knowing how important he was to me.

"I'm sorry I scared you guys last night. Sutton thinks it was triggered by anxiety, and I'm going to work on that, but I also really want you all to know how much I adore you."

"Awwww," Lyla says, but doesn't finish what she was about to say, so I continue.

"I just really want you to know that I love you with all your sadness, all your feelings you can't share yet, all your quirks and secrets." I look right at Matty before continuing, "In fact, there is nothing at all that you could tell me that would make me love you any less. I need you all in my life because without you, I wouldn't feel whole. Okay? I just want to put that out there in case there was any doubt."

Matty's eyes well up, so I'm fairly sure he received my hidden, as well as my overt message. He fans his eyes and then blows me a kiss. I wish he would talk with us about how he feels because I think it would set him free, but it's enough for now that he knows I'm here for him, no matter who or what he feels like.

Now that everyone is acting normal again and started in with any pertinent unit gossip, of course, this is the time the lab technician chooses to invade our airspace.

"Mercy, can I borrow you for a little while?" she asks. If you want my opinion, she shouldn't interrupt rec time. She should have plucked me from the alien spy-inhabited group this morning. Rec time with my friends has been far more healing lately, and that's no lie.

***

It's not until after dinner during reflection group that Sutton summons me to his office. I was starting to wonder if he changed his mind about seeing me every day or if our early morning session was it for today.

When I close his door behind me, he cuts right to the chase, but he doesn't explain why he is still here at a quarter to seven at night when he's not on call.

"All your labs look perfect."

"Gah! You mean no folate deficiency?"

"Very funny, smart ass."

"Am I funny? Or smart?"

"You are both. Distractingly so."

"I distract you?"

"Sometimes, yes."

"Only sometimes? I'll have to try harder." I don't know why I feel so playful. It wasn't that long ago that I was impervious to his charms.

"That's not a good idea. Listen, I'm going to ask you some questions, and I want you to answer them as they pertain to you in the last six months, and only during a wakeful state." He widens his eyes at me as if to drive that last point home.

"Got it."

"Do you have any beliefs of a persecutory or grandiose nature that seem bizarre or implausible to others?"

"No, just the aliens that spy on me and track my thoughts through my pupils."

"Be serious, please, or we will be here all night."

"Okay, then, no."

"When awake, do you hear voices distinctly different from your own thoughts that others do not hear?"

"No."

"When awake, do you perceive things, without any external stimuli, that others around you do not?"

"No."

"Never?"

"You said in the last six months."

"What about ever?"

"I don't think so."

"Do you experience grossly disorganized or catatonic behavior, or have you been told you have bouts of disorganized thinking or jumbled speech?"

"No."

"Do you have problems with goal-directed behavior?"

"Let me consult all my degrees and certifications...."

"Right. Okay, let's move on. I have not noticed any negative symptoms—negative, as in something is missing, such as an ability to express or understand emotions, loss of verbal communication, loss of motivation, things like that."

"Okay?"

"Would you agree with that?"

"Yes, nothing seems to be missing."

Sutton leans back against the couch and drags his hands over his face a few times like he's trying to wash something off. He sits there for a while with his eyes closed, and his head tipped back. I can picture him in a lawn chair with a beer in one hand and his handsome face soaking up the sun. Then he leans forward and rests his forearms against his knees while he clasps his hands together. He is staring at his feet when he finally speaks.

"You do not present with schizophrenia *at all*."

"Wait! What?" I know I heard him correctly, but I did not expect him to say that. Just about anything but t*hat*.

"Mercy, I am going to run this past a few other docs just to make sure I am not missing anything, but don't be surprised if your med cup looks a little different and then continues to evolve. The staff will also become ultra-interested in your thoughts and behavior, as will I."

"You're going to change my meds?" This is a scary thought because I've tried them all, and the side effects can be awful. More than that, I'm afraid of experiencing my psychosis as often as I used to.

"I won't make any changes without discussing it with you first, and any modifications will happen slowly and in a safe manner. But we *do* need to talk about the possibility that you do not need to be on antipsychotics."

"I'm afraid to relapse. The acute phase of my illness is not something I wish to revisit," I say with conviction—and more than a little bit of fear.

"Listen," he leans in so he is very close to me again. "You cannot suffer from an acute phase of an illness you do not have. I'm not at all saying we don't have work to do. I'm just saying we need to take another look at the playbook."

"I'm afraid."

"*Mercy*, you have my word that I will take care of you. I'm asking you to trust me."

"I do trust you."

"Okay then, let me help you."

Chapter 10

When Sutton said he was going to run my case past a few other docs, he failed to mention that I would be presented to an interdisciplinary, collaborative team of doctors and run through a rigorous battery of tests and procedures, as well as endless questions and assessments.

I missed three full days of group and spent a disconcerting amount of time trapped in an MRI machine. They may not be convinced I'm schizophrenic, but I can *promise* you that I'm claustrophobic.

I was supposed to meet with Sutton at 9:00 this morning, but he isn't here yet, so I opt to lie down on his couch and wait for him instead of going back to group. When Sig was here, this office was always closed up and kind of stuffy. Now, it has been infused with something fresh and bright—something that smells good and has blue eyes.

"Thanks for waiting, Mercy." Sutton blows in like a cool breeze and smiles at me so brightly that I feel it in my chest. "Want to get out of here for a little bit?"

I pop up like a Jack-in-the-box, no longer interested in lying down. "Does a snake drag its ass? Of course, I want to get out of here for a little bit!" Now, my smile matches his.

"Go get dressed for hiking."

"You mean, change out of my flip flops and put on a bra?" I ask as I stand up. He drops his head, but not before I see his shy, little boy smile.

"I'm on it," I exclaim over my shoulder because I'm already on the move.

"Mercy?" he calls after me.

"What?"

"Get your letter to Elijah."

***

He drives a Raptor, which looks big and tough if you ignore all the colorful balloons in the back seat. He can't even see out the rear window to the bed of the truck there is so much latex in his way.

"You going to a birthday party, Sutton?"

"Clearly."

"This is a nice truck. Did you steal it?"

"Uh, Noooo."

"What? You dress like a poor college kid. I figured you'd drive some busted, piece of shit car that burns oil and has a squeaky fan belt."

"That's awfully specific. What else did you assume about me? I mean, besides the, *I can't possibly be a real doctor, part."*

Oh crap. He's calling me out on the fact that I think about him. Maybe he knows *he* is the topic of conversation on the unit. I wonder if he also knows Matty did my makeup before our little outing.

"Nothing," I lie. The truth is, we've all speculated about what he looks like naked and how beautiful his perfect girlfriend must be. I bet she is blonde, with fake boobs and a bleached white smile, tan too—pretty much the exact opposite of me—pale and redheaded.

I change the subject, "So what's the plan now that half the MDs in the country believe I was misdiagnosed?"

"I can tell you how I think it should go, but I want you to weigh in too." His arm hangs casually out of the window, and his hair blows all around. He looks effortlessly sexy and tousled. My open window has a different impact because my hair is whipping me in the face and, no doubt, matting together. He looks handsomely windswept; I look like I just survived a hurricane while strapped to a tree.

"I would like to ween you off the antipsychotics and evaluate what medication, if any, is appropriate for your anxiety and panic attacks. A mood stabilizer may also be in order, but I don't like to change more than one thing at a time because I like to be clear about what is doing what. Make sense?"

"I guess it makes sense, but what happens if I start halluc—having more episodes?"

"We will treat those for what they are, and we will get you to a healing place. I was concerned when I went through your file and saw that you were always sedated after an episode. We need to learn from those instances if we have any hope of unlocking your past, and freeing you from all that trauma."

"Speaking of my past, do you think I'm a bad person for forgetting about my little brother?"

"Number one, you didn't forget about him. Number two, you need to realize the human brain is capable of doing all kinds of things to protect the conscious mind, and number three, Mercy, *you* are light years away from being a bad person."

"I've been a paranoid schizophrenic for so long, I don't know how not to be."

"You do not need to worry about labels. All you need to do is be yourself. You have nothing to be ashamed of."

"I feel like I've been hiding a wicked part of myself for my whole life." This happens to be a very introspective moment for me because

75

I've always felt like there was something wrong with me—something dark and unlovable.

"There is your psychosis right there. It's time to accept that there is nothing evil inside of you. No devil to speak of. All that wickedness you cling to? Babe, that was all done to you, and in front of you. You do not get to take ownership of that, not anymore."

Did Sutton just call me, *babe*? It was so fluid and natural; I don't even think it registered for him. I'll tell you what though, it fuckin' registered for me.

***

Sutton parked by a hidden, overgrown trailhead, retrieved the balloons from the back seat, and then a picnic basket from the bed of the truck. Then we hiked our asses straight up a mountainside for over an hour.

It was kind of cute the way he would stop and hold his camelback tube for me to drink out of, but I'll tell ya, he *grossly* overestimated my hiking stamina. Yoga? Sure, all day long—but climbing Everest is not in my wheelhouse. I need a damn Sherpa to haul me the rest of the way up.

"Good lord, Sutton, is this where you kill me and leave me for the forest scavengers?"

"We're almost there. You are doing awesome." Then he stops dead and looks at me like I just offered to piggy-back him up the hill.

"Please tell me you have the letter…or this will be a dual round-trip."

"I have it."

"Good, because any second now, you will see why we hiked all this way." As if on cue, the trail gives way to rocky cliffs and a breathtaking view.

"Wow, this is insane! I didn't know places like this existed so close to home."

"Careful, the trail is a little sketchy over there. Follow me this way. There is a perfect spot for what I have in mind."

"What do you have in mind?"

"Lunch," he says matter-of-factly, "Oh, and some unburdening of your soul." He turns to me and grins, "No big deal."

"Oh, thank God, it will be nice not to have to haul my soul's burden all the way back down." Then I look around and add, "I need to unburden my bladder too."

"Go ahead while I set up lunch."

When I get back from being one with nature, he has prepared a picnic on a huge, flat-ish rock that overlooks the whole canyon. It's the kind of thing where if you get too close to the edge, your perception gets all wavy, so I keep a solid ten feet from the face of the rock. Just so you know, this is something you base-jump off of, not picnic on.

"Oh, holy cow, I figured you would bring food from the hospital…this is, wow. I don't know what to say."

"Say you're hungry because I'm not schlepping this back down the hill," he laughs. He brought all kinds of cut-up fruit and different cheeses, mini-sandwiches, cookies, and flavored sparkling water. He thought of everything.

After we eat, we both lie back on the rock and stare up at the sky. It reminds me of a foster home I was in. They had a pool in the backyard, with a diving board that must have been fifteen feet above the water. I used to sit up there and hang my legs off the end. It felt like I was suspended above the world—precarious but safe. That's how I feel now.

"I like how you treat me like I'm a normal person. You've never made me feel broken or inadequate," I muse.

"It's because you're not broken or inadequate. Everyone has things that make them unique, you are no different. Caring for your mental health is the same as setting a broken bone or treating diabetes."

"It's weird, though."

"No, it's not. Your mental state is exactly what I would expect from someone who's experienced everything you have. So, if you look at it like that, you're totally normal."

"Uhhh," I pause, struck by being called normal for the first time.

"Do you know that I won't drink hot coffee out of anything plastic? Not even a travel mug. And if I don't go to the gym within thirty minutes of waking up, I won't go at all. They're both hard and fast rules. I never waver. Some people would call that weird, but it's quirks like that that make me who I am."

"You think my episodes are quirks?"

"What would you call them?"

"The bane of my existence and a mighty albatross of psychological burden wrapped around my neck for all of eternity."

"Does it have to be, though? Or, with treatment, can you live a fulfilling life? I'm not suggesting you don't tackle it head on. I'm saying, don't identify so much with this perceived brokenness that it's all you see."

"What am I if I'm not broken?"

"You are everything." There is an ache to the words that sounds painfully unscripted. "It's shocking to me that you don't know that. Look at your relationships and the impact you have on people—everyone scrambles to be a part of your world. You're like a shiny pearl inside a filthy oyster."

I smile as I watch the clouds slowly morph into a whispy collection of spun sugar. It's amazing how different you look when viewed through another's eyes. Sutton thinks I'm *everything*.

He breaks my contemplative silence as though he wishes he could reel in his last soul-baring words, "We need to get back to a therapeutic focus."

"God forbid we forget about our therapeutic focus and talk like regular people."

"I wish we were regular people, but I have a responsibility to you as your doctor."

"I prefer you as a regular person."

"Sometimes I do, too, but I have this really meaningful exercise planned for you. I'd like you to attach your letter to Elijah to the balloon strings and send him your thoughts and intentions. I truly believe he will receive your message."

"This afternoon has taken a swift left turn."

"It's time you acknowledged your feelings about him and about his death. Do you think you can do that?"

I remain stock still for a few minutes. For some reason, the idea of my brother getting an apology letter from me feels as raw as a paper cut. It seems depressingly like not enough, but also recklessly like too much, and I'm suddenly not sure if I can.

"Tell me a story about him, a happy one," he prompts. I don't need to ponder very long because I've actually been thinking about Elijah quite a bit lately.

"I remember being so excited for his birth. As my mother got closer and closer to her due date, I slept less and less—I didn't want to miss it, and I didn't know that it takes a long time to expel a tiny human from one's body. Anyway, my excitement lasted exactly ten minutes after he was born because I was so jealous of all the attention my parents gave him. I used to sneak into his room at night and whisper to him that they would never love him as much as they loved me. I would tell him how, pretty soon, they would grow tired of him and forget all about him."

Sutton doesn't say anything I expect, like, *that is typical of a firstborn, or that's pretty universal for a sibling to feel like that.* He stays quiet, so I continue.

"Before too long, my taunting whispers evolved into me crawling in his crib with him. It wasn't long before I was cuddling him and singing him to sleep." I am openly crying now and can't seem to stem the flow. Lately, the flood of tears has been off the charts, but after all these months together, I don't bother hiding it from Sutton anymore.

"I loved him so much, Sutton. *I loved him*, and they took him from me! Worse than that, they made me believe he was evil. I wasn't allowed to cry because I missed him, I wasn't permitted to hate my parents for letting it happen, and I couldn't stop the leaders from doing it to other little boys." I sit up and face Sutton, whose legs are extended out in front of him while he leans back on his hands.

"They turned me into one of them!" I scream before melting into my anguish. He runs his fingers through my hair and directs me to his lap, where I lay my head against his thigh.

"You were never one of them, Mercy." His words hang in the air above us while I cry, and he strokes my hair. Nothing but the breeze and my sobs break through the serenity of the beautiful overlook. Not for a very long time.

By the time my tears and snot dry and my sharp inhales morph into a regular breathing pattern, the sun is getting low in the sky. Sutton whispers so he won't frighten me with the sudden noise.

"I think you are ready."

He helps me stand and attach the letter to one of the balloon strings. Then holds the envelope up to my chest, where he takes my palm and presses it against the letter. Essentially, we are both pressing the letter to my heart.

"He knows you loved him then, and he knows you love him still. You were never liable for his death. It was tragic, but your tiny childhood hands had no part in it, nor could they have stopped it. It's time to release the notion that you could have saved him or that you had any sort of culpability in his death."

I nod, but a fresh stream of tears flows as I sit up and lean against Sutton's chest. He wraps his arms around me and holds me as if he is just as invested in this process as I am, and I adore him for it. He is much more of a friend to me than a doctor. That connection happened gradually, but I've never really seen him in a professional capacity.

"I'm ready," I say after a sniffle. We've been standing like this for at least fifteen minutes, and if I'm honest, I'd mention that I want him to hold me close like this for a lot longer.

"Take your time, Mercy. We aren't in any hurry."

I close my eyes against his chest and say a silent prayer to my brother. Then, raise my hand and let go of the letter. We stand here and watch the balloons on their journey until they are a tiny pinprick in the sky and then disappear altogether.

"They're gone," I say on a tiny breath.

"No, they aren't," he says as he cups the side of my face in his palm. When he continues, we are still gazing into each other's eyes,

"Have you ever heard the poem, *Standing Upon the Seashore*, by Henry Van Dyke?"

"No," I can't help but exhale a laugh. He always knows the right thing to say, and of course, in this tender moment—it's a poem.

"I'm paraphrasing here, but it's about a ship that looks huge and mighty while docked but gets smaller and smaller as it sails further away. Then Van Dyke goes on about how the ship is just as big as it was, it's just gone from sight."

"Oh, how profound. You didn't say it was a *literal interpretation*."

"Hold on, though, the end is the best part," he chides with a sweet smile on his face.

"Because, just as someone says, *it's gone*—the voices from the opposite shore shout, *here it comes!*"

Chapter 11

It's been more than a month since they weaned me off the antipsychotics, and the biggest changes have been the amount of energy I have and the lack of ringing in my ears. I'd like to say my nighttime torment is a thing of the past, but it has been happening on a more frequent basis. Sutton insists it has nothing to do with coming off the Seroquel and everything to do with unlocking my past.

The letter to Elijah was a huge breakthrough for me, however, it is but one step on a long journey. Sutton has helped me to begrudgingly realize my parents were victims in their own right, but my hatred for them still burns bright.

My sessions with him have primarily focused on his rather enthusiastic belief that I suffer from Post-Traumatic Stress Disorder. I don't want to trivialize his convictions, but what I experience during my episodes is so intense and crippling I feel like the paranoid schizophrenia diagnosis is a much better fit.

Don't forget that I have been around people in the grips of psychosis since I entered adolescence. I've seen people scratch their faces bloody to rid themselves of the spiders. I've watched them wet themselves in fear. I've witnessed someone throw a chair through the TV so he could slit his own throat with the shards—simply to appease the voices. I've seen hell through their eyes, so I'm more at home with a label of paranoid schizophrenia because hell is more authentic to what I experience.

I may be in a state of sleep or suspended consciousness, but hallucinations can absolutely happen at night, and despite the conclusions of the medical panel I was paraded in front of, I'm not convinced I should have come off the Seroquel.

Lyla recommends benzos. She says I would sleep like the dead instead of being terrorized by the feeling of imminently joining them. I'm taking her thoughts under advisement because it would be nice not to have to wonder what will happen once I drift off to sleep.

Anyway, since Sutton feels more comfortable calling it PTSD, and I'd rather authenticate it by referring to it as debilitating hallucinations brought on by a paranoid schizophrenic, delusional mind, we have begrudgingly, yet amicably decided to refer to the incidents as *my nighttime sufferings*.

He doesn't want me all hung up on labels anyway—even though he spent weeks insisting that PTSD nightmares are every bit as intense and realistic as a schizophrenic hallucination, and perhaps worse because they are so often replicative nightmares or even exact replays of the traumatic event.

I've rolled my eyes quite a bit at his talk of replicative nightmares because my hallu—nighttime sufferings involve me being burned with acid and my insides exploding. Kinda hard to explain away my lack of scars, and intact bodily systems if I'm "re-experiencing" or having flashbacks to actual events, right?

Yeah, well, that's what I thought. Until tonight. Tonight, my brother was in bed with me. He was coughing and choking and foaming at the mouth. As for me, I was standing on my bed, screaming for someone to help him.

The night nurse walked away with a fat lip and a bloody nose, and when I kicked someone from the code team in the jaw, I was restrained. I'm not talking, held down. I'm saying, I had several grown men lying across my body until my waist, wrists, and ankles were secured. Then, when I was still trying to bite them, they strapped down my head as well.

I'll hand it to them, though, they followed Sutton's explicit instructions, and they did not sedate me.

By the time Sutton storms in, the circus has already left town, and I'm alone with one of the night nurses in my room. When I no longer felt like I could tear through my restraints, and I was inconsolably crying, the nurse had taken pity on me and removed the strap across my forehead, but otherwise, I'm still trussed up. Sutton takes one look at me and then growls a single word.

"Out!" He sits down on my bed and is already undoing my restraints as the nurse exits the room. "Are you okay?" He missed all the carnage, but he's not a bit worried I will lash out. In fact, once my wrists and abdomen are free from the restraints, he pulls me against his body and holds me while I finish draining the well.

I'm not sure if I am crying for my brother, or for being strapped down and unable to even wiggle for over thirty minutes, or if I'm crying because of his kindness. At first, I think it is about Elijah and the helplessness, but the longer he holds me, it becomes more about the kindness—and him.

"Was it the same? The screaming and burning?"

"*No*," I whisper.

"Tell me," he murmurs sweetly into my ear, which causes a weird sensation between my legs. Almost a tickle…or a strange pressure.

"I was trying to get the foam out of his mouth so he would stop choking. I was desperate. Wild."

"I'm sorry you have to experience all that. Are you feeling better now?"

"Why *do* I have to experience it? Can't I go back on the antipsychotics? Or even Benzodiazepines? It's all too much."

"You have a lot of repressed trauma. In order to heal, we have to address all that ugliness. It won't always be like this, I promise. Plus, I've told you, the antipsychotics were not helping you."

"Yes, they were," I pull away so I can look him in the eyes, "All this nighttime bullshit is happening much more often now. You know that!"

"Mercy, listen to me. It's not because I've weaned you off the meds. We are bringing some truly awful stuff to the surface. We have to. We need to drag it out where we can see it, so we can subdue it. It's going to take time, but your mind is healthy. It just needs some serious attention. I want you to think of each night terror as one step closer to getting better. If I give you Benzodiazepines to sedate you at night, we will allow that trauma to hide forever and attack at will. Now, it may be appropriate to treat your anxiety with Benzodiazepines down the line, but I will never prescribe them to knock you out at night."

What he is saying makes sense, I just don't like it. I lean forward again, but this time, my face is against the crook of his neck instead of directed at the wall. I can smell his skin, and it affects me so much I almost pull away—but he brings his hand up so his fingers are in my hair and cupping the back of my head. My heart rate picks up, and that surprises me too. Why is my body suddenly reacting to him so much?

"Can you go back to sleep? Or do you want to talk through some of it—in my office, of course." Sutton is always willing to hash out my crap. At this point, I've lost count of how many times he's been roused from his bed and had to race back here to tend to me.

"I'll try to go back to sleep. Where is Lyla? That reminds me, they said they might have to move her to a different room for her own safety—can they do that? I don't want them to take her away. I would never hurt her."

"They might have to move her for a little while, but not because you might hurt her. It's not good for her own recovery to be frightened awake like she is. It's also hard for her to fall back to sleep once she's up, that's all. I know you would never hurt her."

"I hurt a few of the staff tonight."

"They probably had it coming," he tries to hold back his laugh, but I can feel his chuckle rumble against my body. It makes me press myself against him even more. I like how his chest feels against my nipples, his body against the cotton of my shirt makes them tingle a little, and I can feel them swell. What the hell is happening to me?

Sutton finishes removing my restraints and helps me get into bed. For a second, I think he is about to kiss my forehead, but he doesn't. He tells me goodnight and then walks out of my room.

I still feel funny between my legs. It reminds me a little of that time I brought myself to orgasm. For the first time in ages, I move my hand down there, but this time it feels surprisingly different. This must be what everyone gets so excited about. My body feels alive, and my nipples are literally pulsing. Touching myself feels amazing—the only gross thing is that everything feels wet and kind of disgusting right now. Not enough to stop me, though this feels too good.

Chapter 12

Something happened today in group that has never happened before, and I'm not sure where to put my feelings about it. The new guy happened.

I'm not all that clear about his situation yet, but from what I can put together, his mental health is being evaluated because he was involved in a car accident that killed a young mother. The basis of his length of stay will, no doubt, be determined by whether or not he is suicidal.

He doesn't seem suicidal to me, just really smiley, and he looks at me a lot. I'd say he's a few years older than me—maybe twenty-five-ish, and he is cute. Not handsome like Sutton, but he makes me feel shy when he looks at me. His name is Wes—short for Wesley, and he has strong arms with naked lady tattoos on them.

Anyway, the thing that happened in communications group, was that he and I were asked to role-play. The situation was about some kind of conflict at a gas station—I honestly don't even remember what—and he told me I was beautiful.

The word literally took root and bloomed somewhere deep in my belly. It also made me feel warm inside, between the legs. Right now, I want to talk to my friends about it, but I can't find Matty, and Lyla and Veronica are petitioning the staff for some sort of cross-stitch craft. I'd even talk to Tracy right now, except she's chatting-up the same guy that left the flower blooming in my stomach. *Wes. Wes-ley. The cute guy who thinks I'm beautiful.*

I guess I have to go to my session with Sutton before I discuss the new guy with my friends. I'll need to be careful what I say in front of

Tracy, though, because she looked all giggly and starry-eyed when she was talking to *Wessss*-ley.

"Hi," Sutton says as I glide in and sit down. He sees my smile, but he approaches it more like the pin on a grenade. Not that I never smile; in fact, I find myself smiling at him a lot these last couple of months, but he must sense something about this particular grin because he looks at me with a big question mark on his face. He also looks really sexy the way his hair is still a little wet from his shower.

"Did…did—you shower here?" I ask, my pulse picking up a bit.

"No, I always shower at the gym before work. How are you feeling today?" He is not referring to my dopy grin. I've been through this line of questioning daily since they adjusted my medication. He is purely interested in my state of mind as it applies to the change.

"I feel good. The ringing in my ears is completely gone. I don't notice my mouth being so dry anymore. I have a ton of energy…"

"Any new feelings or symptoms?"

"Uhhhhh, yeah. I mean, sort of." Oh, man, my cheeks are getting hot. I know he is my doctor, but this might be too embarrassing to mention. "Actually, never mind. Everything is fine," I say as I quickly dismiss my line of thought.

He continues to stare, and it makes me uncomfortable, so I picture him at the gym in the shower—head tipped back, rinsing out the shampoo, the water running down his chest and—

"*Mercy*?" his voice sounds low and a little demanding. "That's not how this works. I need you to be completely upfront with me about everything, no matter how small or insignificant you think it might be. I've made some substantial changes to your treatment regimen, and I want to stay on top of everything."

"You're so dramatic. It's not a big deal, and it's probably not even related to my med change."

"Lay it on me," he says. Everything out of his mouth sounds so sexual, he wants to *stay on top of things*, he wants me to *lay it on him*... damn-it, now I'm sweating.

"I just get this weird feeling deep in my stomach sometimes. Actually, more like my pelvis...my, like, low pelvis." I can't even make eye contact with him; it's so awkward to talk about.

"Weird how?"

"It's just a funny sensation between my legs."

"Okay."

"And it...the feeling—it makes my vagina wet." *Jesus-God-fuck, well...there it is.*

"Does it happen when you touch yourself? Or all the time?" he asks, completely tuned in. Dang-it, now I've hooked him, and he will never drop it.

"Definitely when I touch myself," *Oh, hell, I just admitted to my doctor that I masturbate.*

"It's okay, you don't need to be embarrassed, Mercy. Most people masturbate. It's perfectly natural."

"Do you, Sutton?"

"It's not exactly appropriate for me to discuss my masturbatory habits with a patient, Mercy."

"So, you have masturbatory habits, then?"

"None that I can talk about."

"Well then, how do you expect me to feel comfortable talking about mine?"

"I'm your doctor."

"I don't care. All these weird feelings and sensations are new to me. It's not like I have a mom I can talk about it with—My mom left out the puberty and sexual tingles part when she dropped me like a hot sack of shit. So, all this is a little unexpected and scary for me! Do you know I can feel my nipples throb? What the hell is that?"

"That's a perfectly normal sexual response. So is your vagina getting wet." After he answers, I swear I can see his nostrils flare a little. There seems to be a new energy in the room now, but I can't tell if it's reserved...or savage.

"Why, though? Why all of a sudden?"

"It probably has a lot to do with being off the antipsychotics. Decreased sex drive is a very common side effect of the medication." I can actually see him breathing. His measured inhales, his chest inflating—his breaths seem stiff and calculated instead of natural and effortless.

"It wasn't decreased. It was nonexistent. I was at a zero, now I'm at a thousand...I'd really feel more comfortable around, say...two hundred."

"You've never felt any sexual feelings before at all?"

"Nope. Nada."

"Maybe you should run with it. I understand it might be disconcerting at first, but you are almost 21. A healthy sex drive is amazing."

"I don't think it's healthy."

"Now, that's a different story. What do you mean by that, specifically?"

"Specifically? Like what do I think about when I rub myself? Is that what you are asking?... I think about you quite a bit—"

"I mean, are your thoughts immoral or deprav—Wait, **WHAT?**"

"Sorry, I didn't exactly mean to divulge that information. But, to answer your question, my thoughts are not immoral unless you consider picturing my psychiatrist naked in the shower to be immoral or depraved. Do you?" Sutton is very uncomfortable right now; he is shifting all over the place and stammering way too much.

"No, no, it's not immoral or depraved on your end." Now he is running his fingers through his hair and looking anywhere but at me. "It would be immoral of *me* to *act* on that because I'm your doctor. The thing is, Mercy, it's actually common for a patient to develop feelings for their doctor. The problem is that a patient's judgment is often clouded because they are getting help from that person, they are feeling better, and they associate those feelings as sexual or loving. It's called transference. There is a word for it because it is so common."

"I don't know about all that because Wes makes my nipples hard too, and he is most certainly not my doctor. Is that transference? If another patient thinks you are beautiful, and you wonder what it would feel like to kiss him and have his fingers between your legs? You know, see if *he* likes how wet you are?" I boldly refuse to look away from Sutton's discomfort. Transference, my ass. If he had any idea where he falls in my dirty thoughts, I'm pretty sure he would forget he's my doctor.

Okay, I admit, that was a lot to throw at Sutton, but I didn't like the way he couldn't look at me. Just because he consumes my thoughts does not mean I will fall apart if he doesn't return the sentiment. Although, it feels like sometimes he does return it.

Truth be told, I feel a little rejected by him right now. I don't like this feeling, so I'm kind of scrambling to get away from it by lashing out.

"Mercy, please don't."

"Please don't, *what*?"

"Please do not get involved with Wes."

"Sutton, you will be done with me in a few months and can wash your hands of all my pesky *transference*. As far as other men? You don't get to dictate that."

"Mercy, please. That is a bad idea on many levels."

"Are we done here?"

"Not even close."

"Well, I'm done. I'll see you tomorrow."

It's rec time, so I beat a path straight to my friends. Apparently, I'm moving pretty fast, too, because Matty announces that I'm "Comin' in hot!" I dive into a little ball on the couch next to Lyla.

"What's going on, Mercy?" she asks.

"I don't know, I'm all over the place. I think I just had a fight with Sutton. I'm pretty sure I told him I think about him naked when I touch myself, and I *know* I threw Wes in his face to see if I could make him jealous. I'm a complete mess." Then I sit up and wipe the hair out of my face, "And Wes told me I'm beautiful."

"Umm, yeah, the whole group heard that little nugget. We should start there, right? Or do we need to start with Sutton's nakedness?" Lyla asks with a cute little smirk.

"NO WAY! We will not start with *either* of those. Did y'all miss the biggest announcement of all?" Matty exclaims, scandalized. All three sets of our eyes land on Matty's because none of us know what he is talking about.

"Our little fledgling has learned to fly." He looks excited and like he is perched on the edge of something. Still, we all just stare at him.

"Mercy is finally touching herself! Did y'all miss that? Jesus, if I had a vagina, I'd never take my hands off of it. Wait. Was that an overshare?"

"You guys, for real. I'm mostly off my meds, and I swear to God I want to hump everything on the unit."

"Nobody says *hump* anymore, Mercy," Veronica says with laughing eyes. "Hold on, because there are a number of things we will need to address if she is going to finally start liking guys."

"Wait, like what?" I ask.

"I mean, has anyone ever had the sex talk with you? Have you thought about birth control?" Veronica asks as she shoves up her sleeves.

"I know about the mechanics of sex, and I'm a long way from needing birth control. Don't get ahead of yourselves here."

"I agree. We should ease into all that big stuff. How about we start with your eyebrows…and, I'm sure—" Matty's eyes dart down to my crotch and bounce back to my eyes a few times before Lyla tips over into my lap, laughing.

"What?" I ask. Now they are all laughing. "What did I miss?"

***

Matty has convinced a day nurse to allow him to tweeze my eyebrows—as long as we do it right here, by the nurse's station. So, that's what he is doing—ripping hair out of my face. Everyone loves Matty, so he is rarely refused anything. Well, that's not entirely true, he has to use an electric razor, flimsy rubber bands for his braids, and the staff has to stand there and watch him floss his teeth—lest he hang himself with the string.

"Colleen? You know you're my favorite, right?" Matty's voice is a touch higher than normal, so I know he is angling for something from the nurse.

"Matty, I'm er'ones favorite when they want something from me. What can I do for you?"

"I was just thinking, my birthday is coming up, and Mercy here has had, what, a dozen birthdays here?"

"What are you getting at, Matty?"

"I want a day trip to the hair salon."

"I can arrange for someone to come to the unit, Matty. You know that."

"What if Sutt-I-mean-*Doctor* Sutton signs off on it?"

"Matty, this isn't elementary school. We don't go on field trips."

"You're right," he says dejected, as he drops his head. "Why should we get to feel special on our birthday—we're just a bunch of throwaway mental patients."

"**Matthew Edward Hopkins!** Don't you dare tell me you are a bunch of throwaways! There is not a darn thing wrong with any one of you! God made you special, the same way he made me chocolate, and we all get to use our uniqueness for His glory. Do you understand me? Don't nobody get to mope around here, we pick ourselves up, and we try to make the world a better place every day....*talkin bout bein a throwaway*...don't even get me started, Matty Hopkins!"

At first, I was stunned by the tirade, but then I realized she walked right into Matty's trap. Colleen is always telling us we are perfect and made in God's image, and she doesn't let us get away with being down on ourselves. Matty is manipulating the situation, but *day-uum*, he's good at it. He deserves an Oscar because his hangdog look is on point.

"Now, you two listen here. I will *talk* to Dr. Sutton, but that is as far as I am willing to go. Do you hear me?"

"Yes, ma'am," Matty says, still working it.

"And you both know that er'body else is gonna want to go on a field trip too."

"We'll tell them we are off to get root canals," Matty offers reasonably.

"No, sir, you will not. Cuz, we both know you gonna come prancing back in here with a weave and fancy makeup."

This, he smiles at, but he still doesn't look up at her. To be honest, I don't even think his birthday is coming up. Anyway, who knows if Sutton will even sign off on it. Although he *did* take me to the top of a mountain.

Colleen and the rest of the staff go about their work, evidently resigned to the fact that Matty is wielding some tweezers, and no longer at risk of jamming them in his eye or slitting his wrists with them. He is still plucking the shit out of my eyebrows, but we are mostly alone now.

"Matty, if Sutton says yes, you aren't going to cut your hair, are you?" I know how much he loves his hair. In fact, he takes better care of himself and takes more pride in his looks than any of us.

My hair is long, just past my bra-strap, but the most I ever do with it is sleep in two French braids, so it's wavy the next day. I was lucky not to get all the acne the other teenagers did in the juvenile unit, but it's probably because I never wore makeup back then. Now, Matty does our makeup all the time just for fun.

"Of course not, didn't you hear Colleen? I'm getting a weave." All of a sudden, with no thought whatsoever, I broach the subject.

"Do you sometimes wish you were born a girl?"

He stops plucking, but he leaves his arms up and doesn't look away from my eye contact. Part of me wants to take the tweezers and shove them in my own eye just to distract him from my question, but he surprises me when he answers.

"Every day."

His answer stuns me. Not because I haven't thought so for a long time, but because I never thought he would admit it. I recover quickly.

"Then, I think you *should* get a weave."

"You know I can't. There isn't a place in the world for people like me," he mumbles quietly, making my jaw drop open.

"Then, you need to make one."

"I wish it was that easy, Mercy."

"I know it's not. I'm sorry the world isn't ready for your awesomeness."

"Maybe someday."

"Have you ever told anyone about feeling that way?"

"I talk about it with Sutton but never with Sig, and I've never told anyone else." My heart swells at the idea of Sutton making that kind of a breakthrough with Matty. He might be just what this unit needed.

"When we live together, we will do our makeup and play dress-up all day. You can be whoever you want to, Matty, and someday you won't have to hide who you are."

"Okay, but guurl! You need to stay on top of these eyebrows!" We both laugh, and then I risk a tweezer in the eye to pull him into a tight hug.

"I love you, Matty Hopkins."

He kisses my head, "I love you more, Mercy Kavanaugh."

"**MATTY!** You done with those tweezers yet?"

"Ugh, the forbidden embrace," he scowls and pulls away before calling over his shoulder, "*Not just yet, Ma'am.*"

***

Colleen comes into my room right before shift change, which is unusual. Lyla is brushing her teeth and getting ready for bed, so we are mostly alone.

"Mercy, you know Dr. Sutton can't sign Matty off the unit. If things were different, if Matty's case were different, then maybe."

"I know."

"I did speak with the doctor, and it's different for you because there is a transition plan in place. We all want you to be successful when you leave here. That's why Dr. Sutton has all that stuff planned for you off the unit."

"What stuff?" I perk up. I'd even climb that mountain again if it meant I could lay in his lap and have him stroke my hair again.

"You haven't talked about your transition with him?" she asks, surprised.

"Ad nauseam. But nothing about being off the unit."

"He didn't talk about life skills classes? Cooking, driving, paying bills? Nothing like that?"

"He did but, I guess I never—I didn't really think about that stuff being off the unit."

"*Girl*, you know Dr. Sigmund would have kept you under his wing forever. But Dr. Sutton wants to see you fly."

"I know," my words catch in my throat. I am developing intense feelings for him, and it has not one damn thing to do with transference.

"Now, about Matty. We all know how special he is, so I'd like to do something for his birthday. Lord knows this unit could use a little fun. Never mind that that boy's birthday was five months ago. He deserves the world, and I want to give it to him."

"What do you have in mind?"

"A slumber party."

"He can't sleep on the women's unit, and we can't sleep on his."

"Nobody said nothing about sleep. I'm talking about facial masks, nail polish, deep conditioning treatments—all that girly stuff. We'll do it on Monday night when all those silly men feel the need to holler at the TV and beat their chests every time someone scores a touchdown. What do you think? Dr. Sutton already gave me his stamp of approval."

"What do I think? I think I'd like to take you with me when I leave."

"Oh, Mercy, you know how much I love you all. You deserve the best the Lord has to offer." Then she hugs me tight—like, way tighter than normal.

Chapter 13

The next day, when I walk into Sutton's office, he surprises me by standing up from his desk, shoving both hands into his pants pockets, and asking me if I'm ready.

"Ready for what?"

"Your hair appointment at the salon. Matty was very specific."

"*You* are taking me to the hair salon?"

"Yeah, normally, a tech would take you, but alas, one was not available. We only have an hour, so let's hit it."

"But why are you taking me?"

"I'm multi-tasking. This is our session today," he says as he holds the door open for me. I like the outside of work Sutton, this will be fun.

Once we are in his truck and on our way, he asks, "Are there any developments on the Wesley front?"

"Developments like what?" I look over at his profile and wonder if he might be a tiny bit jealous. "He hangs out with us and smiles at me a lot. And he's told me I'm beautiful a few times."

"Are you attracted to him?"

"Of course, me and half the unit. He is cute, and maybe a little bit of a bad boy, all tatted up."

"I want to caution you again about him," he says with authority, while also holding back.

"Why? Is he a bad person?"

"You know I can't talk about another patient with you. I'm just saying you both should be focused on your mental health, not a temporary crush."

"You said it yourself, I'm almost twenty-one, a healthy sex drive is good for me."

"That doesn't mean you should jump on the first guy who calls you beautiful."

"What makes you think I'm jumping on him?" I ask, and if I'm completely honest, it's kind of fun stoking his apparent jealousy. It makes me feel better about the whole transference rebuke.

"I didn't mean jumping on him—"

"Because it would be more like *bouncing*, wouldn't it?" I ask as I bounce up and down in the seat a few times. I have no idea how to have sex, but that's what I'm trying to simulate. Sutton's jaw drops, and he openly stares at me while he should be watching the road.

A few quiet minutes go by before he speaks again, "Please promise me you will have high standards when it comes to men. There is a whole sea of men that will want to sleep with you, but only a tiny fraction of them will be worthy of you."

***

When Matty, Lyla, and Veronica told me I needed to *tend the garden*, I thought they had a razor in mind. I suppose being on a unit where only electric razors are used; I should have known.

For anyone who has never felt the white-hot pain of having your nether region waxed, allow me to explain. Imagine peeling your vagina skin off, and, well, that's it. It's raw and blisteringly painful, and I think I'd rather put my fist through a cheese grater.

When Sutton picks me up, with exactly the same hair, and an additional sheen of sweat covering my body, all I can say to him is, "You were right, Matty was very specific."

"Did you decide not to have your hair done?"

"Trust me when I say, I absolutely had my hair done."

"They decided they couldn't mess with perfection, right?" he smiles and reaches up to run his fingers through my hair, then stops short and settles for tucking a lock of it behind my ear. He has absolutely no idea of the horror I just experienced, but he *did* have to stop himself from touching me—so, that almost makes it all worth it.

"Depends on your idea of perfection, Sutton. Tell me, do you prefer a pre-pubescent vagina?" He stops the truck just before pulling out of the parking lot and gives me a pointed stare.

"What are we talking about here, Mercy?"

"Vaginas. Do men prefer them bare? Or natural?"

"I can't speak for all men, but—How did we get on the topic of vaginas, exactly?"

"I've been on the topic for thirty minutes, and trust me, I bear the battle wounds."

"What the hell went on in there?"

"It's better you don't know."

"Apparently so. Hey, I'm going to stop for coffee, you want one?"

***

Back at the unit, I'm just in time for art. Today, we are shaving crayons and placing the flakes between wax paper. When we have the shavings all placed like we want them, the staff comes around and irons over the top of it, melting the design together. It would be fun, except my friends can't stop giggling about my hair salon ambush.

I wish they would shut up too because Wes is sitting next to me— he saved me a seat, actually. The first time he brushed his hand against my leg, I thought it was an accident. The residual path of his touch blazed hot on my thigh and sent a reminder to my brain about the newly awakened state of my sexuality.

The second time he did it, was no accident. He waited for me to object to the placement of his hand, and when I didn't, his fingers crawled closer to the inside of my thigh. The fact that he is two seconds away from sliding his hand inside the leg of my shorts has my insides fluttering like crazy.

"Wes."

"What?"

"Get your hand off of me."

He pulls it away with a mumbled apology and then makes small talk about how our art should be used as the next Rorschach ink-blot tests. My body is aching to be touched, I even briefly consider putting his hand back on my thigh, but it's not him that I want touching me.

The thought of someone, *namely Sutton*, touching my freshly bare skin with his fingers makes my whole body heat up and dampens my panties. I don't know if it has anything to do with the newly experienced smoothness down below, but I am buzzing with something intensely provocative.

"I just didn't want you to get in trouble, that's all," I lie. "We are not supposed to touch here."

"What if that's all I think about?" he asks, leaning in slightly to make sure I am the only one to hear him.

"All you think about is touching me?"

"Not just touching," he whispers.

"What else?" I ask. I'm probably going to go to hell for this, but his words mesmerize me, and I want to hear more. Even though he is not who I want to hear them from, I want to know what a man fantasizes about.

"Where should I start? First of all, I got hard when I heard you had your pussy waxed." I gasp at his crude language, and only after that do I glare over at my friends.

"That made you hard?" I whisper back. It must not take much to get an erection.

"It made me want to crawl between your thighs and lick your pussy until your legs shake." I freeze for a second. One, that sounds gross, why would he want to do that? And two, he said pussy twice inside of one minute.

"Hey, Lovebirds! What are you two whispering about?" Tracy asks—or sings, whatever. There is also a sharpness to her question and a fire in her eyes that reminds me of her little crush on Wes. Well, she can have him—because I'm setting my sights higher.

I want Sutton to think of me and get hard like Wes does. And when I think of Sutton licking me down there, I damn near pass out. That particular thought, no matter how disgusting it sounded at first, is going to be my masturbatory fodder for months to come—if not years.

"We were just talking about how Mercy's melted crayons ended up looking like a sunflower. Don't you think? Let's see yours, Tracy." He smiles back at me and then gives his full attention to the rest of the group.

***

For now, Lyla and I still share a room because there is not another available bed on the unit. Before her Benzos drag her under, I want to talk. I have so many questions, I don't even know where to start.

"Lyla, if you wanted to make a guy's penis hard, what would you do?" I ask in a whisper. She flips over and looks at me through the dark. She has tried to talk to me about this kind of stuff for months, it's only now that I'm interested.

"What would I do? I'd probably dress sexy and talk dirty. Why, my little apprentice?"

"I can't stop thinking about Sutton. I want him to touch me and do things to me, but I can't be sure he is attracted to me."

"Are you crazy? All men are attracted to you."

"I've never even seen a penis in real life, let alone an erect one."

"Mercy, repeat after me."

"Okay."

"Cock, dick, pecker, knob, Johnson, boner, chub, hard-on." Instead of repeating her words, I laugh into my pillow.

"Nobody says penis or vagina or erection—they say cock, pussy, and wood. You can't be so technical if you ever want someone to fuck you. Plus, Wes would be more than willing to show you his dick in any state."

"I like Wes, but he is not who I want to be with."

"I think he'd be okay teaching you a few things with no strings attached," she snorts. "As far as Sutton goes, he may want to have you for breakfast, lunch, and dinner, but he will never act on it because it's taboo, he's your doctor."

"I don't want him to be my doctor. I want him to teach me everything there is to know about se—I mean, fucking."

"Then, you will have to appeal to him as a man, not as your doctor."

"How?"

"Just like I said, dress sexy and talk dirty. You should wear a short skirt to your session tomorrow and skip the panties."

"I could never do that."

"You couldn't flash him your pussy, but you want him to stick his giant cock in it?"

"LADIES, GOODNIGHT!" one of the night nurses hisses into our room.

"You should at least let Wes finger you," she whispers.

"Oh my God, stop talking about Wes."

"Let's see what Matty and V think tomorrow, but Wes is hot…and Sutton is unattainable. Every woman in this hospital wants to bang Sutton. He is used to batting women away like flies, don't torture yourself."

Chapter 14

When I get to Sutton's office for my session, I plop down onto the couch. Sutton tosses me a bag of cinnamon candies and then walks around his desk and sits down next to me. He hasn't been consistent with the candy, in fact, it's been a while since he had them at all. This small detail has me worried.

"Hey, how are you feeling?" his voice sounds pained. Now I am definitely on high alert.

"Fine. What's going on?"

"I want to ask you about something that has never been noted in your charts over here, either juvenile or adult."

"You are scaring me, and you look like you are about to break open—just tell me what's going on."

"Mercy, were you ever sexually abused as a child?" He looks like he wants to scoop me up and rock me to sleep. What the heck?

"Of course not! Remember? Demonic possession, paranoid schizophrenia…that's plenty to work with, right? Plus, you keep going on and on about my parents being victims too—now you think they sexually abused me? Why do you assume that?"

"I've been looking over some of your medical files from St. Vincent's and noticed something that doesn't sit well with me. It's just that, you were awfully young to present with an absence of hymenal tissue."

"I hope my future husband won't be disappointed, the ole hymen is quite a prize, right doc?"

"You don't recall any type of sexual abuse at all?"

"No."

"Then, I have another question. Are you open to trying hypnosis?" He gently places his palm on my thigh before evidently getting burned by my flesh and yanking his hand back.

"To, like...relax? We already have a group for guided meditation, why do you want to hypnotize me?"

"I wouldn't do it, I know my strengths, and that's not one of them. I would have a colleague of mine step in—but only if you are open to it. It's helpful because it can sometimes help with repressed memories or help flush out specific traumatic events."

"Sounds pretty soul-baring."

"It can be."

"Why am I the only one bearing my soul?"

"Because you are my patient."

"What if I want to be your friend too?"

He smiles broadly, and some of the tightness in his face melts away before he says, "I absolutely consider you my friend."

"Then, I'll try hypnosis, but I'm going to need you to open up to me a little too."

"Mercy, that's not—"

"Okay, we can skip the hypnosis then. I'm not a carnival exhibit, and if this little *friendship* only goes one way, then I'm out. I have a lot to learn about men before I'm sprung from this joint, and it would be cruel to ask Matty...so I'd like to ask you. But if you are not comfortable with that, I'll ask Wes, he sure is willing enough."

"First, why do you bring up Wes all the time?"

"Because Wes awakens a lot of curiosities that I have, and lately, I've been feeling awfully naive when it comes to my sexuality." I don't mention that *he* awakens the lion's share of my curiosities, but I need to feel him out a little more. Lyla is right, he does have to bat women away—I've seen him do it, but even with the whole transference thing, I've never gotten the sense that he is batting me away.

My friends speak of him as though he were a consummate professional. He has never touched any of them, and he doesn't get jealous if they talk about Wes. If I really think about it—which I do, a lot, he is very different with me.

"I will absolutely help you with those curiosities, and try to assist you while you navigate the field of your sexuality, but I have to be careful not to cross the line."

"Then **tell me** when you feel like you are approaching that line, instead of dismissing me altogether, before I've even opened my mouth."

"I'm sorry. You are right. We can talk about anything you want as long as I can tell you when I'm afraid to cross the line," he says with a sigh of acceptance, as though he were caught in a spider's web and getting more stuck the more he struggles.

"That's better. Now, tell me about hard-ons. What makes you get one? How long does it last? What does it feel like? All that stuff." My transition is not a smooth one, but this is part of me feeling him out—figuratively. I want to see how far off track he will go with me.

"I feel like I should speak generally here, and not as though I am answering for myself as a guy, but here goes. In order for a man to make love to a woman, his penis needs to be hard—"

"I know all that, skip to the good stuff."

"It's all good stuff, Mercy," he says through a hundred-watt grin.

"What makes you get one? What do you think about when you have one? How do you get rid of it?"

"Again, speaking generally here, a guy typically gets several erections a day...often more. They can be from seeing something or someone they find sexy, or thinking about something sexy—"

"What would be an example of something sexy you would think about?"

"An example would be thinking about someone doing something sexual to you. Or thinking about doing something sexual to someone else."

"Kissing?"

"Sure."

"Looking at or touching breasts?"

"Yes, both."

"What about licking someone's...clitoris?" I cringe.

"Yes, that would do it too."

"What is the male equivalent? Someone licking your dick?" I purposely ask about *his* dick, not just any guy's dick.

"Licking it, putting it in their mouth, sucking it—"

"Do guys like that?"

"Yes, very much. It feels good, the same as having your clitoris licked." Oh crap, he did the same thing. He said *your* clitoris, not *someone's* clitoris.

"Wes told me he wanted to do that to me."

"Wes better keep his tongue inside of his bold mouth."

"Would that bother you if Wes licked me down there?"

"Yes, quite a bit."

"Why? Because he is a fellow patient or because you don't want anyone to do that to me."

"Both."

"You said it feels good, why wouldn't you want me to experience that?"

"I don't want just anyone to have you like that."

"That's mean, Sutton."

"It's not mean—maybe selfish, but not mean."

"Do you know I'm almost twenty-one, and I've never been kissed?"

"That does not mean you should give that part of yourself lightly." He is so open and honest; it's encouraging me to push him even harder.

"Have you ever thought about kissing me?"

"As your doctor? No. As a man? Yes. But my official answer to that question is, no, you are my patient."

"What about someday when I'm not your patient?"

"I've actually thought about that a lot. The thing is, I don't trust anyone else with your care. You were grossly mismanaged from the start, and I can't bear the thought of someone else taking over."

"Are you attracted to me?"

"Yes."

"Have I ever made your dick hard?"

"As your doctor, no."

"As a man?"

"Yes."

***

I can't get to my friends fast enough. There is so much to talk about, and I feel like I need to spit it all out now, before the songbird, Tracy comes over. She is straddling the friendship group, half in and half out, but I don't trust her with this Sutton stuff—especially because she feels some sort of way about Wes' little crush on me.

Matty, Lyla, and Veronica listen to me spill my guts with their forgotten books left open on their laps and their mouths left open to catch flies. When I finish, there is a collective gasp, and then, like mice scurrying after crumbs, they all start talking at once.

Lyla suggests a code name, so we can speak sort of freely about it, and it's Veronica that dubs the Sutton situation *Bedlam*. But if you ask me, that doesn't sound very covert or stealthy. If anything, it's going to raise suspicions, but whatever.

Everyone has an opinion about how I should play it, ranging from ignoring Sutton and sitting on Wes' face, to an all-out offensive assault on Sutton.

Matty says jealousy is the fastest way to get to him. Lyla and Veronica insist I take the route of straight-up vixen. I myself, have issues with both. Namely, because I don't want to use Wes, and I can absolutely not conceive of being any bolder with Sutton than I already have been. Seriously, just using the terms *dick* and *hard-on* almost turned me into a slab of virgin stone.

"Guys, let's not forget that my meds kept all these feelings at bay until now. I can't go from throwing up in my mouth at the thought of being naked with a guy to suddenly becoming a harlot. Is that an acceptable term, harlot?"

"You don't have to be a harlot for Wes, and he can drive the ship. You can sit back and be all pure and virginal," Matty explains.

"You don't have to be a harlot for Sutton either, in fact, playing it coy and subtle will work better anyway," Lyla states, directly to Matty.

"How about that? A little reverse psychology on the doctor himself. Seriously, you need to approach it as your sweet, innocent self—but with a hearty dose of sex kitten. We'll coach you. It will be perfect." Veronica may be grossly overestimating my sex kitten proficiency, but she makes up for it with confidence in her coaching abilities.

"I can't get away from my innocence, that is a fact, and I'm sure Sutton wants a woman—not a girl."

"Don't worry, Mercy, we will be playing up the fact that you are a woman, and he's already shown interest, so trust me." Lyla's confidence is at a level ten, as well. "First things first though, no more dowdy sweatshirts and workout pants."

"What about my scrubs?"

"Nope."

"So, I can't be comfortable anymore?"

"Absolutely not. Do you think women wear high heels and thong underwear because they are comfortable?"

"I've got to get to my session with my shrink" Matty says as he rises from the couch, slightly distressed at missing the rest of the conversation, and heads to Sutton's office. Within a minute, Wes notices the seat vacancy and saunters over.

"Hey, Mercy. Want to join me in a rousing game of checkers?"

"As a matter of fact, I do," I say as I decide to pepper in a little of Matty's advice too. I can be friends with Wes, and if Sutton gets a little jealous, then that's just fine.

The two of us make our way to the game table under the watchful eye of Tracy. She is developing some angry feelings toward me and has not been hanging out with us much. I would like to convey to her that I am not interested in Wes besides looking at him, but I'm not sure it would temper her dislike of me.

"What do you think of Tracy?" I ask. Maybe if he is interested in her as a backup option, I can point him in her direction.

"I think I'd like her better with a gag in her mouth. Why do you ask?"

"She likes you."

"Oh, I know. Problem is, I don't care."

"You are not interested in her at least a little bit?"

"No, I'm not. Did you miss the memo? I'm interested in you," he says pointedly. Dang, I'm not used to someone being so forward...or so interested.

"So, here's the thing about that. I think you are completely charming and good-looking, but I'm a little hung-up on someone on the outside. I feel like I should just throw that out there."

"Doesn't mean we can't hang out in here."

"I'm not saying we can't hang out, I just want to be honest with you," I explain. He gives me a wolfish grin in response.

"And I appreciate that," he says as he jumps two of my checkers. Somehow, the way he says it doesn't really convey his appreciation. It's more like he will take it under advisement.

"Are you going to watch the football game on Monday night?" I ask as I slide my checker, and immediately get jumped by his. Damn, I need to start paying attention.

"I haven't thought about it, are you?"

"No, we are throwing Matty a birthday party—he doesn't know, so don't say anything."

"Will there be birthday cake?"

"I kinda doubt it."

"What about pie? I'd love to eat some cherry pie." He doesn't take his eyes off mine as he slides a checker into place. "King me, Cherry."

"Why do I get the impression you are not talking about dessert?"

"Because I'm not."

"Okay, weirdo. So, are you coming to the party? Or watching lame football with the dudes?"

"Oh, I'm coming to the party," he says assertively, then adds, "Listen, if I could score a birthday cake, would you do something for me?"

"Does it involve touching your penis?"

He drops his chin to his chest and gives a sort of snort-laugh. "No, but I wouldn't turn you down."

"What would I have to do?"

"How about, skip wearing panties for the party?"

"Now, *you* missed the memo."

"I'm not sayin' you have to show me or anything. I just think it would be really sexy. And my sister bakes a mean birthday cake."

"I'll think about it. King me."

***

After a horrible loss at checkers and nearly a whole puzzle, I've decided that Wes is a great guy. Not my guy, but a great one. It turns out he was the passenger in a drunk driving accident that killed a young mother. He struggles with it because he fed his buddy shots all night before getting in the car with him. That's a lot to have on your conscience.

He is here voluntarily, which I told him is a good place to start, but I don't have any words of wisdom for him—even after clocking all kinds of time here myself.

He should talk to Colleen. Even though she doesn't run any of the groups, she has a way with words. Plus, she backs everything up with God's weigh-in, so her nuggets of wisdom are all the more powerful. Colleen would tell him that he can't change the past but, he can choose to move forward and make a positive impact on the world every day. I think that's where he should focus his energy, and I told him as much.

Chapter 15

On Monday, Wes certainly delivers on the cake. It's a two-tier creation that may or may not have originally been for a little girl's Frozen birthday party. It's blue and glittery and dusted with shredded coconut made to look like snow. There is also an Elsa cake-topper suspiciously close to the cake, but no longer on top of it.

The staff, no doubt encouraged by Colleen, has also delivered. They have supplied a cucumber facial mask, a manicure set, some hair chalk designed to make bright pink and blue streaks in your hair, and some scented lotions. Let's not forget the men, they will be distracted from the concurrent festivities with popcorn and orange Fanta. That seems fair enough.

I have heard that Sutton will be in attendance this evening, as well. Which is unusual because he will stay late now and then, and he is always on call for when I suffer in the night, but a full evening basking in his glow sounds pretty amazing. I don't know where he plans to ally himself, with the guys or us, but I have been sucking on nervous excitement all day.

In case you are wondering, I haven't decided about the panties—or the lack of panties, I should say. Wes' sister brought the cake to visiting hours, and in a way that obligates me to go without. However, I never fully committed to the trade-off, I merely said I would think about it.

I don't want to give Wes the wrong idea, but if I'm honest, he has loosened up a bit since I told him I am interested in someone else. He has respected the boundary and now sits aptly in the friend zone.

Since I've admitted to my friends that I'm hot for Sutton and spoken my secret to the universe, the wheels of fate have been in motion. On the advice of my friends, I have presented myself, not as a vulnerable patient, but as a sexual being. I've seen Sutton put aside his doctor persona more and more, but damn-it, he still feels a responsibility to me as his patient. His morals have been tested, but they haven't exactly wavered.

There are times that I zone out when he is talking and hone in on his lips. I'm endlessly curious about what it would be like to be kissed by him, and I feel an almost primal need to be touched and explored by his mouth and hands.

I've been staring at the same paragraph in my book for thirty minutes when Matty plops down next to me. He has just come from his session with Sutton, so there are a million ways our conversation might go.

"I heard it's my birthday today."

"Yeah, one for the record books, apparently."

"V said Sutton will be in attendance. You know what that means, right?" he asks as he conspiratorially scooches closer to me so he can keep our conversation quiet and just between us.

"That he will get overtime? What the heck are you saying?"

"Just that he won't be here in a professional capacity. Do you think he gives a shit about watching Monday night football with all these clowns? He will be here casually, so it will be a perfect time to flirt with him."

"Matty, I don't know how to flirt," I hiss, more in fear than anything.

"Lord have mercy, MERCY. You really are a baby deer, aren't you?"

"I prefer the term, novice, but I'm a quick learner, so hurry up."

"All I want you to worry about for tonight is looking hot—don't worry, I got you. And you need to smile at him no less than five separate times. There is an art to it though, you need to let him catch you staring at him. Then you smile and turn away shyly...but only briefly! Then you look back and do it again. After an hour or so of that, you let him catch you looking at him, but you don't look away, you *wink* at him."

"Matty! That's bush league, I flirt more than that in my sessions with him."

"I know, but asking about his cock-stands is too overt. I'm saying you need to appeal to the predator in him, he is stalking you right now. As soon as you look vulnerable, you will start running—and he will chase you down. Got it?"

"And you don't think winking at him is too overt?"

"Not at all, it's playful...and it sets a trap that he can't help but walk into. Plus, remember, he won't be here as your doctor. Now, where are we with Wes? I heard Lyla talking to him about breaking you in a little, here and there."

"WHAT?"

"Shhhh, I didn't say you had to serve him up your V-card, just shake off a little chastity, maybe learn how to kiss with your tongue."

"Lyla asked him to *break me in* here and there? What was she thinking?"

"Her heart is in a good place. Listen, this might be hard to hear, but you need to understand that it's not all that attractive to be a girl when Sutton wants a woman."

Matty's words scorch themselves across my brain and leave a charred path in their wake. I have never thought about the fact that Sutton most likely will not want to teach me everything from the ground up. There is truth to Matty's words. I am a girl, and Sutton most certainly wants a woman.

***

While we are all in daily reflection group, the nursing staff makes an attempt to decorate for Matty's *birthday party*. They do the best they can within the parameters of the hospital, which means, no latex balloons, no ribbons to hang ourselves with, and no banners—for the same reason.

They have utilized a single roll of crepe paper streamers, and in order to maximize the effect, they have only placed them over our little area of couches by the windows, where we read and gossip about Sutton.

Speaking of Sutton, he is not here yet, but my friends have done my hair and makeup, and Lyla has dressed me like her own personal doll. Which translates to me breaking about five different dress codes *and* calling all kinds of attention to it from the ten pounds of makeup Matty dipped me in.

We don't actually *have* mirrors on the unit, but we have these metal-like trays above our sinks that serve as mirrors. So, besides feeling like my face cannot breathe through the occlusion of spackle and facial contouring, I'm not entirely sure how I look. My hair is fluffier than I like it, but that may be because it's brushed and styled. Usually, I leave my hair wavy and just run my fingers through it because I like it all piece-y and separated—not beaten into submission.

My clothes are one hundred percent Lyla's, even the thong that's currently riding up my ass crack. She decided that I would *feel* sexy wearing a pretty bra and panty set, which would be fine, except that the lace bra is chafing my nipples, and the ass floss will remain wedged inside my crack for the duration of the evening. I'm also wearing a skirt that is too short and revealing for the pale state of my legs and a shirt that feels too small for me because Lyla's skin-tight style is not even in the same zip code as mine.

As ridiculous as the outfit is, it was all sufferable until she demanded I take off my Chucks in favor of her sandals. The shoes are cute, but they don't fit, and I can all but promise you I will trip and leave a lip-skid down the hallway at some point this evening.

Now that it's dark outside and I can see myself in the reflection of the window, I sort of like what I see. I don't so much like the look on *me*, but if I saw someone else that looked like I do, I would think she was pretty.

One of the meatheads watching the game calls out to me from across the room, "Where ya headed, Mercy? You're all dressed up, with no place to go—Well, I've got somewhere for you to be. Why don't you come sit right here next to me?"

"No thanks, short-timer. Your hand down your pants will have to do."

"Maybe my lap would suit you better?" he tries again. I open my mouth to respond, but that's as far as I get.

"Maybe you should shut the fuck up!" Wes yells as he stands up and charges toward him. Two different guys extend their arms and bodies to prevent Wes from getting any closer to the loudmouth.

"What's the matter, puppy? You think defending Mercy will bring back that innocent woman you killed?" Now, no less than five guys stop Wes' launch toward the instigator.

Both Lyla and I are already in motion to retrieve Wes when one of the nurses asks if she needs to turn off the game in favor of the home shopping network. The boys heed the threat and calm right down, and we swoop in and lead Wes by each bicep back over to the estrogen heavy side of the room.

He is ramped up and still has murder in his eyes when we roughly push him toward the spot on the couch next to Veronica.

"Easy, tiger, that jug-head only wants to put the focus on you in order to deflect his own issues. Repeat after me, I will not give him the power to disrupt my recovery," Veronica says as she stiff-arms him into staying put.

He is panting with rage, but he repeats her as well as he can with his teeth clenched, "I will not give him the power to disrupt my recovery."

"Good. Now, say it again."

"I will not give him the power to disrupt my recovery."

"Excellent, now look at Mercy and tell her she looks beautiful."

"Mercy, I'll be jacking off all night thinking of you."

"Awww, you're so sweet," I say before I laugh out loud. I don't think anyone has ever masturbated to thoughts of me before. It's kind of a potent thought. I'm starting to realize I have a tiny bit of power over some men in that way. Too bad it's the wrong one.

"I still might accidentally on purpose pop that douchebag in the jaw," Wes says, only partially distracted by us.

"Revenge is beneath you. How about you try living your best life, and forget all about him? Huh?" Matty says perfectly before he adds, "I appreciate this cucumber face thing, but look at all these synthetic ingredients. I'm not putting this crap on my face."

There is enough nail polish for each of us to have our own, but while Veronica, Lyla, and Matty do their toes, I fumble with the hair chalk because my skirt is too short to put my heel on the seat of my chair like the others.

"I think my hair is too dark for this to show up, want me to give you some pink and blue streaks…or, more like pink and blue tips?" I ask Wes.

"Only if you have to touch me to do it," he says with a smile. We have all accepted this kind of talk as normal for Wes, so it doesn't bother me. He isn't skeevy about it; he is more teasing than anything.

I'm standing in front of Wes, trying to open the tube of hair chalk. In order to be close enough to reach his hair, I'm straddling him. Actually, not— the stance is from more of a distance, and technically, only one of his legs is between mine.

"Wes, this is the perfect opportunity to show Mercy your cock, none of the staff can see you," Lyla says. I jerk my face over to look at her because she did *not* sound like she was kidding.

"You know you want to see it too, Ly," Wes says, completely undisturbed by the suggestion. "What do you think, Mercy? Want to see a dick for the first time?"

"Why am I all of a sudden everyone's pet project?" I ask, avoiding the question entirely. The truth is, I do want to see it. I want to see it soft and hard. A girl should have knowledge of these things.

"You are not a pet project. Think of it more as a survival guide. You don't want to pass out the first time you see one of these hogs, do you?" Wes asks. Matty's words blaze across my mind again, *Sutton wants a woman, not a girl.*

"I'm pretty sure you can't just whip it out right here," I point out, as I squeeze a little sticky, blue chalk onto my fingers.

"I have more finesse than that," he says as he shifts his position a little. I know he is maneuvering himself out of his jeans, so I am suddenly very interested in putting blue chalk on the tips of his hair. That, and my cheeks are blazingly hot, so I don't want to face anyone.

"Mercy, look—I can't stay like this forever, I'm going to get busted," he says, halfway between amusement and general concern about getting caught. I look down. He has it in his hand. It's less aggressive than I thought. Completely non-threatening.

"Okay, I saw it. You can put it away now."

As he tucks himself back in, Veronica asks, "So, what did you think?"

"It looks like the pictures from human anatomy class, but floppier and more circumcised." Everyone chuckles at that. I don't know what I was expecting, but maybe more bells and whistles.

"*Mercy?*" Wes whispers, "Are you wearing panties? My sister brought the cake."

"Kind of. It's a thong, so I'm not sure if that counts."

"I showed you mine, now you show me yours."

"There is no way to do that without getting caught," is what I say, but the part I keep to myself is the, *no fucking way am I showing you mine.*

"How about you let me touch it then?" he asks as his fingers tickle the inside of my thigh. Then, slowly, they make their way higher, and under my skirt. I open my mouth to stop him, but it's someone else's voice I hear.

"**Mercy!**" it's Sutton, and the baritone of his voice trickles down my back and melts in my panties. "Do you have a second? I want to discuss that life skills class we talked about earlier." Wes' hand is long gone, but I let go of his hair in slow motion, before turning around even slower. I'm not sure when Sutton arrived but based on the sharpness of his tone, I'm pretty sure he saw Wes' hand under my skirt.

Matty rumbles the first few notes of Taps under his breath, "*Dun, Dun Dunnn.*" I shoot him a glare and swallow my heart back down my throat.

When I get to the nurse's station, Sutton explains how we have to squeeze all these life skills classes in, or I won't complete them before I leave here. They are the night nurses, and like me, have no idea what he is talking about.

"If we hurry, we will be back in time for cake," he says while casually leaning on the nurse's station. Then he says to one of them, "I don't actually know how long the class is, but since it's an evening one, I'm assuming it's accelerated." Then he looks at me and says, "You should put on some different shoes."

"I wouldn't want to be late for my life skills class, Dr. Sutton. My shoes are fine." My voice wavers a fraction, but only because I can see the fire in his eyes. He can hide it from the nurses behind the concerned doctor veneer, but I can tell he's ready to burn the place down. I don't dare look back at my friends—or at Wes. Purely out of self-preservation, I start walking.

"Where are we going?" I ask as Sutton slams down the elevator button.

"I told you, life skills class." Then he clams up because the doors open, and there are other people on the elevator. I can see his jaw knot up and release in a rhythmic pattern. I know he is pissed, but he won't look at me.

Weirdly enough, we take the elevator to the basement and then step off. He gives me a series of frosty looks as we make our way down the empty hallway, and then a wave of his badge in front of the sensor opens the automatic doors to the bowels of the hospital.

"This is kind of shady, isn't it, Sutton?" I ask. He gives me no sort of reply beyond a grunt and keeps walking down the long corridor.

"Sutton?" I stop walking and cross my arms across my chest the way a defiant teenager would. Standing with one hip popped to the side, I hold my ground as Sutton wheels around and charges back toward me.

"Yes, Mercy?" he asks, his patience holding on by a thread.

"I asked you where we are going. Fume if you must, but at least tell me where we are headed."

"Your life skills curriculum requires you to know how to do laundry before being released. Don't you think you should learn how to wash your clothes?" When he asks this, it sounds smug and hateful, mostly because he has his teeth clenched and looks like he would rather dispose of me through the laundry chute than teach me anything at all about separating lights and darks.

"Yeah, but are you sure the catacombs of the state hospital are the appropriate place to learn such things?"

"Let's go, Mercy. You are not in a position to be too choosy at this point," he says as he grabs my elbow and encourages me to start walking again. This hallway is exactly what you picture when thinking about the basement of an institution—flickering lights, concrete walls, and all.

I can hear the hum of machines in the distance, which only intensifies the dank basement setting. However, I can also hear the muffled sound of voices, so I know we are not completely alone down here.

When Sutton finally stops walking and waves his badge at the sensor next to a set of large double doors, I realize he is serious. The automatic doors open up to the humid expanse of a giant laundry room, complete with wretched florescent lighting and rows of industrial-sized washers and dryers. Throughout the vast room, there are cream-colored canvas carts that range from empty, to brimming with soiled hospital linens. There are also oversized stainless steel folding tables peppered about. I get the distinct impression that the room bustles with activity during the day, but has been stripped of the usual chaos at this hour.

Before I'm completely finished taking in the room, Sutton backs me into one of the folding tables and crowds me out of any personal space.

"What the hell are you doing, Mercy?" he asks, somewhere between a growl and a plea. He is looking down into my eyes because he is so close to me. I don't know how to reply to his question because every time I inhale, my chest inflates to the point I actually touch his body.

"*Learning to do laundry, apparently*," I whisper on a cautious breeze.

"That's not what I'm talking about," he clarifies as his eyes dart around the room. There is a jumble of voices somewhere beyond the row of machines, but no one is in sight. "With Wes. What the hell are you doing with Wes?"

"It's not what you think. He is teaching me things," I attempt to explain, but my voice is a shadow of itself.

"Mercy, remember when you asked me to be open, but to tell you when I was afraid of crossing the line?"

"Ye—" I start, but don't get the opportunity to finish because his mouth is on mine. He puts his hands on my waist and lifts me to the metal folding table before stepping between my legs. I gasp at the sudden kiss, or maybe the coldness of the table against the backs of my thighs, but my eyes also flutter closed, and I kiss him back.

I've imagined kissing him so often, this feels like a dream. It also feels surprisingly natural, even when he slips his tongue into my mouth. I can feel him let up his grip on my waist with one hand, but only to entwine it in the hair at the back of my head. He crushes my face into his.

The act feels possessive on his end—however, completely needy on mine.

He backs off slightly and speaks against my mouth, "This is one of those instances where I'm afraid I might cross the line," then he is back on my lips. I always figured tongue kissing would be sloppy and a little disgusting, but it's not. Not at all. I'm afraid I might not be doing it correctly, but it feels right.

My body is screaming with all kinds of warning alarms. His kiss is affecting me in ways I wouldn't necessarily expect, but I can only assume the amount of sexual frenzy I'm emitting is within the normal range.

"I want you to cross the line," I pant as I embarrassingly press myself against his body. This is all very new to me, but it's so perfectly savage that all I can think about is discovering more about the demanding hard-on in his pants.

"You don't want Wes' fingers between your legs anymore?" As he asks the question, he drops his hand and within a second, has shifted the fabric of my panties to the side.

I moan into his kiss when he touches my bare skin. It's flooded with warmth, and the discovery seems to incite something unchecked within him.

After a few minutes of wild kissing and a healthy familiarity with my newly waxed region, he tries to back his head away from me. I'm not done with his lips, so I close the space again. This time the insistence of the kiss is mine.

"I want your fingers. Not his," I pant between kisses.

He pushes my legs wider apart with his free hand while the fingers between my legs continue to explore my body. When his thumb finds my clitoris and rubs it purposefully, a throaty groan escapes my mouth. He swallows down my excitement as he continues to kiss me with a recklessness I have never known.

I can feel the exact moment when the angel on his shoulder speaks louder than the devil. He pulls his hand away from the moistness he created and steps back as if I slapped him.

"Mercy, I'm so sorry. Jesus-fuck, what have I done? I'm sorry, Mercy, I'm sorry." He is raking his fingers through his hair and watching his feet as they pace three steps in one direction and then back.

"Don't say you're sorry! Say you want me, you asshole!" His revulsion with the situation hits a chord deep in my consciousness and hacks away at my hotly contested self-respect. He is disgusted right now. I learned how to kiss and nearly came on his fingers—and he is disgusted.

I drop my head down as I adjust my skirt back into place. He takes a step toward me and lifts my chin. He may be expecting the tears of a broken, fragile woman, but he gets my barely contained rage. I can tell my eyes are flickering with it.

"Mercy, this isn't about you. It's about me. I will not let you make it about you."

I laugh, but it's really more of a cackle, "Sure, Doc. Why would you be any different from everyone else? Huh?"

"You do **not** understand, and you are reading this all wrong, Mercy!" He is kind of shouting right now, and his snarky tone surprises me. "I am so completely torn about wanting to be with you, but also wanting you to get better. I don't know heads from *fucking tails* right now! I *do* know that I can't have both. And you know what? Sometimes, sick fuck that I am, I want you so bad that I don't care if you get better! What do you think about that—especially coming from *your doctor*?" His words are hot and hateful, and they ring with self-loathing. He has never sounded less like a professional, much less, like a doctor.

"Why can't it be both?" I challenge, clouding my fury with words.

"Why?" now his laugh is a cackle. "Because it's unethical AS HELL, that's why." Now he stops pacing and stands rooted to the ground, chest puffed out, and ready for battle.

"Then why don't you teach me how to do the stupid laundry, and we will forget the whole thing happened," I say, just as angry as before. He plants his palms on either side of me and leans in close again. This time it's not for a kiss. This time, he looks like he wants to rip my head off.

"You should report me. Kissing you was an extreme lapse in judgment, and I can understand if you don't trust me with your care—or anyone else's care for that matter."

"Screw you, Sutton! Show me how to work these machines, and we can be done with this." I shove him back a step and hop down from the stainless-steel table. He closes the space between us again and sets his glare acidicly on mine before he answers.

"I don't know how to use them."

"Then how do you propose I learn that particular life skill?" I shoot back, having summoned as much sarcasm as I can muster.

"Laundry is easy. Mindless even. You separate the whites from the colors, toss in a detergent pod, and push start." He still hasn't backed up, which is aggressive for someone who supposedly feels bad for what he just did.

"Fine. Now let's go eat some frickin' birthday cake, *Doctor*."

Chapter 16

My friends have a lot to say when I get back, but I can't risk telling them about it. Wes, having felt the tug of testosterone, had wandered over to watch the football game while I was gone. Tracy, apparently having felt the tug of Wes, now cheers and shouts at the refs with the rest of them, so it's a little hard to justify my clamped-shut mouth.

Matty, Lyla, and Veronica knew something was wrong the moment I stepped off the elevator, and the fact that Sutton made a beeline straight to his office didn't go unnoticed either. Something about my laundry story didn't quite ring true, so each of them called bullshit in their own way.

Matty crossed his arms over his chest and cocked his head to the side while squinting his disbelief in my direction. Veronica tapped my knee three quick taps while saying, "Nice try." There is zero chance she bought the explanation. And Lyla pinched her lips together while giving a slow nod, the non-verbal cue indicating that we will be discussing my big, fat lie once we're alone in our room.

I can't tell them. Never mind my progress toward a healthy mind; Sutton is their doctor, too. Despite my initial assessment, he is working wonders through this wing of the hospital. I don't think Sig ever had a real handle on the people here. His understanding of their problems was very one dimensional. He would medicate Matty's depression, but never try to understand why he might be depressed. And Sutton wasn't here two weeks before he started breaking through Matty's iron curtain.

Veronica is even making progress with her OCD, though she's been mighty resistant to the Cognitive Behavior Therapy that pushes her so hard and so often. Sig treated her for anxiety, but something like OCD requires more than just medication. Enter, Sutton. Now, the doors are blown off, and she is making noticeable progress.

I would also be remiss in not mentioning Tracy. She has opened like a clam. She now shares some pretty horrific stuff in group and is starting to process some intensely bothersome childhood abuse. Abuse we all suspected, but somehow sat just below the surface of her consciousness. Turns out, she used the singing to disappear from herself. Imagine that. Having to escape from traumatic events by going so deep in your own mind, you lose touch with what is happening to your body. Yeah, all of us are a little more tolerant of her singing now. As well as feeling like a bunch of judgmental assholes.

Anyway, Sutton did all that. He has accomplished more in a few months than Sig did in years. I can't take all that away from my friends. They need Sutton as their doctor. If I pull back the curtain and reveal him as a man and not a God, it would never be the same.

That's how I feel one minute anyway. The next minute, I want to tell them everything and divulge every detail. To hell with everyone's progress. I want to analyze every second of what happened and come up with a game plan for moving forward.

The honorable part of me would back down and show all kinds of restraint as his patient. But the newly unleashed hedonist in me says, screw it, green light. For now, all I can do is stick to my laundry life skills class story and try to derail everyone by bringing up something juicy from earlier.

"Can you believe Wes showed me his dick?"

"If Sutton didn't crash the party, you could have seen it hard too. He had a semi when his hand was up your skirt. Only needed about ten more seconds," Veronica says before cutting to the quick. "So, when do you think you'll tell us the truth about your little sojourn with Sutton?"

I think about her counting everything before I answer. "Honestly, he took me to the laundry room, showed me how to separate the lights and darks, tossed in a detergent pod, and that was all," I say, trying like hell to keep looking her in the eyes.

"He didn't even stay for cake. Must not like sugar," Matty says with a knowing glint in his blank expression.

"Or he already had some sugar," Lyla points out, to an enthusiastic round of head nods.

Chapter 17

That night, after Lyla fell asleep, I cried into my pillow for an hour before resurfacing with a new steely resolve. I was even able to maintain that resolve this morning through breakfast and group. Now, it sits heavy on my shoulders as I make my way to my session with the sexy doctor. I've come prepared too—for war or submission, I'm not yet sure.

I walk in and sit down. Sutton remains standing behind his desk, arms crossed. Besides the very physical barrier of his workspace, there is a less obvious barrier behind his eyes. But it's a roadblock just the same.

"Don't bother with apologies, Sutton."

"Mercy, I'm not sorry. I've put my job and entire future on the line, but I'm not sorry I kissed you."

"Okay, then. Why the standoff?"

"Because it can't happen again."

"Suit yourself," I say as I lean against the back of the couch and open my thighs past the point of decency. I'm wearing the same skirt as last night, but this time, I skipped the panties. I've come to the conclusion that I want him more than I need him to be my doctor.

I still haven't discussed him with my friends, but in the beginning, Lyla said to dress sexy and talk dirty, and Wes said it's sexy to forgo the panties. So, I'll start there.

Sutton notices my spread legs, and for a few minutes, time stops altogether. The fact that I know he is looking at my body intimately right now is enough to twist my carnal tingles into a tightly coiled snake. The act is lewd. It's salacious. It's so brazenly over the top; I can hardly contain myself. I have never flashed my body in this way, and shockingly, the deed has as potent of an effect on me as it does on him.

"*Mercy*," he whispers before licking his lips and going mute.

"I want a new doctor, Sutton."

"No."

"I'm serious. If I have to choose between my mental health and you. I choose—"

"Don't say that. It might kill me, but we have to get back on track. Mercy, we *have* to." His eyes are pleading with me, but they still blaze with fire.

"I don't want to. I want you to touch me here," I say as I drop my hand between my legs and widen my thighs even more. He gawks for a solid minute before he answers. His voice is broken apart, but his rejection is stitched back together before presenting it to me.

"Dr. Gingham will run your session tomorrow. He specializes in hypnosis, and I think it will be helpful. I'll be here for support and to take some notes, but the session will be his tomorrow." He drags his gaze up to meet mine.

"That's all for today, Mercy. You can go join the group."

***

When I get to the rec room, I see Lyla and a hospital porter carrying her stuff down the hall, and my anxiety spikes. She can't move rooms now, I've only just decided to tell her everything about Sutton.

I stop moving my feet and feel my lips go completely numb. My attraction to Sutton was just handed back to me in the form of scorched rubble, and now they are taking Lyla from me. I'm trying to process the enormity of my feelings all in the space of a few seconds.

My frozen demeanor must set off a distress flare because Veronica hurries over and slips her arm through the space beneath my elbow, then walks me to our couches by the windows.

"This is only temporary, Mercy. In a few months, you can sleep on top of Lyla if you want to. What you are feeling is not a permanent condition. Breathe, it's only for a short time. Breathe, this is only temporary."

Thankfully, Veronica's whispered mantras are lengthy enough for me to get a handle on my face. I have to control my emotions, or I will find myself under all sorts of scrutiny. The truth is, no one knows about Sutton, so I have to act accordingly *only* about Lyla's room change.

"I guess a bed finally opened up, huh?" My words indicate stability, but my voice doesn't sound like my own.

"I can see the anxiety written all over your face. Do you want me to do a guided meditation with you?" Veronica asks. She still hasn't unlatched her arm from mine, and I swear she can tell something bigger is at play.

"I'm fine V. Isn't it almost time for yoga anyway?"

"Mercy, did he hurt you?" she asks, and it cracks my heart open. She knows I should still be in session with Sutton, and she has always been so tuned in to everyone else's state of mind.

"Not like you think," I whisper as my throat dries out.

"Honey, did he try to force himself on you?"

"No. It's the opposite. He rejected me," I say flatly, resigned to my new situation.

"I'm sorry, Mercy. If it's any consolation, I don't believe he would have rejected you if he wasn't your doctor. You know? He can't really dip his cock in a vulnerable patient and still keep his medical license. There will be hundreds of men available to you in a few months. You can take your pick of them, just hang in there, okay?"

"You're right. Thank you." I'm saying all the appropriate stuff, but Veronica can see right through it.

"Do you want me to tongue my Ativan and give it to you tonight?" Her offer is sweet but unexpected, so it makes me laugh.

"No. I can handle a little rejection. Like you said, I'll have tons of other options in a few short months.

**

I feel four or five sharp cracks from what feels like a whip or the pierce of angry snakebites and then jerk awake. I'm soaked with sweat, and my sheet is wound around me as if to restrain me from fighting back against the angry mob. There are spots on my body that still burn with wild intensity under the moonlight, but upon further inspection, nothing remains to speak to the residual pain. Not a single burn, welt, or wound exists. But the nightmare is real.

I'm fully awake but can't speak to the presence, or lack of angry men in my room. Their hatred has followed me into wakefulness. I can still remember their bearded faces and the ominous chanting. I can hear them now.

I've never heard them clearly before, but now they sit between my ears and harass the quiet I know exists. They scream at me to renounce the wickedness that compels me. They spit on me and slap my face. I scurry into the corner of my bed, but they persist. Then I feel it. Another piercing bite. The pain is indescribable, and it pulls from me a tormented wail.

"Stop! Please, nooooo!"

Chapter 18

I've hardly slept. The threat of the men returning had me huddled in a ball all night, shivering from the persistent dampness of my clothes. My numbed-mouth pleading hadn't elicited the same response as screaming in the night, and the empty bed next to me offered no comfort.

I needed Sutton. I needed him to talk me down. To hold me and explain away the terror. But he was nowhere to be found. Lyla was gone too. It's clearer than ever before, this psychosis is mine to bear. Now, I'm all alone to face the hallucinations, and the thought of them being a figment of my sick mind is too crippling to acknowledge.

I've never knowingly hurt a soul, I don't even kill spiders. How is it possible that I would create this horror, only to unleash it upon myself? All morning, I have sipped my coffee while landing on the realization that I am exactly where I belong. The little crush on Sutton was a distraction from the fact that I am sick.

The problem lies in the fact that the devil inside is only harmful to me. I can never lead a normal life or hope for normal things. I am a monster for turning on myself like this. In the past, everyone feared I was a danger to them, or their children, or to the staff, but the truth is, my brain only wants to destroy *me*.

When I pad into Sutton's office, it's with the understanding that a mental institution is the best I can hope for. With a mind that routinely sabotages body and soul, there is no hope for me.

"Good morning, Mercy. This is Dr. Gingham. He will be guiding you through some relaxation and focused attention techniques today. We talked about this before. He is going to utilize an approach called Regression Therapy, which is a treatment that focuses on resolving significant past events believed to be interfering with a person's present mental and emotional wellness." Sutton delivers this information with the utmost professionalism and not an ounce of moral conflict, making me feel incidental and stepped over.

I nod a cursory hello to Dr. Gingham before taking my seat. He seems a little put off that I don't shake his extended hand, but he recovers by shoving it back into his pocket and staring at me.

"Dr. Gingham, would you please give us a minute?" Sutton says without taking his eyes off of me.

"Of course, just let me know when you are ready to begin," he says as he shuts the door behind himself. Sutton immediately squats down in front of me.

"Mercy, is everything okay? Are you still comfortable trying hypnotherapy?"

"I want to go back on antipsychotics. The hallucinations are becoming pervasive again, and I just want to shut them out. I haven't slept, I'm anxious all the time, I'm dep—"

"Mercy, I'm not going to blindly throw meds at you. Antipsychotics are not the correct course of treatment," he says as he slowly shakes his head. When he continues, it's with less strain to his voice, "What happened last night, and why wasn't I called?" The tenderness in his voice allows the tears I have been fighting to breach my lids.

"Because I'm all alone. You can't help me anymore."

"Stop, don't say that. You aren't alone." He leans in and pulls me against his chest. Holding me tightly, he strokes my hair and coos into my ear, "You are not alone. I'm right here."

I pull away and lightly tap his forehead, "You are with me *here*. I want you *here*," I finish as I lay my palm on his chest, over his heart.

He places his hand over mine before he answers, "Mercy, you have me here. Can't you see that? You are all I think about, but I'm desperate to see you through this, so I can still look myself in the eyes. I have turned your treatment a hundred and eighty degrees in the opposite direction. I have taken a decade of your mental health care and dumped it out on the floor. How can I not see you through to the other side? I would be a monster if I followed my heart."

"Then, be a monster."

"You don't know what you are asking."

"Then hypnotize me, and let's be done with this."

"I need to clear up one more thing before Dr. Gingham comes back," he says as he places his fingers beneath my chin, raising it and directing my gaze into his.

"The next time you spread your legs for me, it needs to be when I am no longer your doctor. Do you understand?"

"Why do you say stuff like that to me?"

"Because you need to know the effect you have on me. And you also need to know how important my job is. Mercy, you *can* heal from your past. You need to trust me. But you also need to know I am not a robot. I'm asking you to play nice—for now."

"Whatever you say, doc."

"Don't dismiss my feelings like that, Mercy."

"Why not? You dismiss mine just fine. In fact, I thought that's what this was all about. Right? Dismiss feelings, heal my schizophrenia, rinse, and repeat."

"Mercy," he almost growls. "I can't be your doctor and your lover."

"Who said anything about love?"

"Are we going to keep talking in circles, or are we going to figure out what's causing your nightmares?"

"I'm ready when you are. Go ahead, fix me," I say petulantly.

Sutton exhales a loud breath before standing and walking to the door and calling Dr. Gingham back in. Once we get all the pleasantries out of the way, he directs me to lie down on the couch. Sutton perches his ass on the windowsill while Dr. Gingham moves the desk chair closer to where I am.

"Mercy, I will be inducing a trance-like state in which you'll have heightened focus and concentration. You will remain in complete control. Regression therapy focuses on areas of conflict and other potentially negative aspects of your life. The goal is to isolate the causes of negative emotions and determine their cause in order to better address them. Does that make sense?"

"Sure, I guess."

"Hypnosis is simply a tool that can help facilitate various types of therapies and medical or psychological treatments. You see, through a trance-like state, we can achieve a heightened state of awareness, open the door to the unconscious mind, and help find the conflict, turmoil, or hidden pain. Through this process, we can reveal the invisible connections between events and feelings. Regression can be very healing and transformative."

"Great."

"Do you have any questions for me or for Dr. Sutton?"

"Not about hypnotherapy."

"Excellent, then I'll just dim the lights, and we can get started."

"I'd like for you to focus on my voice. You find the cadence of my words to be soothing, so as I guide you into a state of deep relaxation, each word draws you deeper and deeper into a tranquil state. I'd like you to take a deep breath for the count of five, hold it for eight, and then release it for a count of ten. Again, in for five, hold for eight, and release for ten. One more time, in for five, hold for eight, and release for ten. As you feel yourself let go and completely relax, I'd like you to visualize a staircase. Each step you descend brings you a hundred times deeper into your relaxed state. Let's begin."

Chapter 19

Sutton:

Watching Dr. Gingham induce Mercy into a state of deep relaxation borders on ridiculous. He has spent nearly thirty minutes walking her down some stairs and then going through each body part to individually relax each one.

His hypnotic suggestions don't seem to have an effect on me because I am decidedly, not relaxed. In fact, I'm more tightly wound than before because all I can think of is how badly I want to abuse her trance-like state.

She has become hypnotically pliable, and all I can think about is asking her to take off her shirt. I think I could alter the relaxation technique to have her become a hundred times more relaxed with each piece of clothing she removes. Hell, I'm getting hard just thinking about it.

I wonder if I could hypnotically suggest she make out with me up against this windowsill and then forget about the broken ethics of it and leave feeling completely free of whatever trauma in her past landed her here.

She will be my undoing for sure. Besides the fact that she is strikingly beautiful, her stone-cold innocence is what makes me want to bend her over my desk and teach her all about men and their erections.

The irony in all this is that I wrote my dissertation about transference and counter-transference. Can you imagine how hard fate is laughing at me right now? My entire future is on the line, and all I can think about is how many sexual positions I can introduce Mercy to.

A cough from the resident hypnotist redirects my focus from the way her shirt snugs up across her chest to his pointed look. Did he just ask me a question?

"I'm sorry, Mercy. Can you repeat that last part?" he says with wide eyes and a chin sweep that directs me to her face.

"Purity rites. You asked why I didn't like the sect leader. That's why."

"Mercy, as if you were watching it happen on a television screen, I'd like for you to elaborate on the purity rites. What did they entail, exactly?"

"Unmarried girls have to go with the Prophet so he can administer the rite of purity. If he finds us impure, it means we are not a true Believer, and we will be cast out to live and eat with the animals."

"And what does it mean to be *found pure*?" Dr. Gingham looks at me with disgust in his eyes. I think we both know what it means.

"I'm not sure."

"Does it mean the girls are virgins?"

"I don't know that word, what does that mean?"

"Mercy, how old are you right now?"

"Six and a half," she answers in a small voice. I launch myself off the window sill, and in three long strides, I'm almost by her side. I'd take her hand if this asshole would sit back down and get his hands off of me.

Dr. Gingham boldly shakes his head and walks me backward a few steps before he holds his hand in front of my face, indicating that I need to stop. When he sits back down next to her, it takes him a minute to collect himself.

"You're doing great, Mercy. I'd like you to go back to the day you received your purity rites. Can you do that?"

"Yes."

"Tell me what happens during this time."

"I'm crying because I'm afraid of the Prophet, and he is squeezing my hand. Mama is crying too, but she isn't making a sound. He takes me into the church, but it's empty. No one is singing or praying… There is a back room… It's behind Jesus on the cross." Her breaths start speeding up, and I want to go back in time and castrate this fucking pedophile.

"Mercy, you are completely safe from this man, he cannot hurt you."

"No. I'm not safe. He is a bad man."

"You are watching what happens on a screen."

"But he is hurting my hand. He's squeezing me and dragging me into the little room. There are others here." She is becoming agitated, and I want this to stop right now. There is little doubt she was sexually abused as a child and that her "hallucinations" are a direct correlation of such. I don't need the gory details in order to help her.

"Who are the others?" Doctor hypnosis asks.

"Mr. Fitzgerald. Mr. Calloway. Mr. Stands. And Mr. Williams. They are smiling at me and telling me not to be afraid. They are trying to make their faces nice, but I don't like them."

"What happens next, Mercy?"

"They're all holding me down on a table. Mr. Calloway lifts my dress up, and the others pull my legs apart."

"—Great job, Mercy, you can leave the hidden room now. Those men will be fed to the pigs later, and you will never have to worry about them ever again. Go ahea—"

Dr. Gingham gets right in my face and growls at me to shut my mouth. He is almost purple with anger, but I don't care. I've heard enough.

"The goal here is to isolate the source of her negative emotions and determine their cause in order to better address them! Now, you can either leave the room or sit quietly on your hands, and keep your mouth shut!" he grinds out, right in my face and hardly audible otherwise. For such a slight man, he is a scrappy little dude.

I thought this was a good idea before. Now, I'm having a hard time remembering why I thought so. I open my mouth to say that's all for today—she is *my* patient, after all—when she speaks.

"The Prophet says I have to repent. I need his help. He says that only he can save my soul. He wants to fix me with love. Love, he says."

"Okay, Mercy, we can come back to that at a later date. For now, I'd like you to imagine a brightly lit stairway. You feel completely safe and secure, and you realize that there is no danger associated with the staircase. In fact, you want to go up a few stairs."

"Okay."

"These particular stairs represent years, so each step you take advances you a year at a time. I would like you to take two steps up the stairs. Can you do that for me?"

"Yes."

"Are you eight years old now?"

"Yes."

"Is this a happy time for you?"

It takes her several minutes to respond, but when she does, her forehead knits with tension, and her breathing becomes evident in the rapid rise and fall of her chest.

"No. No…it's not a happy time."

"I want you to take another step up the staircase. Now you are nine years old. Is this a happy time for you?" He knows this was the year of her life she was abandoned at St. Vincent's—just before her tenth birthday, and this asshole is asking her if it was a happy time? What a dick.

"I will never be happy again."

"What do you see?" he asks, as though he can't see the tears pooling in her closed eyes. It's all I can do to stay quiet.

"His face is red, and the vein in his forehead is sticking out. He is really close. His breath is hot, and he is screaming at me."

"What is he screaming?"

"Child of satan! In my name, I cast out the devil!"

"Mercy, I'd like you to notice a doorway to your left. The door is warm and welcoming, and you understand that when you pass through the door, you will leave any feelings of fear and anxiety behind you. Go ahead and walk through that door. When you close it, any lingering adverse emotions completely drain away. You feel utterly relaxed and revitalized, and when you wake up, you will have no recollection of any residual strain or discomfort from your session. I'd like you to take several deep breaths. With each inhale, you become more alert until you are ready to open your eyes."

She blinks her eyes a few times and then looks over, first at me, and only then, at Dr. Gingham. She sits up and runs her fingers through her hair, as though embarrassed to have drifted off. All I want to do is hold her and make sure she is okay, but seeing as that's professionally frowned upon, I will refrain from doing so. At least until this guy is out of my office.

"Did it work?" she asks, with no discernible memory of the events that just took place.

"I think it went as well as can be expected. How do you feel?" Gingham asks while I bite my tongue.

"I feel rested, but I'm not sure that's what we were going for," she says with an embarrassed giggle.

"Well, I'll tell ya, the thing about regression therapy is that it can help point to some areas where we should focus. It's not a treatment, it's a tool, and I feel very confident that I can help you."

"Great. I look forward to the help," she says as she turns and cuts her eyes at me. Was that a non-verbal dig? Is she insinuating that I can't help her? What the hell was that?

"This type of therapy has several goals. The first is expression and release of emotions previously repressed. And the second is relearning or reprogramming the subconscious mind. It will take some time, but I've had some extraordinary results with this kind of thing."

"So, we need to do it again?"

"Oh, yes. Today was just a cursory glance. If it aligns with your treatment goals, I'd like to see you twice a week," Then he looks directly at me and annunciates, "In *my* office."

"Alright, I'm game. I believe I have nine a.m. available most days," she says, sweetly. Saccharine—sweet, that is.

*The fuck? 9:00 is **my** time.*

"Actually, I will have to get back to you on that, Dr. Gingham. Thank you for your time, we'll be in touch," I say as I shuffle him toward the door.

"Dr. Sutton, may I have a word with you in the hallway, please?"

"Of course."

When I follow him out of my office, I'm suddenly aware that most psychiatrists would not have been so possessive over a patient. I wish I'd had enough sense in my head to have realized that sooner.

After the door closes and we're alone in the hall, he speaks. "I acknowledge that some medical doctors tend to see things in black and white, and don't always accept the many shades of gray, but I'd like you to give me an opportunity to work within the confines of that gray area, to unlock her subconscious mind. What may seem like cut and dry childhood abuse to you can have a distinct role in her current affairs. There are lingering effects from her childhood trauma that can't even be quantified at this point."

"I agree with you. I'm just a little worried about all the anxiety and trauma this will bring to the surface, that's all. There is little doubt she's been through hell."

"Agreed. Will you let me help her?"

"Uhhh," okay, so he is not on to me and my lecherous ways after all. He thinks I doubt his ability to do the job. "Yes, I suppose we can give it a few sessions before we assess the efficacy of it...but I'd like to be present durin—"

"Absolutely not. With all due respect, doctor, I'm highly respected in my field, and my track record speaks for itself. Believe it or not, I am equipped to handle anything I may uncover."

"I'll speak to my patient and get back with you. Thank you for coming."

When I face Mercy in my office again, she wastes no time before asking, "Who is Mark?"

"Huh?"

Chapter 20

My hallucinations are back with a vicious vengeance since going off the antipsychotics. The men are with me almost nightly. The soaked sheets are commonplace. My throat, raw from screaming, is now standard. What wasn't standard was the slap to my face that drug me from the abyss.

She apologized after she did it. I think it surprised her that she actually struck a patient. But the ridiculous thing was that I didn't recognize it wasn't part of the hallucination—and I fought back until a rather large orderly dragged me into the hallway.

Now, I'm sitting here in nothing but a t-shirt—the last clean *and* dry article of clothing to my name, while my damp sheets are stripped and my bed re-made. Both the nurse and orderly keep their leery distance, but *I'm* the one who got hit. Well, technically speaking, the nurse did too, but that was reactive, and I'm certain there is a protocol for handling delusional patients, and I'm pretty sure slapping them isn't part of it.

If I wasn't ruminating in angry feelings right now, I'd mention to her that I'm not planning on telling anyone that she smacked me. So, she can stop worrying about losing her job. I might even take credit for the handprint on my cheek if she plays her cards right.

"Everything ok in here?" Sutton asks, obviously getting faster at springing from his bed and racing back to the hospital to peel me off the ceiling. Good, maybe when he gets sick of having his sleep interrupted, he will put me back on the antipsychotics.

I get it, he doesn't want me to be schizophrenic, but this is getting ridiculous. I had gone months between hallucinations. Now I have several a week. That's not the kind of progress I want to make.

"She was screaming for Mark Sexton," the nurse says, omitting the part about her handprint on my skin. Both Sutton and I look away from each other, snapping our necks to look in her direction.

"What?" I ask.

"Who is Mark Sexton?" Sutton asks at the exact same time. Of course, he focuses on the other man's name on my lips instead of the fact that I clearly need to be medicated.

"Don't worry, Doc, he's probably just one of the hallucinations that pin me down and drip acid on my skin—I seriously doubt he's boyfriend material at all."

"Thank you, you two. I'll have a look at your reports in the morning," he says, all but dismissing them from the room. I'm still a little bitter about the slap and the manhandling me out of the room like a two-year-old having a temper tantrum, but I'm *really* mad at Sutton.

"All of this is totally unnecessary. Why do you persist?" I ask, challenging him for the umpteenth time.

"Who is Mark Sexton?"

"For fuck's sake, Sutton!" I jump up from my spot on Lyla's former bed and begin to pace the room. "Why do I have to suffer like this? Do you get some sick pleasure from seeing me unravel?"

"The only pleasure I'm getting right now is from you waving your ass at me—are you even wearing panties?" he asks, as my mouth drops open and stays there.

"I'm not going to dignify that with a response. Sutton. I. Want. A. Second. Opinion. You are hell-bent on me not being schizophrenic, and I want to know why?"

"Because. You. Are. Not. Schizophrenic. Oh, and you've had about eight second opinions, so are we done with that yet? Still want a new doctor, Mercy?"

"Don't you know how hard it is to go through this? To suffer like this almost nightly? Listen to my voice! This rasp is not because it sounds *sexy*—it's from screaming for my life!"

"Come here."

"Why?"

"Because you need a hug, and I need to be the one that gives it to you."

"You want to get fired or something?"

"Do you think I don't know that one of them slapped you? They are writing their reports and covering their asses right now. I would be less surprised to see the Tooth Fairy come through that door than one of them," he says with total conviction.

This is the Sutton I want. The man that desires me, not the doctor that pushes me away. Instead of sitting down next to him where I was before, I take a seat on his lap and rest my chin against his shoulder. His embrace feels strong but tender. Not doctorly at all.

"How did you know one of them slapped me?"

"First, by their demeanor. Then by the evidence left on your cheek. I could lift fingerprints from that," he says softly, overlooking his anger for now. One of his arms drapes over my thighs while his palm cups my t-shirt covered butt. The other hand is buried in my hair, holding my head against his body.

"Do you remember anything from your session with Dr. Gingham?" he asks.

"Not really. Did I do anything embarrassing?"

"No, honey. You were perfect," his words are pained, but their impact is far less noticeable than his touch because now he slides his hand under my shirt to touch my naked ass. The gasp gets stuck in my throat while my eyes fling open. I welcome his desire and crave his touch, it's the boldness that surprises me.

"Mercy, I don't know what to do. You have some past trauma that needs to be addressed. There is some really ugly stuff locked away in your subconscious."

"What are you saying? Stuff, I don't remember?" I pull slightly away, the perfect distance for him to close the gap with a kiss.

"Can we go to my office? I'm about to cross the line."

"First, let's talk about *how* you would cross the line," I probe, before cocking my head to a perfect kissing angle. I see his Adam's apple bob as he swallows hard.

"There are a thousand different ways."

"Show me one," I press.

His hand moves from my butt and finds more neutral ground on my thigh. Before my disappointment can manifest, he glides his palm under my shirt and up the side of my ribs. The tickle of his touch is so intense it makes me feel like I have to pee.

"*What are you doing to me?*" he whispers as his thumb finds the bottom swell of my breast. I don't answer his question because I can't, and he isn't looking for an answer anyway.

When his thumb swipes over my nipple, all my insides clench. His eyes flit between boldly looking me in the eyes and then drifting achingly to my lips. I would lean forward and kiss him, were I not paralyzed with how freakishly tingly my whole body feels. It used to take me thirty completely committed minutes to awaken that part of myself—now, his cautious touch is nearly enough to get me there.

His thumb gains tenacity and begins to assertively drag my nipple back and forth. At this moment, I would concede everything to him. Such a simple touch, but it's fogging my brain and presenting as more stimulation than I thought possible.

"Tell me what those little gasps mean, Mercy," he mumbles into the space between us.

"I...It's...I think I'm getting close—" his fingers close around the bud of my nipple and simultaneously pinch and tug.

"You think you're close to coming? Right here on my lap?" his words are provocative, and the last ones I hear before everything spills over, and I'm awash with something more complex than a simple orgasm.

"But, I've hardly touched you," he chuckles, and he's right, but it's not just his touch. It's the potency of my need for him. It's the raw and savage emotions I harbor. It's wanting him so much, but being kept at arm's length. It's never having felt the loving touch of another, and now, having that touch burn through my skin. For once, not to harm, but finally to re-build.

"Put some more clothes on. I'll see you in my office in five." That's it. That's his reaction. I'm having some sort of profound experience, and all he can think about is getting out of the temptation of my room.

"No."

"What did you just say?" he asks with surprised amusement.

"I said, no. I'm not your complacent doll to play with on a whim. You don't get to start fires and then stand back while the forest burns down."

"How very poetic. But I'm still your doctor, and we have some work to do before you go back to sleep." He closes that statement with a kiss that's delivered like his own slap to my face. In fact, his anger—or sexual frustration meets mine head-on. The kiss itself isn't angry, it speaks more to the unfairness of all this.

I can feel his erection against my hip, and I long to see it, or even just know what's causing it. Is it merely my half-naked body that is turning him on? Is this always what happens when he kisses someone? What is behind it?

"I can feel your hard-on," I say after breaking the kiss for a second.

"Yeah? Well, you'd have to be in the next room to miss it."

"Tell me what's making you hard right now," I urge.

"Are you serious?" he asks as he completely breaks the kiss.

"Yes, tell me," I say, a little embarrassed to be wondering such a thing.

"Ummm, my hand on your tits, the fact that you just came on my lap from nipple stimulation alone, the idea that within five seconds I could have your legs spread open and be caressing your g-spot, the knowledge that at any moment, I could lay you down on the bed and—"

"So, I am just a doll you like to play with." It comes out not as a question but as a deflated statement.

"Do you really think that?"

"I'm starting to, yes."

"Then, let me show you something," he says as he turns me away from him and leans me back against his chest. He widens his knees so that my legs spread scandalously open. The whole thing takes a matter of seconds and leaves me stunned. He is absolutely demonstrating how easy it would be to take me if he were so inclined.

"Did you see how easy that was? Can you sense the proximity of my cock to your open body?... Do you know *why* I'm not fucking you right now?"

"Why?" I pant. He's right, if he were to free his erection right now, it would nestle against my nakedness. The whole thing is making me feel giddy and impulsive. I rock my body against his hardness and groan with the sensation it sparks.

"Because, you are **not** a doll to play with," he grinds out against my ear. "Would I jeopardize my whole future to play with a **doll?**" he sounds angry, so I stop rocking my hips and murmur,

"I want to be your *dollllll.*"

"Is that right, Mercy? You want to be my doll? Nothing but some perky tits to play with and a warm body to sink my dick in? Is that all you want to mean to me?"

"I want you to be a man, Sutton."

"Would a man throw away his medical license just to touch you here?" he asks as his fingertips find the neediest part of my body. The spread open part. The part that begs for his touch. "Hmm? Would a *man* do that?"

I don't know how to answer him. His fingers have made contact, but they lack full commitment. I'm panting with the proximity of his touch and the impugning breath against my ear. When I begin to writhe around on his lap, he drags his middle finger through my crease and then taps it against my clit a few times. Each tap is like a brazen challenge— or a threat. I'm not sure which one.

"Yes," I finally answer.

"Is that right? A man would give up his medical license? To, what, *finger* you? Get the fuck off my lap, Mercy, we have work to do."

Chapter 21

I'm still sulking over last night as Sutton grumpily walks me to the other end of the hospital for a session with Dr. Gingham. I'm not even sure why he feels like he needs to hover over me. I'm perfectly capable of taking the elevator and locating suite 425. Actually, the pedestrian bridge to a different building annex threw me for a minute, but I still would have managed without a guided tour from my brooding doctor.

I clamp my arms across my chest, he digs his fists into his pockets, and neither of us says a word. It's a step down even from where we were last night in his office. Then, I had my arms *and* legs crossed while my foot swung wildly up and down. He had simply pointed out that the motion was my body's valve for anxiety. Then he had the gall to ask me if I wanted to talk about my anxiety. My eyes became poisonous little slits, and I had actually hoped for a bolt of lightning to come through the window and strike that pompous look right off his face.

He is a sexy little fucker, but not so sexy that I don't want to see if he comes harder with my hands around his throat. *He* is the medical doctor, and look how much damage he is causing my fragile sexuality. While pushing the notion of subconscious childhood sexual abuse, he wants to ignore the damage he is currently causing and dredge up a bunch that doesn't even bother me—what is the psychology behind that?

"If at any point you feel uncomfortable discussing anything with Dr. Gingham, I want you to feel completely free to pull the plug and end the session. Ok?"

"Why? Because now you are worried I will say something about you? Out you in some egregious way? You are a real asshole, you know? You're so worried about how my illness will blow back on you that you can't even see beyond your own selfishness. Why don't you just go fuc—"

"Actually, Mercy," he grinds out, "I was more concerned with the men in your past holding you down and raping you while you were a child." Then he turns on his heel and storms back the way we came.

"All the way down the hallway. It's the second to last office on the left," he shouts, without even turning around to say it.

Now, why would he say that? Psychiatrists don't get to lash out and say whatever they want just so they can hurt you. He should know better than that.

As if! Wait. Does he think the angry men in my hallucinations are holding me down so they can rape me?

What the hell is that all about?

***

After my session with Dr. Gingham, I feel like I just did hot yoga for three hours. I feel utterly relaxed and wrung out, but I also feel rejuvenated and like skipping back to the unit. That is, until I see my pouty doctor with his shoulder propped against the wall, waiting outside my hypnotherapist's office.

"Is this the Sulky-Express back to the psych ward? Because I think I'll wait for the next one," I say, and I'm mostly unmoved by the slow, unintentional smile that he seems hell-bent on concealing from my view.

"Oh, it's the Express, alright. Straight to the medical board for sexual misconduct," he mumbles under his breath.

"What was that? Hmmm? You got something to say, Sutton?"

"Yeah, I've got something to say, Does Dr. Gingham want to speak with me before we head back?"

"Nope. Actually, I believe he said that you should go pound sand."

"Pound sand?"

"Maybe he didn't exactly say, *pound sand*. But he definitely didn't say he needed to talk to you," I say as I breeze past him. I love that he is so put-off that Gingham may have disparaged him in any way. His mouth is still frozen open in shock.

"Mercy, wait," he calls after me as he pushes off the wall and catches up to me in three strides. "We need to talk about some stuff."

"Are you sure this is the best place for that kind of talk, Sutton?" I ask, indicating the hospital corridor we currently stand in.

"I'm talking about your patient care," he says, and I can't help but snarkily laugh out loud.

"Oh, is that what we're calling it? Patient care?"

"Yes, that's exactly what we're calling it. That is the most important thing right now, and I intend to follow through. Mercy, stop," he says as he grabs my arm and stops me in my tracks, forcing me to face him. "I'm sorry, I said that to you before your session. I was angry and lashing out, but it would have been more appropriate for me to bite my tongue off than to say something like that. I'm sorry. I promise you, I will never speak out in that manner again."

"Humph," is all I can get out before I resume walking. The truth is, I forgot all about what he said. I'm still marinating in his indecision between being a man and a doctor.

"I have about twenty-five minutes before I see my next patient. Do you want to go to the cafeteria and get some coffee? Or we could speak in my office, of course."

"Fine. Coffee."

Neither one of us talks again until we sit down at a table that still needs to be wiped off. Evidently, Sutton prefers the privacy of the table to actually having a clean one.

"We haven't talked about Sig in a while," he says cautiously, and I almost spit out my first sip.

"Sutton, do you have any idea where I'd be if I didn't bury all my little abandonments? I don't want to talk about Sig. I prefer to move on with life. Why do you insist on circling back to this every couple of weeks?"

"Because abandonment is a major crux in all this. It's one of the contributors to your anxiety. You've never learned to properly deal with it...or any loss, for that matter. It's time to address some of that."

"I don't want to call him. I don't want to write to him—"

"What would you do if you could? Regarding, Sig?" he asks.

"I don't know—throw fine china at his head? Does that count?"

"So, you're angry?"

"Yeah, genius. I'm angry."

"Because you believe he abandoned you, correct?"

"Uh, yeah," I say, exasperated.

"It seems to me that he loved you quite a bit—in a fatherly way," he delivers this statement casually, but it lands like a poison dart. I don't respond to him. I can't.

"Mercy, I've shared with you that the board asked him to step down. He didn't leave by choice, nor was he given an option to do it gently. He did his best to do right by you. I'd like you to step away from the anger briefly and acknowledge how devastating the loss of another parental figure was for you."

My mouth is moving, but all it's doing is gulping for air like a dying trout on the riverbank. Sutton is about to flick a match onto the kerosene-soaked rubble of my life, and it will burn for months.

"I want you to start looking at different perspectives when it comes to interpersonal relationships. It's important to dignify them instead of automatically jumping to the one that feels *safe*. To you, anger is safe, right? Anger can't hurt you. Anger puts you on the offensive, and you're able to beat back all those other pesky emotions that you think make you weak and vulnerable, right?"

I'm still dumbstruck that Sutton has dragged this out in the open in such a blisteringly raw way—over coffee, no less.

"Sutton, if I were to step away from my anger like you suggest, I would never stop crying. The well of sorrow inside me is *bottomless*, don't you see that?"

"Mercy, you never completely grieved for your brother. You haven't mourned your parents. You've been in a constant state of flux, refusing to deal with the pain—and you don't think all that affects you? You're afraid to open your heart, for fear it will be crushed and handed back to you. That is evidenced by the fact that Matty, Lyla, and V are your first real friends. You've been keeping all these incredibly valid feelings of sorrow and loss masked, and by doing that, you are inadvertently hanging on to them. Don't you see? Now, and arguably since childhood, you've been manifesting these repressed emotions in some vivid, highly destructive ways."

"I don't know how to change. A leopard can't change her spots."

"No, she can't change her spots, but she can adapt to her environment. She can either go through life angry that the Hyenas always try to steal her prey or get proactive and drag the Gazelle up a tree."

"I don't—I don't even know what to do with that comparison," I admit. I appreciate his commitment to it, I just don't know how it applies to me.

"It's easy, babe," he whispers. "You can stay put and deal with the Hyenas, or you can do something about it." He glances down at his watch and then scoots his chair back. "We've got to get back, but I still want to get a session in today because—" he seems timid to finish his statement, so I sit up a little straighter because I instinctively feel like I need to brace myself for what he is about to say.

"Veronica is leaving," he says gently.

Veronica is leaving?

You would think I'd have a solid understanding of the rotation by now. People come, people go. Insurance runs out, people evaporate into the world. Beds open up, beds fill again. It's a constant cycle, and the door never stops spinning. It's no surprise that my friendship group is dismantling, but that doesn't change my reaction.

My eyes flood with tears because I'm not ready. We've made all kinds of plans for the four of us to get a place together, but in my world, plans change, and dust sifts. People disappear. Veronica is leaving, and she is taking a part of me with her. Part I may never get back.

"Listen to me," he urges, as he risks placing his palm on top of my hand, in full view of the bustling hospital cafeteria. "It's going to be okay. Your circumstances are fluid. It's not as though you two will be kept apart by logistics like in the past. You can maintain a friendship with her even if you don't know exactly what that will look like yet. Okay?" He is so soothing he has an immediate calming effect on my spiking anxiety.

I'm still mad he wants to pretend last night never happened, but everything about me wants to latch on to him and never let go. In a world full of rules and constraints I have to contend with, I have no choice but to accept things as they are. He can be my doctor instead of my boyfriend if he must—I'll take him however I can get him. I just don't want to ever be without him.

I nod my head, afraid to answer him with shaky words as he takes my hand and stands. He lets go of me as soon as he realizes what he's done, and then, after clearing his throat, says, "We need to double-time it back to the unit."

***

When I approach my friends after returning to the unit, there is a crackling static to the air—as if they were talking about me and all of a sudden have to change the subject.

"How was hypnosis?" Matty asks.

"Fine. Why are you all talking about me behind my back?" I question, getting right to it. As usual, my hurt presents as anger. They all start talking at once, but it's Matty's voice that gets through.

"Simmer down, we were just saying we are glad you have Sutton to lean on because Veronica is leaving this afternoon, and I have less than a week before I have to return to work, or they won't hold my position anymore. The floor dynamics are changing, that's all."

"You're leaving in less than a week?" I ask, and it sounds like a distraught plea.

"Only if I want to keep my job and not wind up penniless and on the streets," he says with a smile that softens his words. "Plus, your days left are in the double digits now."

"I'm not as excited as you two. Why are you guys so amped up to leave?" I don't understand their brimming excitement. Don't get me wrong, I want to leave too, but I'm terrified to do it.

"I need to get back to normalcy and decent food."

"Matty, this *is* normal."

"Ha! This isn't real life. This is therapy and starched sheets," Veronica chimes in."

"Mercy? Please come to the nurse's station," one of the RNs calls over to me. I'm thankful to walk away from my friends because the mood has shifted. Instead of being comfortable and happy here, all of a sudden, they are ready to kick open the doors and go storming out. My state of mind can't handle that at the moment. In fact, I'm going to see if Wes wants to play chess after I figure out what the nurse wants. I can't be around people with one foot out the door right now.

"Do you need to see me?" I ask one of the new nurses as I approach the reception desk.

"Mercy, this is Mr. Donaldson. He is your driver's ed instructor."

"My driver's huh? What?" I ask as I automatically stick out my hand to shake his.

"Let's go, young lady. We have quite a bit of ground to cover—so to speak."

Well, okay then. Looks like I'm learning how to drive right now.

Chapter 22

Today has been a whirlwind of emotions with lots of feelings to process. But, despite the imminent departure of two close friends, my predominant emotion is glee. I drove a car for the first time in my life, and that makes me feel like I really can survive on the outside.

My driver's ed instructor lectured at me for forty-five minutes and then gave me a quiz before allowing me to drive around some orange safety cones in a deserted parking lot for fifteen minutes. It was amazing.

Now, back on the unit, pink-cheeked with bloomed excitement, another emotion stomps on my joy and spits in its mouth. Panic. V is saying goodbye to everyone and already has her personal belongings back. She is leaving right now. As in, RIGHT now.

After a tear-filled goodbye, I waste zero time in beelining straight to Sutton's office. It's not time for my session yet, but I don't care. I feel empty, and he fills me back up. I need him right now.

I'm not still crying when I knock on his door, but I know the tears will flow at the slightest provocation. Thank God his "In Session" light is not lit because I'm not sure it would even stop me at this point. When I open the door, he is standing by the window dictating notes into his phone.

He doesn't speak, he simply opens his arms while I close the space between us. He holds me while I cry, softly caressing my hair and murmuring sweet things into my ear.

After many minutes of crying, I step back and tug a few tissues from the box on his desk, and blow my nose. Strangely, the sadness feels less pervasive now, like he took some of it from me.

I don't need to explain what happened; he already knows. He even tried to prepare me for it this morning.

"I have something for you," he says as he steps aside to flip the switch on his desk that illuminates the red light outside, indicating he's with a patient.

"You do?" I ask, stunned.

"Yes, but it comes with some rules. What do you want first, the gift or the rules?"

"Such a kill-joy. Give me the rules, I guess."

"One. You can't talk about it outside of this room."

"Okay."

"Two. You can't talk about it outside of this room."

"What is this, Fight Club?"

"You saw the movie Fight Club?" he asks, surprised and maybe a little bit impressed.

"No, I read it, of course. What is this, Fight Club?" I repeat. He smiles and shakes his head.

"Three. You can only use it in here, and only *after* our session."

"Oh my God, is it a vibrator? Please tell me it's a vibrator. Lyla and Veronica act like they are the best things ever invented…Is it? A vibrator? Ly says you have to name them, her's is the silver bullet, and V's is The Hulk—they both have others, but those are their favo—"

"It's not a vibrator, Jesus, Mercy," he says as he slowly shakes his head and tries to hide his amusement. "Now, I kinda wish it was, though." He hands me a box that he pulls from his desk drawer. It's not wrapped, but it has a yellow bow on it. Yellow means friendship, right? Too bad I'm going to paint it vibrant red at some point and give it back to him.

"Can I open it?"

"I certainly hope so, it's pretty useless if it stays in the box."

When I take the ribbon off, I already know what it is because the box shows a picture of it. Sutton gave me an iPhone. I'm speechless as he guides me to sit on the couch and then follows suit, sitting right next to me. After I turn it on, he prompts me to set up facial recognition to unlock it, and I start to feel a little drunk with power…even if he keeps it in here, he can't unlock it to see what I've been up to.

"I love it, thank you."

"You didn't even see the best part. Go to your contacts." When I do, I see he has some already set up. Matty, Lyla, Veronica, one that says, *not Wes*, and one that says, maybe someday. I laugh.

"Are you, '*maybe someday*'?"

"No, that's Sig. I'm, '*not Wes*'—and don't you forget it. Go ahead, text Veronica," he encourages me with a nudge. He guides me through the process, and eventually, I tap out a message.

Me: *Hey Veronica. I miss you already.*

When she doesn't respond right away, I say, "This thing doesn't work, is it too late for the vibrator?" We both laugh, and I slyly work my way onto his lap. When I hug him tightly, he returns the sentiment—for about ten seconds. Then he stands up, deposits me back on the couch, and walks over to stand behind his desk, looking flustered.

"Let's get to work, shall we?"

"Do you have a boner?" I ask, holding back my giggles. I like making him squirm, this is awesome.

"Not yet. But we actually have some work to do, so put away the phone for now. And definitely wipe that mischievous grin off your face."

"Great, let's pack up the laughter and happiness, so we can drudge up some painful memories," I say sardonically.

"Now, that's the spirit!" he says excitedly—though terribly sarcastic as well. "I want to start with Mark Sexton. You scream out his name in the night, a handful of the staff can attest to that. He is clearly of some importance."

"I don't know who he is. I've tried to remember him, but I don't," I say emphatically. Dr. Gingham is really interested in this guy as well. If he were that important, I'd remember him—bottom line.

"I've done some pretty exhaustive research from your hometown all the way up to this very hospital. There was a Taylor Sexton in your hometown, but he died shortly after you were born, and from what I can tell, he never married or had children. All records of Sextons at St. Vincent's didn't correlate with the years you were there. And there were no foster family placements or even prospective foster families by that name in your file. As far as this hospital, there was a labor and delivery nurse named Molly Sexton, as well as a Radiologist named Peter Sexton, both here at various points, but no one that you ever came in contact with. I'm completely stumped. Obviously, this guy is hugely relevant, yet there is no record of him anywhere."

"I don't know what to tell you. Maybe he is not a real person."

"What, like a ghost or an imaginary friend?" he asks, unconvinced.

"Noooo. Like a hal-luc-in-a-tion," I say with extra emphasis.

"I don't buy it. Do you ever remember any drifters or seasonal workers? Any circus' or carnivals ever come to town?"

"Ha! Circus or carnivals—as if the Believers wouldn't have thought the devil himself had come to town."

"Tell me more about the Believers."

"I don't remember a whole lot, I was young."

"You said before the leader was a Prophet? So, it was believed he could communicate directly with God and convey His messages?"

"Yes."

"What else do you remember about him?"

"He had bad breath and was missing some fingers on his hand. I hated when he touched me with that gross hand. I was afraid of it and of him."

"When did he touch you with his hand?"

"Every time he tried to cast out the demons." I can feel beads of sweat form around my hairline, but I'm not too sure why. For some reason, this feels like unfamiliar territory.

"Can you explain how he attempted to cast out the demons?"

"At church. There was a box." Now, I'm visibly shaking, and I don't know why.

"Mercy, tell me about the box."

"The paint was chipping off of the wood. It was old. There was a room hidden in the back of the church, too. That's where they kept the box. It was always so cold back there." Inexplicably, I shiver. I haven't thought about that box in a very long time. Death is inside that box.

"I want to talk more abo—"

All at once, the speaker on his desk phone crackles to life, and a panicked voice escapes. "Dr. Sutton, we have a code blue at intake." He stands up immediately but remains rooted to the floor. I can see the conflict all over his face. He knows he has uncovered some sort of riddle from my past, but he has pressing obligations as the unit psychiatrist.

"Mercy, there's a medical emergency. I have to go. I need... can we—"

Now we can hear shouting. Intakes are generally fairly smooth, but every once and a while, we get a particularly volatile one. Sounds like that's the case now.

"I'm sorry, Mercy. I have to go."

He leaves me sitting on his couch, with absolutely no regard for the knot of anxiety that sits heavily in my gut. I feel like the ghosts from my past are in the room with me, blowing their icy breath on the back of my neck. Logically, I know I'm alone. The problem with that is that schizophrenia is not logical. I can almost *smell* the Prophet. It's like I can feel his scratchy skin against mine all over again. On one hand, I'm afraid to move for fear I'll trigger an instinctive chase. On the other hand, I've got to get the hell out of this office.

I need the hum and clang of the busy unit to distract my mind from thoughts of the Prophet. Dragging that man out into the light was a terrible, terrible idea.

Chapter 23

I'm naked. I'm shivering. And every few seconds, they douse me with more Holy water. The Prophet is shouting. Two men are holding me down on the altar, and the rest of the men and women are dancing and spinning around. The spectators are working themselves up into a mob induced frenzy, and the energy in the room is absolutely frenetic. There is a crucifix pressed into my forehead so hard I can already feel a bruise forming. Even the tight clench of my teeth is not enough to detract from the pain.

"In my name, I cast you out!" The Prophet exclaims, over and over between outbursts of, "So sayeth the Lord!" His face is nearly purple with religious zealotry and fundamentalist fervor. Through blasts of angry spittle, he continues to rant, "The gospel preaches the word of Mark sixteen, and we, as His True Believers, shall heed His word! The five signs and wonders of His grace will show us the way! Out Devil!"

My teeth are ready to shatter from the quaking of my jaw, but the yammering prayers all around me offer no peace. I can't see my mom and dad anywhere, though I can hear my mother's cries from deep inside my bones. It sounds arthritic and pitiful, as though she knows she is about to lose another child to the church.

"Mark sixteen! So sayeth the Lord!" Then, the old, decrepit box is dragged into the room, and all the noise is drowned out by the sound of my own screams.

"Mercy! Wake up! You are safe, It's me, Sutton. Mercy! Mercy! **Wake up!"**

I wake like I've just breached the surface of the ocean, having been anchored to the bottom of it. The gasp is immediate, and the need for oxygen burns my lungs.

"Mark sixteen! So sayeth the Lord. Mark sixteen. Mark sixteen," I babble as my bladder lets go.

Consciousness is slower to the surface. The gentleness of Sutton is enough to keep me under, but the acrid smell of urine cuts through the room. My humiliation is so profound that I can't bring myself to acknowledge that I've just wet the bed. I know where I am, but I'm terrified to open my eyes because I know the box is here.

It feels like hours go by before I finally have the courage to open my eyes. I have to know if it's still here. Sutton isn't afraid of it, and I'm safe in his arms, so I'm going to look. I have to know if the box is still here.

"Are you okay, sweetheart?" Sutton whispers. The room is dark, save for the part illuminated by the long, thin window on my door. Light shines in from the hallway, but only a sliver of it impacts the darkened space.

"Where is the box?" I ask, my voice dusty and parched.

"You were having a nightmare, Mercy. There is no box."

"It's in here. I can feel it," I insist.

"No, honey. It's just you and me. You are safe."

"I'm not safe."

"I promise, you are."

"I peed."

"It's okay, Mercy. You were terrified. That is nothing to be ashamed of. It's a testament to the level of fear you felt. When you are ready, I'm going to have one of the nurses come in and help you get cleaned up. There is something I need to do in my office."

"Don't leave me," I plead so quietly it's almost not even audible.

"I'll never leave you. I will be right here after your shower, okay?"

***

When I finish getting cleaned up, I sit on Lyla's bed with my knees shoved up under my sweatshirt, and arms hugging my balled-up body. Paula, the nurse, has finished changing the sheets, but my humiliation remains, somehow imprinted to the bed.

Sutton isn't back yet. He said he would be here. My hair is freshly washed, and the dampness of it is causing my sweatshirt to stick to my back. The gummy feel of it is only trumped by the soreness in my mouth. I brushed my teeth again—hard, like I wanted my gums to bleed.

I hate this dark side of myself. My own mind is such a traitorous place to dwell. I've never known such treachery. The worst part is that I've turned on myself. The caverns of my own mind have sown this despair.

"Want some help blow drying your hair?" Paula asks. I shake my head stiffly, but fast. I don't want her in here. I'll keep post all night if I have to, just like this—but I'm waiting for Sutton.

After twenty more minutes and three room checks from the nurse, Sutton finally comes back in. I'm still huddled inside my stretched-out sweatshirt, and my hair has begun to dry in ropey clumps that hang limply down my back.

My self-loathing is interrupted by his brash and fluid movement through my room. He grabs the fresh blanket off the bed, and in the same motion, he wraps it around me and helps me to stand.

"Mercy, come to my office! We've had a major breakthrough—I know who Mark Sexton is!"

Chapter 24

My face is stoic when he shuts the door to his office, but when he grabs my cheeks with both hands, it stuns me to attention. His office is fully dark, with the tiny exception of a sliver of moonlight that slashes across his desk. It dulls when he switches on his desk light instead of the brash overhead fluorescent light.

He pulls me against his body, then wraps his arms around me. "Everything is going to be okay," he says as he tightens his hold, in an attempt to offset my shivering.

"Lie down on the couch, we ha—"

"Will you lie down with me?" I ask, and it sounds like the loudest thing I've ever said. There is a short pause before he toes off his shoes and then moves to the couch. When I lie down next to him, he gathers me safely in his arms with my head tucked under his chin. I can smell him, warm and intoxicating.

He begins gently, with barely a murmur, "Mercy, did the Believers talk about signs and wonders?"

"What do you mean?"

"Mark sixteen. It's a passage from the Bible, and verses 17-18 are particularly poignant."

I'm not sure what to make of his words, but instinctually, I tense up. I know there is truth to what he is saying, but it feels transient and fleeting instead of something I can fully grasp.

"And these signs shall follow them that believe: In my name they shall cast out demons; they shall speak with new tongues. They shall take

up serpents; and if they drink any deadly thing, it shall not hurt them; they shall lay hands on the sick, and they shall recover."

His words are an echo from the past. A rigor in my bones. It's true though, and admitting such a thing is like breaking through the uppermost crust of deep snow—fragile, and once you fall through, there is no stopping until you hit the ground or it swallows you.

"Does any of that sound familiar to you?"

"*Yes.*"

"Casting out demons and drinking poison?"

"*Yes.*"

"Did the Prophet do those things to command obedience?"

"They were thought to be gifts endowed by the Holy Spirit."

"So, he spoke in tongues and performed faith healings as well?"

"The signs were a test of faith."

"Mercy, was your faith ever tested? With snakes?"

"*Oh, yes.*"

"You were forced to *take up serpents*, as a child? What did that entail?" he strokes my back like a lover and holds me as though he knows I need his borrowed strength.

"They held me down. Then the Prophet would cast out the demons, and everyone inside the church would sing and pray and dance around like they were the ones possessed. I was scared because of the demons inside, but nothing compares to being stripped naked in front of the congregation and having them dump the snakes out on my body."

"Everyone believed the snakes would rid you of the demons inside?" he asks softly as if he is afraid to spook me into clamming up.

"Snakes were seen as incarnations of demons. If a church member was a true Believer, they had the Holy Spirit within them, and would suffer no harm."

"Were the snakes venomous?"

"Some of them."

"Were you ever bit?"

"Many times… I think—I think it feels like—I think that might be the acid I feel on my skin, or maybe the whips." My voice is timid, and the realization still feels more like an echo than reality, but on some level, I know it to be true.

"What would they do after you'd been bitten? Did they have anti-venom? Did they take you to a hospital?"

"Believers don't seek medical treatment because they place their faith in God to heal the afflicted."

"I'm so sorry, Mercy," he says as he kisses my head and then tips my chin up to kiss my lips. You've been through so much."

I want to languish in his kiss, but I feel like a faucet that's been left on, I have to continue. These memories—these remnants of the past are like the tar in a smoker's lungs. They are the tangible residue of a repressed childhood, and sooner or later, I'll need to face the damage. It's unavoidable, the wreckage is all around me.

"One time my face swelled up so bad, I couldn't see between my eyelids, but the worst part was how tight my throat would constrict. It felt like I could only breathe in one oxygen molecule at a time."

"And when you survived, did they stop all the devil nonsense? Did they believe the demons were cast out, and that you were healed by God?"

"No. Because my episodes persisted." And then I add, as if the lethargic epiphany has finally taken hold, "Sutton, my hallucinations were because of my past. The schizophrenia—"

"I know."

"It's all—"

"Yes, it is."

"Sutton?" I ask as I tip my head back to look him in the eyes.

"What?"

"Teach me how to forget," I whisper.

"It's a part of you. You can't forget, but you can heal. You can address the PTSD, and your anxiety—and Mercy?"

"What?"

"The only thing I want to *teach* you, is how to love."

Chapter 25

Sutton saves me from my seven-billionth wellness group therapy session when he struts in like a Hugo Boss model and waves me over to him. Everyone takes strict notice of his presence, but he does stuff like this all the time, so no one suspects that I'm any different from anyone else. Certainly not that I'm the girl who spent the wee hours of this morning wrapped around his body and making out with him on the therapy couch.

"What's up?" I ask as I approach him at the nurse station. His face is unreadable, but is extra scruffy, thanks to me. I probably still have the matching rash on my own.

His smirk mirrors mine when he answers me, "All kinds of stuff. Come with me." We walk to his office with me wondering if he was making an erection reference, but he squashes that thought as soon as he shuts the door and turns on the in-session light.

"Remember that step-down facility we talked about?"

"No."

"That residential, transitional service? The one funded by HUD Section 811? The facility I've been trying to get you into for months?... The one we've discussed on at least five different occasions?"

"Oh, you were serious about that?"

"Of course, I was serious. You need to transition from a hospital setting to being completely self-sufficient. That's where this program comes in."

"You mean the halfway house? Matty said only addicts and criminals live in halfway houses."

"I'm not sure Matty is our expert here. This is a fantastic opportunity for you to step down to a less restrictive environment. The program is in a residential, sub-acute setting. You would have your own bedroom—It's the perfect place for you. And a room finally opened up."

"What about you?"

"I'm good, I have a condo downtown," he says with a teasing smirk. He can't seem to understand why I'm not excited. In fact, why the hell is he so happy?

"Will you still be my doctor?"

"Oh, that. Yeah, there are all kinds of PHP—Sorry, partial hospitalization programs that we would put in place. In that case, you come to the hospital for part of the day and then go back to the step-down facility."

"And my nightmares?"

"The place is staffed 24 hours a day. It would be a safe environment for you. Obviously, we can address all that stuff with the—"

"*All that stuff?*"

"I'm not minimizing the nightmares, Mercy. I'm trying to tell you that you have a room in a *house*. With a kitchen and laundry room—you can have your computer without having to check it out from the nurse's station."

"Great," I say, but it's delivered flatly, so Sutton cocks his head in a questioning manner.

"Mercy, this is the best-case scenario. The other option is to wait until you turn twenty-one, and then show you the door. Is that what you want?"

"I want my friends. And I want you," I say. His voice softens in response to my admission.

"Trust me, you will have a much better opportunity to keep in touch with your friends in a residential setting. As far as me, I will still be your doctor because all your clinical treatment will occur off-site…as in, back here, on the unit."

"Okay."

"You will work with a social worker as far as community integration. So, that person will handle the stuff like driver's ed, gainful employment, bank accounts—all that tedious stuff. You will also start seeing a psychologist in addition to myself and Dr. Gingham, that's all part of your transition plan. Why do you look like you are about to cry?"

"What are you talking about?" I ask, but even I can feel my chin quivering, and my eyes filling with tears.

"Listen to me. Matty is out in four days, and Lyla isn't far behind him. Do this. Move into the step-down facility. Go have lunch with your friends. Get your driver's license. Find a job. And in between all that, continue to have your sessions with me. This isn't an eviction, I'm offering you some freedom from these walls." At some point during his explanation, he took my hand, and is still holding it now.

"What if I live with a bunch of assholes?"

"Well then, I guess you will have to learn how to deal with assholes. That should be a life skill class in itself. The world is crawling with them."

"When does this all happen?"

"Not right away, there isn't even a social worker assigned to you yet. But soon, okay?"

"I'm afraid."

"No, Mercy. You are brave. That's what it's called when something scares you, but you do it anyway."

Chapter 26

Brave, my ass. This isn't brave. This is mopey and pathetic. Now Matty is gone just like Veronica, and Wes threatens to walk out on a daily basis. Truth be told, I think the staff would watch him do it too. He has been somewhat of a troublemaker on the unit and probably equates to a heckler at a stand-up comedy club. He has even worn out his welcome with Colleen, and that says *a lot*.

Group therapy sessions have been infused with his hysterical showboating of the highest order, and are the only reason I even attend anymore. Who would have thought group therapy would be such a comic relief? Wes has given a very boisterous voice to all of our inner monologues. He says what we all think, and when it comes to things like aliens monitoring pupils and government tracking devices implanted beneath the skin, well, sometimes it's funny to watch the drama play out.

Lyla is my only other friend left because the songbird, Tracy, hates me and avoids me at all costs. Lyla and Wes are amazing, but without the whole group, the whitewashed walls simply ring hollow.

Lyla is obsessed with filling my head with fool-proof ways to seduce Sutton during my sessions. I think she has made it her personal goal, not to get better herself, but to get me to cough up my V-card before she leaves.

Her ideas are lofty, considering my novice state. I'm not saying I am completely opposed to them, only that they are not for amateurs. The tactic that I happen to be the most comfortable with requires me to smuggle my new cell phone from Sutton's office, and somehow ditch the watchful eyes of the staff, so I can snap some racy selfies.

Proceeding as if that were actually possible, Lyla has already started strategizing my attack. More accurately, she has spent rec time sketching out salacious poses and slutty outfits and then walking me through the plan like an offensive line coach running plays.

I'm not entirely sure I'll be able to pull it off, but even with all the potential obstacles, it still makes more sense than her other idea, which is lying naked on Sutton's desk with my legs spread and an inviting tilt to my smile.

Needless to say, Lyla is a level ten with guys, whereas I am more of a negative three. And recently, without Matty and Veronica's sometimes conflicting input, she has reprised the role of my sexual Jedi Master. Rec time has taken a drastic detour away from the fictional world of books and has sped headlong toward more of the verbal pornography type.

Having listened intently to Lyla's explicit how-to's and erotic play-by-plays, I can finally say I have a comfortable grip on a wide variety of sexual acts—and a permanent buzz down below.

The knowledge that at any moment, Lyla could be released from her state-sanctioned stay, or I could be introduced to my transitional social worker, hovers like a guillotine. I know Sutton made it possible for me to keep in touch with my friends, but somehow, I know it will never be the same. And I am terrified.

Any moment now, my life is going to become virtually unrecognizable.

Chapter 27

"How have your sessions with Dr. Gingham been going?" Sutton asks, all fresh-faced and sexy. He has no idea I am picturing his tongue on my nipple right this very second.

"Good, I guess. He seems to think I'm making progress," I answer as I shift my position on the couch and then shift again.

"You haven't had a nightmare in three nights, I would consider that progress. Especially because of the heightened anxiety from Matty leaving and your looming change of placement." God, his lips are perfect. He even slow-licks them to torment me.

"I think it helps me to understand where they come from, you know? Before, I just felt like my mind was turning on me. Now, I don't feel so crazy. I don't feel normal—just, not full-blown crazy."

"I'm glad I could help you with that. We still have a lot of work to do, though."

"I disagree. Can I use my phone now? I'm dying to find out how Matty is doing."

"We are like, three minutes into your session."

"So? Can I have it for a little while?" I push. He sighs.

"Sure." He gets up, almost reluctantly, to retrieve my phone. It's still in the box. My fingers are itching with the need to check on Matty and see what new stories Veronica has for me. The last one almost made me wet my pants I was laughing so hard. In a nutshell, her cat was pissed that she left him for so long, so he totally destroyed her apartment and taunted her roommate endlessly. I really need to meet that cat. I think I love him already.

"Fifteen minutes, okay? We have work to do."

There is nothing new from Veronica, but I quickly tap out the seduction plan, just in case she wants to weigh in. I'm sure she will find the racy selfies rather bush league and try to encourage something far more daring, but that's fine with me. I need all the help I can get.

In my text to Matty, I tell him about the halfway house and how I'll be rubbing elbows with addicts and criminals soon. I also tell him I miss him terribly and not just because I have to do my own makeup now.

Anyway, after that, I don't really have anything to do with my allotted fifteen minutes, so I decide to text Sutton. He looks to be checking his email, or something equally boring, so I'll go ahead and spice up this session.

Me: *The capabilities of this phone are fairly limited inside of fifteen minutes. Now I'm back to wishing it was a vibrator. That seems like a better use of my time, don't you think?*

As far as Sutton is concerned, I'm texting with my friends, so he has no problem fishing his phone from his pocket and stealthily checking the incoming text. He snorts on a stifled laugh before tapping out a reply.

Not Wes: *I can think of quite a few ways to better use this time.*

Me: *Is that sexual innuendo? Or do you agree about the vibrator?*

Not Wes: *I can't say I disagree about the vibrator. But I was referring to cognitive processing therapy, or perhaps some prolonged exposure techniques.*

Me: *No thanks, I'm going to ask Veronica to send me something that vibrates. Anyway, did you know this phone has Solitaire?*

Not Wes: *If I can't interest you in a little CPT, how about some good old fashioned, psychotherapy?*

Me: *No than—*

Then there is a knock on the door, and we both scramble to hide the evidence of my phone. I drop it between my thighs and pinch them closed while Sutton shoves his into his pocket. When he looks up at me, I toss him the empty phone box, he drops it in his drawer and then with a look of begrudging solidarity, he walks to the door and opens it.

"Dr. Sutton, I'm Hilary Eades. I'm the social worker assigned to Mercy Kavanaugh. So sorry I'm late." Picture a frazzled kindergarten teacher that has completely lost control of the classroom and has kids swinging from the ceiling fans and the walls covered with paint and toilet paper—that haggard image, that's Hilary Eades. My new social worker.

"Nice to meet you, Hilary. Please come in." He shakes her hand and then gestures her into his office.

"This is Mercy Kavanaugh. Mercy, say hello to your social worker, Hilary." Then he gives me the stink-eye when I don't stand to shake her hand. Normally, I would have conformed to the demands of social etiquette, but my phone is between my legs, and I'm trying to smuggle it out of here.

The next forty-five minutes are a rundown of my new life, new responsibilities, new expectations, and new living situation. My social worker clearly has a mountain of other cases because she delivers the information with a flurry of hand motions and in a bullet-pointed format. Her hair is in disarray, with more strands free from the bun than are contained, and her files are no better.

In fact, if this is the woman I'm supposed to trust my immediate future with, I think I should manifest some paranoid delusions and keep my ass right here. I am no more ready for this than I was when my parents dropped me off at St. Vincent's.

In a not so subtle hint, Sutton thanks the social worker for her time and gets up to show her out. I think he can read my lack of faith in her as easily as if it was written across my forehead, and tries to minimize the damage.

I have enough sense to shove the phone up my sleeve while he is moderately distracted with the formalities of her exit. I can't say I expected the selfie plan to materialize this easily, but I may not get another chance, so I'll have to proceed without Veronica's input.

"Mercy, despite what you just witnessed, this is a good plan. Do not make a judgment about the placement based on the obvious fact that Hilary pretty much mainlines caffeine straight into her veins. She will help you get on your feet, and then all you have to do is check-in with her."

I want to scream at him, *why have you forsaken me*? But instead, with contraband up my sleeve, I just nod and try to determine if he has chest hair by analyzing how his shirt lays against his chest.

"It's going to be great. Trust me."

***

Lyla was caught off guard when I told her I got the phone, and then had spent the rest of the day fretting about how to sneak her slutty outfits to me.

In the end, the bra and panty set that she had built the plan around, were in her dirty laundry. So, she was only able to bring me lacy black panties and black high heels that have no place on a mental health unit. They worry about dental floss on this floor, and here Lyla is, post suicide attempt, with lethal heals attached to her shoes. No shoelaces though—so, there's that.

After dinner, some rec time, and daily reflection group, I have roughly thirty minutes to shower and get ready for bed, so the clock is ticking. However, I remain frozen in front of my open drawer because I still can't bring myself to go completely topless.

Finally, I grab one of the white tank-tops I sleep in, a hoodie, and sweat pants, then add them to the pile of Lyla's stuff on my bathroom counter. There is no lock on the door, but I'm also not on the staff's radar as far as being a danger to myself, so they should leave me alone.

I put the black panties and high heels on, and it's enough to confirm that I'm not ballsy enough to completely expose my chest. I add the tank top and snap a few pics. They are not very sexy, certainly not worthy of being Lyla's protégé. Then, I have an idea, so I slip off the shoes and turn on the water.

After a fast shower, I wring out my hair and as much of the tank top as possible, but the way the wet fabric clings to my body has me shivering and feeling anything but sexy. I snap a few pictures, then a few more.

The 'mirror' in the bathroom is more like a metal tray on the wall, and it doesn't really serve to accurately portray my reflection. The images on my phone, however, are as clear as day. It's almost shocking to see myself, nipples at full salute and clearly showing through the nearly transparent, wet tank-top.

I play around a little with the ropey strands of wet hair and then grip the bottom of the shirt, so my mid-section shows too. Then I get back into the tub and lie down before putting the shoes back on.

Now, the pictures are down-shots of my body and actually capture the cute panties and sexy shoes. I'm not gonna lie, posing in a wet bathtub while trying to look sexy is harder than you'd think, but I manage to get a few good pictures. Before taking the freezing cold tank off, I tug it down and take some even more revealing shots.

Through chattering teeth, I finally peel off the damp clothes and put my sweats on. After squeezing as much water as possible from the wet fabric, I place them at the bottom of my hamper, then brush my teeth. When I pull the hood up and over my damp hair, then unzip the hoodie partway, it looks unassuming but undeniably sexy because I'm topless underneath. So, I adjust the fit, pose, and click, then I unzip more, pose, and click. Then I unzip it completely, pose, and click.

When the nurse pops in to check on me, I'm already in bed wearing head to toe sweats. I'm clutching the phone under my pillow and freakishly paranoid that all of a sudden, someone will call me, and the phone will ring out like an air-raid siren.

"You need anything, Mercy?" the nurse asks.

"Nope, I'm good," I answer too loudly. "Night."

"Alright then, Goodnight."

I can actually hear my heart beating, it's that loud. I didn't really think about the ramifications of getting caught with a phone. Before now, it was all fun and games. But if I get caught, Sutton will get fired, and probably lose his medical license.

I wait at least an hour before I risk sliding the phone from under my pillow. Even then, it's at a snail's pace and transfers directly under the blanket. When nothing happens, and no one is alerted, I curl my body around it and scroll through the pictures.

I pick one with the wet tank top that only shows the bottom half of my face, and send it to Sutton before I change my mind. He can't get fired if no one can tell it's me, right? His reply is almost immediate.

Not Wes: *Fucking hell!*

Me: *Are you mad?*

Not Wes: *I probably should be.*

Not Wes: *Jesus, that's hot!*

Me: *So, does that mean you're not mad that I kept my phone?*

Not Wes: *I can't possibly be expected to process emotions right now, all the blood that normally nourishes my brain is presently hardening my dick.*

Me: *Did that picture give you a hard-on?*

Not Wes: *Yeah.*

Me: *Show me.*

Not Wes: *Are you crazy?*

Me: *I have more pics, that one was pretty tame…*

Not Wes: *I'm going to hell.*

Then, after a few minutes, he sends a picture of himself shirtless with his bottom half under a white sheet. He is obviously in bed. The most shocking part of the picture is that he is griping his sheet-covered erection while it is aimed straight up his prone body. *Holy shit.* The sight of his bare chest and erotic pose has an undeniable effect on me. I pinch my thighs together, trying to relieve the pressure—or maybe to create it, I'm not sure.

Not Wes: *Your turn.*

I send one of the bathtub ones, mostly panties, and legs but the black lace and scandalous shoes pack a decent punch. I'm also feeling bolder now that he has reacted positively, so I send the one where I'm tugging down the tank and exposing my tits more—still only half a face, but I'm biting the side of my bottom lip, and the shot turned out really sexy for someone who isn't particularly sexy.

Not Wes: *Baby…*

Not Wes: *I'm so afraid of you getting caught with the phone.*

Me: *I'm being careful.*

Not Wes: *I need to hear your voice. Call me after safety check.*

Not Wes: *Don't get caught.*

Now, I wait. I'll have to wait for the nurse to poke her head in and confirm I'm not at risk. After that, I will have roughly thirty minutes before she does it again. It takes every ounce of self-control I possess to keep the phone under my pillow. All I want to do is stare at the image of Sutton's bare chest and the comfortable way he holds his erection.

It seems so natural, his hand on his penis. I bet he is touching it right now…and looking at my photos. The thought is heady, and I can hardly sit still and pretend to sleep I'm so drunk with power.

I'll have to commit that image to memory because I know he will make me delete it. The phone itself is bad enough, but any link to him—especially this type of exchange will ruin him. He is my doctor, he is probably ten years older than me, and he is in a position of trust. Whatever this is between us, is taboo on many levels. Not just taboo, I think it's illegal.

After bed check, I wait another five minutes before bringing the phone to the edge of my pillow. I block the light from the screen with my body, the blanket, and my pillow, but it still feels risky because the stakes are so high.

But he wants to hear my voice.

The call barely rings through before he answers. His voice is gravelly, and the whisper of it rumbles in my bones and brings a triumphant smile to my face.

"Mercy, hi."

"Hi," I say, as quiet as possible while still emitting sound.

"God, you're fucking sexy. I have a hard enough time getting my mind off of you without these images."

"Good because I can't get my mind off of you, ever," I admit. It's easier to say since I have to do it so quietly, but this is the first time I feel absolutely free of his moral dilemma. He is not my doctor right now, and I am not his broken patient.

"Tell me what you are thinking about," he prompts.

My thoughts are hazy and disjointed, but after a few false starts, I simply say, "Sutton, you make me *feel*." I know it doesn't make any sense, so I try again, just to be clear, "I feel like I've been numb my whole life, and now I have these pockets of joy with you—I feel like you are unlocking compartments of my heart that I've let wither and die. Does that sound dumb?"

"It doesn't sound dumb at all," he says, and I can tell he has a smile on his face. But before he has a chance to psycho-analyze what I've just said, I jump in.

"*Send me another picture*," I whisper.

"You are making it very hard to keep a professional distance," he murmurs. There is angst in his voice, like he is still trying to do the right thing.

"I'm not interested in a professional distance. Tell me, you want me."

"No." The word cuts through me, and my heart squeezes to a halt.

"*Why?*" The sound of my voice conveys my heartache, and I wish I could take it back.

"Because then it will seem like I only want your body. Mercy, the truth is, I want your heart."

It takes a few seconds to register his meaning, then I simultaneously choke on a sob and squeeze my eyelids shut. I don't respond because I can't, I'm too overwhelmed with emotion. After a few minutes, he speaks gently into the phone.

"Get some sleep, Mercy. I'll see you in the morning."

"Okay," I manage to get out.

"Sweet dreams, beautiful."

Chapter 28

I'm not taking any chances this morning. I don't dare leave the phone in my room, hidden or not, so it's like having a ticking time-bomb strapped to my chest. Well, not exactly my chest. It's down my pants, and that's just as bad. My jeans are so tight, I probably have an iPhone menu screen imprinted on my skin next to my hip, but I can't risk it sliding down my leg or poking out of a pocket.

I'm jumpy too, because I can't unload the thing until my session at nine, so that means I have to make it through breakfast and group therapy without anyone noticing the not-at-all anatomically correct rectangle pressed against my abdomen.

What I should have done is turn it off. I have it set to silent, and all the notifications are turned off, but I can't help my irrational worry that the thing will start ringing in my pants. I'd have to fake a coughing fit and run to the bathroom.

I'm also nervous because I know my days here are limited. My wacky and overworked social worker, Hilary, said it would take a couple of days to get the room cleaned up once the other occupant moved out, but does that mean tomorrow? Next week? A month from now? Who knows?

I have not at all come to terms with moving into the halfway house, or, excuse me, *the step-down facility*. I will be one of five residents, three males, and two of us females. From my understanding, the people who live there are high functioning adults, but they have various challenges—either mentally or physically.

I do have to participate in the house meetings, and I'm expected to clean up after myself, but I get the impression I can leave the premises.

Hilary made a big deal about the nearby bus stop, and the sign in—sign out sheet by the front door. She also said the other residents had jobs and that I would be expected to get one as well.

I didn't bother to tell her about my computer that was donated from the university so I could get my graphic design degree a few years ago. Or that I've made a decent amount of money doing freelance design work. I also didn't feel the need to tell her I won't be taking the bus to work because I can do it in my pajamas while sipping coffee.

***

Eagerly, I go to my nine o'clock standing appointment with Sutton about fifteen minutes early. His *in-session* light is on, so I pace the hallway for a while, and then slide down the wall and sit on the floor to hug my knees.

After last night, all I want to do is take him by the hand and walk straight out of here and never look back. I want him with a hunger that gnaws and consumes. I can seduce him with my body, but he wants the broken parts too. *He wants my heart.*

The door finally flings open and a short-timer storms out of his office. The guy looks like he has been abused by life and left angry and resentful by his need for resilience. I know the feeling. I used to sit in that office and feel the same way.

I walk to the doorway and ask timidly, "Everything okay in here?" He looks up at me and smiles. It's impossible to know what went on in the last session, but it feels like some of the energy has been sucked out of the room.

"Things are starting to look up already," he says from behind his desk as he stands up. After I close the door behind me, he holds out his hand.

"Give me the phone." His voice is firm. I guess I'm dealing with Doctor Sutton this morning. There is no trace of longing in his tone, not like last night.

"No. I still get fifteen minutes."

"That is supposed to be *after* our session. And I feel like your privileges may need to be revoked," he says with a grin that he tries to suppress.

"I didn't have a nightmare last night. And I didn't get caught with the cellphone. So, I think I've earned a few minutes to catch up with my friends before I have to submit to my grueling therapy regimen."

"You have ten minutes. Go."

Truth be told, I don't have anything new to report to Matty or Veronica, and I don't have any new texts from either of them. So, instead, I look over the selfies I took. Funny enough, I'm still wearing the same zip-up hoodie, with nothing underneath.

I decide to send Sutton the unzipped sweatshirt shot. The one with my back arched, face turned to the side, and my arms bent back behind my head. It was a Lyla pose, and an explicit one. It also leaves nothing to the imagination. The others I sent were certainly provocative, but my nipples were at least covered—mostly. This pic is all me.

After I hit send, I keep my head down with my face pointed at the screen, but my eyes never leave Sutton's face. His head is tipped down as well, but his gaze meets mine when he feels the vibration from the text notification. He keeps his eyes glued to mine while he retrieves the phone from his pocket.

I can't help it, my cheeks are on fire. I know *exactly* what he is about to see. We have nearly an hour in here, hidden behind his in-session light, and I've just fired a shot across the bow.

He looks at his phone. There is silence, and a long pause before his eyes find mine again. He waits, doesn't say a word, just stares at me. Then I start to toy with the zipper of my hoodie. As soon as he can tell there is bare skin underneath, he snaps.

"Mercy, come over here."

I do as I'm told, and he rolls his chair back from the desk, so he can stand. He places his palm on the side of my neck and cheek, as if he needs to hold me in place while he looks penetratingly deep into my eyes. And, just when I think he is going to kiss me, he leans in and murmurs into my ear.

"Do you have any idea how inappropriate it is for me to conduct psychiatric sessions with a raging hard-on?" His cheek brushes against mine as he speaks, and the sensation is electric. I don't respond because my lungs have cramped up, and a ticklish shiver runs through my body.

He closes the tiny space between us and asks, "Can you feel what you do to me?" I can feel the hardness of his erection as if it were an extension of myself.

"*Yes*," I whisper.

"Can you imagine the filthy thoughts that kept me up all night stroking myself?"

"Tell me," I pant.

"No. But one day, I'm going to show you." Then his mouth is on mine. It's not a quick kiss, it's one that says he's just getting started. When his hand finds my sweatshirt zipper, a chill runs up my spine. I felt the same sensation last night over the phone when he whispered in my ear. It's like a thousand butterfly wings graze my skin all at once.

The needy effect he has on me is purely anticipatory, but my nipples are already hardening, and the hairs on the back of my neck are standing on end. He unzips the sweatshirt, one tooth at a time, and when the hoodie hangs open and free of any attachment to itself, his hand slides up my bare stomach.

The warmth of his palm and the confidence behind his touch will leave a mark on my skin for decades. It compliments his kiss with perfect synchronicity. At this moment, I can see our future together. Long after this institution is behind us, we can have a life together, and I have never wanted anything more. Nothing from my past has prepared me for this. All the want and desire to belong is nothing compared to how badly I want to find my place with Sutton.

When his hand finds my breast and his fingers gently pinch my nipple, I gasp against his lips. The sensation and the boldness, too shocking inside of this tiny moment. But when he slides the sweatshirt off my shoulders and begins to kiss his way down my neck, my thoughts get blurry.

"Touch me, Mercy," he whispers on an exhale as he nibbles my earlobe. I realize for the first time that my hands, presently on his waist, are clenching fistfuls of his shirt, but are otherwise idle.

I'm so consumed with the riot he incites inside me, I have neglected to reciprocate his touch. Lyla and Veronica, and Wes, for that matter, have all coached me in the art of touching a man, but I'm also very good at reading cues, and evidently, Sutton is good at directing my novice hands.

When I drag my palm up and down his erection, he groans, and that's all I need to confidently move forward. I undo his pants and slide my hand down the front of them. The feel of his bare skin is both hot and silky, and very, very hard.

"What are we doing, Mercy?" he groans with something that resembles despair. It's enough to make me stop stroking his conflicted dick.

"What?"

"This is wrong, Mercy. We have to stop."

"Why?"

"Because I'm your doctor. This is completely unethical. I need to use this time to transition you to the step-down facility, not to contemplate bending you over my desk."

"Why do you always do that to me?"

"Because I'm conflicted as hell."

"I'm getting sick of your untimely bouts of morality," I say as I yank my hand out of his pants and back up enough to shrug my sweatshirt back into place. I'm angry, but I'm not sure it's at him. I know he is trying to do the right thing, and I should be more accepting of his commitment to my mental health—but I'm not.

"I only wish my bouts of morality happened before I stepped so egregiously across the line. I'm sorry. Neither of us wants these boundaries, but they are here. We have to respect them, they are in place for a reason."

"Sure, doc. Whatever you say. Let's get to work on my transition." Now, I *am* angry at him. I zip up my shirt and sit heavily on the couch. He must be getting used to my piss-off-and-die face by now.

"In two days' time, you will move into the facility. They have arranged for your transportation back and forth to the unit, so you can continue your therapy work. I've arranged for you to take your laptop with you even though there was some opposition and claims that it was donated to the unit, but in all honesty, that thing is a dinosaur, and you should get a new one anyway."

"I hate how easily you shut me out."

"Trust me, Mercy, there is nothing about this that is easy for me. Least of all, shutting you out."

"Your actions say different."

"Then listen to my heart."

"Your heart is misleading."

"My heart is the most honorable part of me left."

"Sutton, your honor is hurtful, and I can't trust it."

"You're wrong, honor is the only thing that never lies."

We stare at each other for a few minutes, a standoff of wills. He challenges me to disagree with his honor assessment, but I'm all done arguing in esoteric circles.

"Are we done here?" I ask, but I'm already standing.

"Sure," he says in defeat. He doesn't even object when I take my phone with me.

***

For two days, I sulk and opt-out of all group activities. Lyla and Wes can't even get me to shake off my funk. It's not just Sutton, it's leaving the place that for all intents and purposes has been my home for a decade. It's leaving the amazing staff—most of all Colleen, I can't even think about not seeing her anymore. If Sig was a father figure, Colleen was my mother, and with me only showing up for psychiatry and hypnosis appointments, that relationship will wither from neglect.

My appointments with Sutton are purely obligatory, and I have only participated in the most perfunctory fashion. On his end, it's cognitive behavioral therapy as usual, and he hasn't asked about the phone or referenced it in any way.

I turned the power off two days ago after storming out of his office, with only half a thought to preserving the battery, but he gave me the box and charger during my next session with him, and I've still left it powered off.

I don't know if it's because I'm punishing him for pushing me away, or if I'm trying to preserve the part of me that will go insane if we keep up the sexy back and forth banter over text. Either way, it's not enough to know he wants to be with me if he is not willing to make the necessary sacrifices to enable the possibility.

He doesn't have to be my doctor, and nobody will follow up with me after I evaporate from the system. The fact is, we could make it work if he wanted it bad enough. It hurts my soul that he puts so much emphasis on all the factors that keep us apart because one thing that I will never get used to, is people letting me go.

Those are my scars, bone-deep and impossible to heal from. I've survived being possessed by the devil, an upbringing in a cult including horrific abuse and ritualistic sacrifices, almost losing my life in multiple snake handling ceremonies, and living with paranoid schizophrenia. But all of that pales in comparison to willfully and purposefully being discarded.

I always come up short when weighed against the consequences. My parents weighed keeping me against their beliefs. Every foster parent weighed me against the damage I could cause to their family. Sig weighed, breaking the rules against keeping in touch with me. And now Sutton has weighed his ethical conscience against having a life with me.

Perhaps tearing me down is necessary before each new phase of my life. Maybe if I go into the step-down facility as a shell, they can fill me however they see fit, before tearing me down when they finish with me. That's what has happened all along, I was torn down by the cult and then filled up with paranoid schizophrenia to play a role in the world of mental hospitals. Now, I'm being groomed to fit in on the fringe of society in a halfway house.

This sense of constant reprogramming feels like the biggest betrayal of all, and Sutton has dutifully played his part. And me? I have played my role, as well. They were all just labels, but I accepted them all—and I wore each one like a crown.

Chapter 29

Today is the day Hilary will take me from my home and deposit me among strangers to carve a life out for myself. I could hardly force a smile at my unit going-away party last night, even when presented with a giant box of chocolates and a card that the whole staff wrote really sweet things in.

I've spent hours, if not days crying on shoulders and sobbing into my pillow as the countdown to my departure ticked by. Colleen has done her level best to piece me back together and remind me that when God closes a door, he always opens a window. Too bad I feel like the window He opened leads to the abyss.

Roughly ten years ago, I arrived with nothing but a child's broken mind and the clothes on my back—and the potent fear of the unknown. Now, I've acquired some clothes, books, and an archaic laptop, and I've even hung on to the fear, but there is something disheartening about seeing your entire life fit into a few bags.

As I wait for Hilary, fear and dread have me by the throat. My new life starts today, and I'm not ready. Not even close. This is what the condemned must feel like after their final stay of execution has been denied. Any and all sense of optimism has vanished, only to be replaced by complete and utter desolation. Nothing that even resembles acceptance has scurried across my path.

When Hilary enters the unit, I stand, acknowledging my own human frailty, and walk to the future.

***

The mechanical way Hilary approaches this transfer is generic and a testament to the hundreds she has done before. Her lack of enthusiasm is beyond repair, as is her personality.

She prattles on about house rules and chore lists as I watch the city life blur in my tears. But when she mentions Sutton, I tune in to what she says.

"Dr. Sutton has seen to refilling your scripts, but it will be up to you to stay on top of your meds. You will be expected to take them on your own—no one is going to hand you a paper cup with your pills."

I turn back to look out the window. It's been five minutes, and I'm already sick of her patronizing tone.

"Dr. Sutton has also briefed the staff on your nightmares, so your care should be pretty seamless. I've had cases where the nightmares were so bad, the person had to wear restraints to bed. So, let's see how a few of your episodes go, and we can always make adjustments to your care plan."

"Are you suggesting they restrain me at night?"

"I'm merely pointing out that care plans can be adjusted to fit an individual's needs. You have to understand that the safety of the staff and other residents is a particularly high priority."

"Noted." I tune her out for the rest of the drive because she is somehow unaware of the level of discomfort that sits between us. She seems to be going through some sort of checklist, and proving by the minute that her job has slowly robbed her of the altruistic nature she once possessed.

When we get to the house, she unbuckles her seatbelt and exits the car while I remain seated and note how unremarkable the place truly is. Other than the wheelchair ramp, there is nothing that sets the dwelling apart from the rest of the suburban homes lining the street. No neon signs to announce our shortcomings, no empty cans in the front yard, or cars propped up on cinderblocks.

"Here it is, Home Sweet Home," Hilary attempts to draw some warmth into her voice, but it falls just as flat as everything else she says.

"Yep, here it is."

When we ring the doorbell, we are greeted by a woman who introduces herself as Theresa. She is unremarkable, like the house, and due to my woeful state of mind, I decide she is the cornerstone of mediocrity.

Theresa gives us a brief tour, ending with my room. Dejection has weighted itself heavily to my feet, so I'm slow to enter my new space. There is a twin bed, a small dresser, and a nightstand. The curtains are sun-bleached, but they somewhat match the burnished gold of the bedspread. The entire place smells faintly like a musty basement but also like something has been sprayed to mask the staleness.

"Marv is napping right now. You will meet him soon enough though, because it's his turn to cook dinner tonight," she says as she points to the closed door across from mine. "I hope you like mac and cheese, it's his specialty."

"Okay," I say, more as a verbal pause than anything. It is mildly disturbing to have an unknown man living across the hallway from me. Men and women have their own hallways in my old unit. Bedrooms were never commingled.

"Follow me, and I'll introduce you to Marcella. Now, you're going to think she is hard of hearing, but she can hear just fine. She just likes to pick and choose what she listens to."

"I see," another verbal pause, instead of asking, *what the hell?*

"Colton and Vince are at work right now, but you'll meet them this evening. Colton is the nicest man you'll ever meet, but he's got some tics that might take some getting used to. And Vince, he's a big ole' teddy bear, but he's afraid of his own shadow, so don't expect him to say much to ya at all."

Marcella's room is upstairs, so we follow Theresa to the door with a sign that says, *Keep out, I have a big stick.*

"Who is it?" a cranky voice asks from inside the room.

"Marcella, I'd like you to meet our new friend."

"Make it quick, I'm a busy lady."

Theresa opens the door, and we follow her through a beaded curtain that hangs in front of the door. There are tapestries on every wall, and one on the ceiling, which mutes the light and creates a somber ambiance.

Marcella sits cross-legged on her bed with her palms pressed together against her chest. She looks to be deep in a meditative trance and is chanting the mantra, *Ommmmmmmmmmm.*

"Marcella, this is Mercy."

"*Ommmmmm.*"

"Don't ya want to say hello?" Theresa prompts.

"*Ommmm.*"

With a shrug, Theresa walks out of the room. We follow, but I can't resist tossing over my shoulder, "Good talk, Marcella."

Hilary and Theresa continue to discuss schedules, and my goals and objectives while I contemplate running out the front door. Theresa seems nice enough, but I hate it here and would rather do cartwheels in traffic.

"I'm not feeling well. I'm going to go lie down," I announce before I turn to retreat to my new prison cell. At least I can shut the door and hope to be left alone.

Hilary objects because she wants me to acquaint myself with my *off-premises* schedule, which translates to driver's ed, psychotherapy, and job interviews. Thankfully, Theresa interrupts.

"It's okay. This is a lot to take in. Leave her be."

This makes me want to hug Theresa, but I don't even turn around. Once I'm alone in my room, I close the curtains and curl up on the bed. It's stiff as a board, and it crinkles from the plastic mattress cover on it. I hate it here, and I can't cry hard enough to wash the sadness from my system. I guess it's just a part of me that I will have to get used to now.

Once empty of tears, I take my phone from my backpack and power it on. I do not have the intestinal fortitude to explain my situation to Matty or Veronica, and Sutton put me here, so fuck him. All I care about is checking my PayPal account balance.

I've had money for years, and because I never really bought anything, it's just sat there. The university noticed my knack for graphic design when I was working on my degree, and since then, I've done all sorts of work for them. Marketing brochures, postcards, booklets, banners, posters, flyers, information packages, financial aid packets, career fair pamphlets—you name it, I've done it for them.

When I can't log in to PayPal after the tenth or eleventh try, all pretense of self-preservation crumbles, and I submit once again to wringing the tears from my body.

***

It's full dark outside when a knock on my door wakes me with a start. My eyes are swollen from crying, and the last thing I want to face is my new living situation and questionable roommates. I roll over and tuck myself against the wall.

"Mercy? It's time for dinner. Will you come join us?" Theresa says from the other side of the door.

"I'm not hungry."

"How about you just come say hello to everyone?" she says in a conciliatory tone.

"No." I try the word on my tongue. I have the freedom to use it here. I like it.

"Just for a couple of minutes?" she pleads.

"No."

"How about I make you a plate? Just in case you get hungry later."

"Thanks, but no." I figure, I'll eat in the morning with Lyla and Wes before my session with Sutton. Or, maybe I'll never eat again—I will certainly never sleep again, not here. I would never feel comfortable having a nightmare while living in this place.

I stare absentmindedly at the wall all through dinner and well into the clanking of dishes being washed and put away. With any luck, the house will quiet down soon. I wonder how many other people have stared at this very spot feeling the very same way?

Someone pounds on the door and then opens it right up. My room is dark, but the hallway light is on, so I can see him in shadow. Then he flips the light switch on, and I have to squint my eyes against the bright light.

"I brought you some macaroni and cheese. Everyone likes my macaroni and cheese. Why don't you want to try my macaroni and cheese?" He is a big man, and my immediate impression of him is Lenny, from Of Mice and Men.

I'm so stunned he opened my door and is standing in my room; I don't know how to react. I do know that he scares me. At first glance, he seems cognitively or developmentally disabled, but he has a sharp look in his eyes that reminds me of a wolf. That look tells me he is shrewd and that first impressions can't always be trusted.

Just then, Theresa intercepts him, "Marv! It is not okay for you to barge into another person's room like that. Tell Mercy you are sorry and go sit down. Wheel of Fortune is starting."

He looks at me with predatory eyes and a slight quirk to his lips, "Sorry, Mercy, but everyone likes my macaroni and cheese." His demeanor is off, his expressions are inappropriate, and his words seem to mean something else. There is no doubt about it, he is terrifying.

I've been around mental disabilities for a long time, and I can't shake the feeling that Marv's are disingenuous. He leaves my room slowly, deliberately—while looking back at me with complete contempt.

My heart is pounding so hard in my throat, I can taste it. That man sleeps across the hall from me, and it looks like he wants to acquire a little mercy of his own.

Nighttime falls all around me. Hours pass since Marv walked into my room as if he were entitled to do so. I haven't moved from my bed. I'm hugging my knees and watching the doorknob while the space around me goes numb.

An hour or so ago, Theresa knocked on my door to say goodnight and to ask if I needed anything, but it's been mostly quiet ever since. I am still on high alert, and I don't see that changing.

I must have nodded off for a second, but something brought me back to full awareness. Then I hear it. Something is scratching at my door. It's a slow, deliberate scratch. On the other side of my door is Marv, I know it. Marv and his violent, feral eyes.

I look around my room for something to protect myself with, but there is nothing. I unplug the lamp, plunging myself into darkness, and wind the cord around the base of it. If he opens my door, the best I can do is hurl it at him. Then I hear something besides the scratching.

"*Mercy.*"

"*Merrrrrrrcy.*"

"*Mercy, come out and play.*"

I jump up and push the heavy dresser against the door. Then my bed. The sliding furniture makes a little noise, but not enough to wake anyone up, and not enough to stop the torment on the other side of the door.

I'm shaking when I call Sutton. I have no idea what time it is, but he answers right away.

"Is everything alright, Mercy?" he asks in a rush. His voice is kind and concerned, and it breaks me.

"*I'm afraid,*" I whisper as my eyes dart around the room.

"What are you afraid of?" I can almost hear a smile in his question.

"Marv. He is outside my door."

"Wait. What?"

"He is right outside my door, taunting me…can you hear that? That's him."

"Is your door locked?" he asks, all of a sudden feeling the gravity of the situation.

"I don't have a lock on my door."

"What do you mean, *you don't have a lock on your door?*" he asks, angry at something.

"I put all the furniture in front of the door."

"Has he tried to open it?"

"I don't think so."

"Do you want me to call the police? Do you want me to—shit, I can't come. It would be too suspicious. Mercy, tell me what to do, I'll do anything to keep you safe."

Silent tears are running down my face. He won't come. He wants me to be safe, but not at the cost of rescuing me himself. The weight of my situation is sinking in. I am on my own.

"Mercy, say something. Who is in charge there, anyway? This is bullshit!"

"Never mind," I manage to get out. "Everything is fine. I'm overreacting. Goodnig—"

"Wait! Mercy, be serious. Are you in danger right now?"

"No, I'm fine. I just have to get used to a few things, that's all."

"Are you kidding me right now?" he asks, exasperated, but not yet relinquishing his sense of panic.

"Sutton, I'm fine. Just putting old ghosts to bed."

"Are you sure?"

"Yes. Goodnight." I hang up before the sob breaks free, then I go sit in the corner of my room furthest from the door. For the rest of the night, I watch the doorknob and cry.

There is no more scratching.

Chapter 30

I haven't slept all night, so when I walk back into the hospital I used to call home, it's with the dreary haze of exhaustion. Sutton hustles me into his office before I can even grab a muffin or say hi to Lyla.

Last night was a powerful reminder for me of where things stand with Sutton, and I would rather not linger in his ambivalence any longer. Right away, I lie down on the couch. I'll submit to his cognitive-behavioral runaround, but I'm going to do it while I rest my eyes.

"What the hell happened last night?"

"Mercy?"

"Mercy?"

***

I wake up starving. When I sit up, I realize I'm alone in Sutton's office. The lights are out, and the blinds are drawn. He has also covered me with a blanket that smells like him.

I feel like I'm back where I belong—not in Sutton's office, but here, with Colleen and Lyla. Then I stretch and readjust myself on the couch, settling in, and deciding to milk this reprieve for all it's worth.

Not ten minutes pass before Sutton checks on me and realizes I'm awake. He shuts the door, and then scoots me over and sits down in the same motion.

"Start talking."

"What do you want to know? That place is a nightmare. The people are at best, rude, and at worst, psychopaths. I'd be safer living under a viaduct."

"Let's go then," he says as he stands and extends his hand.

"Go where?"

"To the facility. I need to check this out."

"Uh, okay."

We step out into twilight, which in itself is surprising. I must have slept all day. No wonder I'm so damn hungry.

"What the heck time is it?" I ask.

"Almost 5:00."

"What about all your sessions?"

"The hospital is a big place. I managed."

"And now?"

"What? Now I'm done."

I decide not to fight the losing battle about going back to the facility. Sutton is accustomed to stoking my anxiety like a bellows and then putting out the fire. It's called exposure therapy, and I'm quite familiar with it. The fact that my nerves have eaten a hole through my stomach by the time we pull up to the house has no visible effect on Sutton.

He takes the key from my shaking palm and then unlocks the door. After pushing it open, and with a sweep of his hand, he says, "Why don't you show me around."

My plan is to take him straight to my room, but there is an obstacle along the way. That obstacle is Marv, who is sitting on the couch in plain view, furiously masturbating with his pants around his ankles.

He tips his head back and locks eyes with me, but instead of stopping at the intrusion, he picks up his pace.

"*Ahhh, Mercy, yeah,*" he moans. Just before he spurts ejaculate all up the front of his naked body.

Sutton is frozen in place with his mouth hanging open, so I grab his arm and yank him into motion behind me. I have to push hard against the door to my room because of the furniture. I squeezed out this morning, but it has to open more to allow Sutton to come in.

"What the fuck was that?" he asks, indicating with his thumb over his shoulder.

"That's Marv. He was pissed I didn't eat the Macaroni he made for dinner, so he sat outside of my room all night scratching on the door and moaning my name." I deliver all this with a, *we've been over this already* tone.

He listens as he looks around at the stacked furniture and coiled lamp, then he looks back at me with fury on his face.

"Who is in charge here?" he grinds out as he turns to shimmy back through the door. I follow on his heels, straight to the living room, where Marv is thankfully dressed now.

"Mercy, do you want to try my macaroni and cheese?" Marv asks as he tips his head back like before when he looked at me.

"Listen, buddy. If you say one more word to her, I will have you thrown out of here. You got that?"

"I bet *Big Man* wants my macaroni and chee—"

"What's going on?" Theresa asks from the open doorway, before wiping her feet on the mat and stepping inside. Her lungs are lined with tar, and she brings with her the heavy odor of cigarette smoke.

"Not much, we are just headed out for a quick bite to eat, and homeboy is over there bustin' a nut on the couch. See ya in about an hour," Sutton says as he all but drags me down the front steps.

He drives recklessly for about six or eight blocks before he pulls over and rests his head against his forearms on the steering wheel. I know better than to say anything. I know last night's phone call is running through his mind right now.

After a few minutes, he leans back in the seat, face tipped toward the ceiling, eyes closed. When he opens them, he looks directly at me and says simply, "I'm so sorry."

I nod and lie, "It's okay."

After that, we don't talk, and I don't ask him where we are going because I don't care.

Chapter 31

When Sutton pulls into an underground parking garage, it occurs to me that he is not, in fact, taking me for a quick bite to eat. He unbuckles his seatbelt and then makes eye contact with me.

"Don't ask."

We take the elevator to the eighth floor without speaking, but his eyes remain on mine the whole time. As we walk down the hall, I have questions, lots of them. And concerns too, like, how pissed is Theresa going to be that I didn't sign out on the sheet? She didn't really have a chance to object to me leaving, but it's still a fire I will have to put out when I get back.

"Did you have something better in mind?" he asks as he unlocks the door and pushes it open.

"Is this your place?" I ask, still rooted to the ground. "I was thinking more like a hardware store—for a door lock. And maybe a cheeseburger the size of my face."

"Why would you need a door lock?"

"Um, because Marv is a sociopath, and he likes to hang out on the other side of my door."

"You say, *my door* as if you are going back there," he says as he turns on some lights and walks into the kitchen. "What sounds good for dinner? Oh, wait, you said you want a cheeseburger. Let's order from Carl's, their burgers are—"

"What is this? Are we playing house now?" I ask with a sweep of my arms and an elevated voice.

"We can call it whatever you want, but you are not going back there," he says as he crosses his arms and leans back against the counter. He looks pretty relaxed for being the last person Theresa saw me with before I go missing.

"And you?"

"Me? I don't care what we call it."

"Sutton! Theresa *saw* me leave with you."

"She doesn't know who I am. I'm not worried about her at all. When do you check in with your social worker next?"

"Tuesday. She wanted to give me a few days to settle in."

"You're settled all right, right the fuck out of there."

"This isn't funny!"

"Listen, you should keep your appointments with Dr. Gingham and me, but otherwise, you should be fine. It's an imperfect system, what are they going to do if you don't go back? Send out a search party? Haul you in?...*Force* you to use government funds?"

"What about my stuff?"

"You can get new stuff."

"What about my *computer*?"

"Yeah, you definitely need a new computer."

"But my computer has the programs I need. Photoshop is really expensive."

"You're right. You need your outdated Photoshop. I guess I'll have to take you back," he shrugs and then takes a big step toward me before swallowing me in his arms.

"You really are insane if you think for one second I'm going to allow you to go back there," he mumbles directly into my ear. The sheer emphasis of his rumbly words warms my body from the inside out.

My arms close around his waist, and I return the hug. Even though this is the part of his push and pull that he pulls me in and makes me feel like I'm drowning in happiness. I know the push will follow on its heels.

"You strike me as a better roommate than Marv, but do you have any sleepwalking tendencies or masturbatory habits that I should know about?"

"What? And take away all the mystery?" he laughs. "Let me order some food, and then I'll show you around."

I take a look at my surroundings. He has a nice sized kitchen with a row of stools lining the bar countertop. It has a very masculine look to it, with cherrywood cabinets and dark stone countertops. The living room is flanked by a row of patio doors, but it's dark outside, so I can't see beyond them.

The living room has a fireplace—which I've always wanted, and it looks like he walked into a furniture store and said, *I want that display* because it looks so editorial and un-lived in.

"Dinner is on the way. Now, for the grand tour. Kitchen, living room, and bedroom," he says as he points to each area. "Annnd, that should do it for the tour."

I haven't seen the bedroom yet, but he didn't speak of it in a plural context, and I sincerely doubt there are bunk beds behind that door. This should be interesting.

"I need to shower, but I don't have any stuff," I say, immediately thinking about how badly I need to shave before I share a bed with him.

"I'm sure I have most of what you need, but I can stop and pick up the rest after work tomorrow. Go ahead and take a shower, I'll see if I can find anything that will fit you," he says as he walks into the bedroom.

"Clean towels are under the sink."

"Got it," I say as I notice the bathroom isn't exactly separated from the bedroom. There is a wide-open archway instead of a door, and the same dark cabinets and countertops inside. My pulse speeds up when I look at his bed. This is where sexy doctor Sutton sleeps. This is where *we* are going to sleep. Unless, of course, he has an attack of ethics, which is likely.

"Here's a t-shirt and athletic shorts, it's the best I can do on such short notice," he grins at me while I take them from him. "I'll be out here Google searching medical misconduct and kidnapping charges," he says as he turns and walks back into the living room.

It feels incredibly strange to take my clothes off in a bathroom with no door, and with Sutton so close by. But what is even weirder, is his shower. There are three different options of bronze showerheads and three protrusions from the glass tile that should be knobs, but that don't make any sense.

One knob-thing controls all three heads depending on how far you turn it, so I run through all of them a few times before I realize it's not controlling the temperature. It takes some trial and error with the other two knobs before I find a good temperature, but I still don't know which one is responsible for it.

The shower floor is covered in smooth, black rocks that match the niche in the wall that displays Sutton's products. All of his toiletries smell rugged and manly, including the shaving cream that I use liberally. It's almost enough to grow a penis while I'm in here. I'm not complaining though, it smells like Sutton.

I get out of the shower and wrap a towel around my body and another one around my hair. I really want to brush my teeth, but Sutton uses an electric toothbrush, and I'm not comfortable snooping through his stuff.

"Food's here," he says through the bedroom door as he opens it just enough to announce dinner.

"Sutton? Do you have an extra toothbrush?" I call out before he shuts it again.

"Are you dressed? Can I come in?"

"Yeah."

"You said you were dressed. This is a towel," he says as he walks over and hooks a finger on the towel right between my boobs.

"I meant, I'm covered," I say as a tingle begins to hum between my legs.

"My dick doesn't care about semantics."

"No? But does it have an extra toothbrush?" I say, smiling like a jackal at the mention of his dick.

"Sort of. I have replacement heads," he says as he opens a drawer and gets one out. While he gets the toothbrush ready for me, I consider dropping the towel, but I'm too hungry to think about seduction right now.

***

After we ate and cleaned up, Sutton messed around with my phone for a bit while I halfway watched TV and halfway worried about him searching for my sexy pictures. When he handed it back, he had added a couple of apps.

"You need to continue to come to your appointments and driver's ed, and all that stuff, so I connected your phone to my Uber account. All you do is type in where you're going, like this," he shows me how to use the app, while I focus entirely on the side of his face, noting how chiseled his jaw looks when he talks, instead of looking at the phone screen, but I get the gist.

"And here is the Amazon app, I linked it too. Order anything you need, it will arrive in two days."

"That's really sweet of you, but I have my own money. I just need to figure out how to get into my PayPal account."

"I can help you with that, but I want to do this stuff. I like taking care of you," he smiles. I think he is going to kiss me, but the look on his face passes. Before my disappointment can register, he is already pulling up PayPal.

Five minutes later, my account summary is open on Sutton's laptop and in front of me. The balance is right around what I expected, which is good because I have a lot of expenses coming up—rent, furniture, a computer, Photoshop...

"What are all those transactions?" he asks, trying not to be nosy but not able to help it.

"What do you mean? I had to qualify for FCA to stay in the system until I turn 21. I did it by staying in school and doing freelance work."

"This is all graphic design work?"

"Yeah. Mostly travel brochures and some marketing for the University."

"You are amazing. You know that, right?"

"I wouldn't say *amazing*, I just had a lot of time on my hands."

"No, you are definitely amazing. But listen, we seriously need to talk about this little arrangement we have here."

"Is this where you tell me you are going to sleep on the couch?"

"Not a chance, lady. But this little situation needs to be kept between us. I have to go to work as normal, and you have to proceed as though the step-down facility didn't work out, so you moved in with a friend. If you can arrange to check in with your social worker *at* the hospital when you are there for therapy work, that's even better. Tell her you moved in with a friend, and if she needs to see where, take her to Matty or Veronica's. That's it. There can be absolutely no connections made between us beyond me being your doctor."

"So, you expect me to sleep next to you all night, and then go have sessions with you every day at 9:00 as though nothing is unusual?"

"Yes."

"What if someone sees us together outside of the hospital?" I question with raised eyebrows.

"You are my patient, we are doing some exposure therapy," he shrugs.

"You have thought of everything, haven't you?"

"Nope. I still fully expect this to crash and burn all around us."

"We can minimize that by finding me a new doctor."

"You already know how I feel about that."

I sigh, "Yeah, I suppose I do."

Chapter 32

I get the distinct impression Sutton is stalling about going to bed, which is right on par with his clashing morals. I'm starting to fall asleep on the couch and no longer know what show we are watching, so I get up and announce the obvious.

"I'm going to bed. Goodnight."

"Goodnight." The word rings hollow, and it makes me wonder if he plans to sleep on the couch. I can't worry about that, I have driver's ed at eight in the morning. I also have a three o'clock interview at a grocery store that I have no intention of going to. Hilary has lined up a bunch of crap for me to do, but she is swamped with other cases, so hopefully, she will lose interest in me soon.

I consider ditching my appointment with Sutton too, but that will complicate matters and draw all kinds of attention to my absence. It would force him to put something in motion regarding my whereabouts, and that can't happen. Not while we are shaking up.

I don't bother turning on the bedroom light before I climb into his massive bed. I also don't take off the tightly cinched athletic shorts because I have nothing on underneath. *Dang, this is a big bed*, it makes me want to sleep like a starfish.

I sprawl out at first, but soon enough, I get to tossing and turning. Sleep was at my door, but I chased it away fretting about not being at the facility...Matty not texting back yet...truant job interviews...Sutton eventually sleeping next to me...

When he finally comes in, I'm still wide awake, but I don't let on. I want to see how he plays it. He brushes his teeth, which is more than I did, and then quietly pulls back the covers. Lifting the comforter disrupts the warm little cocoon I'm tucked in, and a rush of cool air claims the space.

Then Sutton gets in bed and promptly turns his back to me. Well, I guess that answers my question about how he is going to play it, he's obviously going to be a saint.

***

When the alarm on my phone wakes me up at 7:00, Sutton is already gone. He left a sticky note on the bathroom mirror that says, *I made you some coffee, help yourself to anything*. He also left a lone key on the bathroom counter, right next to my Sonicare replacement head.

I get ready and put yesterday's clothes on. The coffee tastes buttery and smooth, but I usually take my meds in the morning, so it only reminds me that I don't have them. I'm down to a mood stabilizer and something for my anxiety, neither one important enough to go back to the halfway house.

When I get to the hospital for my appointment with Sutton, I'm a little late because driver's ed is an hour, and Uber doesn't care that I'm double-booked with back to back appointments that seem to overlap.

Right away, I find out that Wes is gone. He checked himself out yesterday, and Lyla's mom is visiting, so I don't get to see her either.

"Mercy! I was worried about you. You're late," Sutton says from the nurse's station the very moment my face rounds the corner.

"The only way I could have been on time is if I teleported here. Plus, you said there would be growing pains with all the changes—this feels like a growing pain to me, not a reason for that look on your face."

"Fine, a growing pain. Let's go to my office," he grumbles. I legitimately think he was worried about me. His whole doctor-patient facade is firmly in place, but I can read the relief all over his face.

Once in his office, he flatly refuses to deviate from my highly regimented mental health treatment and is in no mood for the playful antics I employ to throw us off course. If he held me at arm's length before, now he practically has me in another room.

When I finish up with my boring appointment, I go visit Colleen. To be honest, I'm kind of surprised by how much this doesn't feel like home anymore, but she will always be a part of me. When we speak, I completely gloss over the fact that I'm on the run from the halfway house, and then walk out of the unit like a regular person.

I still have some conflicting feelings about Sig that swirl around my head and keep my anger running hot. I think someday I will reach out to him, and perhaps we will be able to have a relationship, but for now, I can't release him from keeping me sick. It's hard to imagine what the last ten years would have been like had he set me free.

Sutton has his own anger toward Sig but I think he absolves him of that because of his fatherly role in my life. He says that, much like my foster parents over the years, Sig was not equipped for my complex situation, and he did the best he knew how to.

To be clear, I don't think Sig deliberately misdiagnosed me, or tried to hobble me in any way. In the end, I think Sig loved me more than he wanted me to get better. Which, incidentally, shines new light on some of Sutton's inner conflict. Sutton wants me to continue to get better and to be free of my past, even at the cost of his feelings for me. It's frustrating—yet commendable.

I do believe I will be able to accept Sig's shortcomings and forgive him for how he unintentionally shaped my life, but I'm not there yet. For now, I have some living to do and some years to make up for. And because group therapy is no longer required of me, my next stop is the bank, because I have some shopping to do.

***

What started out as shopping for a toothbrush and underwear, turned into a full-blown spending spree. Colleen directed me to a store where you can buy everything from makeup and hair products to trash cans—and everything in between.

I spent an inordinate amount of time picking out bra and panty sets, but V and Lyla would be proud. PJ's took some time too, but only because I'm crafty, and plan to make some changes in Sutton's bedtime attitude toward me.

After another hour or so of picking out jeans and shirts and shoes and dresses, I headed to the makeup section to make Matty proud as well.

I'm not going to say I went crazy, but it's hard to pick out only one nail polish when you are standing in front of a wall of them, and really, do women actually need all those options when it comes to feminine hygiene?

However, the tiny bit of restraint I *did* happen to show was in the electronics department, and only because trying to decipher what processing speed, RAM, and connectivity I require these days, was about to make my head explode.

Anyway, my Uber driver was very helpful when he realized I had a full cart to load into the car, but not as helpful when it came to hauling everything inside. For that, I'm on my own.

I get inside the building without struggling too much with all the bags lining my arms, but while I wait for the elevator, an angel descends.

"Can I help you with all that?" a guy asks. He is sweaty and has earbuds dangling from his neck, so it's clear he just worked out.

"Um, okay. Are you sure?"

"Absolutely," he says as he lessens my load, "Which floor are you headed to?"

"Eight, please."

"I live on the eighth floor too. Which one is yours?" he asks as he pushes the button.

"812."

"812? Isn't that Travis' place?"

"Travis?—Oh, yeah, Travis! …I just met the guy, so I always forget his name," I scramble to recover from not knowing Sutton's first name.

"Although, he doesn't look much like a Travis, does he?" I muse.

"You guys just met? So, you're not together?" he asks, his spirits brightening.

"**NO**," I say, too forcefully, "We aren't together at all," I'm scrambling again to come up with something believable now… "Travis is friends with my brother, and he's doing him a favor by letting me stay here for a few days, that's all."

"Oh, good. I *mean*, that's nice of him."

When I unlock the door, I turn around to thank him for his help, but he speaks first.

"I'll help you get all this inside, and then I'll get out of your hair," he says as he walks straight into Sutton's place. He puts his load down on the kitchen counter and then takes the bags from me and does the same.

"I'm Ben, by the way," he says as he sticks out his hand.

"Nice to meet you, I'm Mercy. Thanks for your help."

"Anytime." He lets go of my hand slowly, "I'm not sure how long you're in town for, but I'd love to take you out sometime if you're up for it."

"Uh. Sure… Yeah. That sounds great." I'm clearly going to have to get faster about thinking on my feet. I sound like an idiot starting every sentence with a verbal pause.

He types my number into his phone while I mentally chastise myself. He is so nice, and I'm not *at all* used to being asked out, so I can hardly be blamed for not thinking of a reason to turn him down fast enough.

When he's gone, I glance at the microwave clock, it's not quite 3:00. Now, it's time to figure out how to do laundry. Sutton has a stackable washer and dryer, so I load my new clothes one by one as I pull off the tags.

I'll have to remember to take the lacy stuff out before I put it all in the dryer, another lesson learned from Lyla. A wash cycle takes fifty minutes, and I have no idea how long stuff takes to dry, but hopefully, it's done before Sutton gets home.

Now, I'm off to shower and get ready with all my new, fun stuff. Maybe this time, I'll figure out the shower knobs before scalding myself.

Chapter 33

When Sutton gets home, my clothes are in the dryer—except for the delicates, which are hung up neatly to dry, and I'm wearing a clean t-shirt of his and sitting cross-legged on the bathroom counter, experimenting with my new makeup.

"Independence suits you," he says with a smile as he leans his shoulder up against the archway wall between the bedroom and bathroom.

"Yes, but does this sparkly eyeshadow suit me?" I ask as I turn to face him and bat my eyelashes.

"Absolutely."

"Well then, that's all I care about," I say as I lean closer to the mirror to apply mascara.

"You've been busy, now I see why you ignored my texts," he says as he studies my bare legs and the section of his t-shirt that covers my pantyless state. Apparently, he doesn't realize that I can see him in the reflection of the mirror. Really, going commando right now was not for his benefit. I just didn't want to put on the same underwear from yesterday and this morning—you can only turn them inside-out once.

"What texts did you send me? I wasn't ignoring them, I'm just not used to checking my phone," I say, still tending to my eyelashes.

"I just wanted to check on you. You've been unleashed into the world, and I didn't know if you were sinking or swimming."

I scoff, "Oh, please. We both know I'm not the type to sink."

"You're right about that, but do I need to buy stock in Target? Or have you exhausted your desire to shop?"

"I'm good for now."

"Okay, well, I'm going to have a beer. It's Friday, and I'm not on call this weekend. Do you want one?"

"I don't know…should we add supplying alcohol to a minor to your growing list of felonies?" I tease.

"*Right,*" he grunts, as he turns and walks out of the room.

"Just kidding, supplying alcohol to a minor is not a felony!" I shout after him, then erupt into giggles.

When I finish with my makeup, I drag my fingers through my damp hair, then hop down to go find Sutton. He sits on the couch with his forearm draped across his eyes. I shouldn't have pointed out my underage status because that is one of his moral dilemmas, but it was too funny not to.

I leave him alone to brood while I fold my laundry and then look through the kitchen for something to cook for dinner. I find a bag of pasta and a jar of spaghetti sauce. After reading the directions, I decide a monkey could prepare this meal, then put a pot of water on the burner to boil.

When I sit on the couch by Sutton, he doesn't even lift his arm off his face when he says, "Your phone keeps buzzing, sounds like your friends are gearing up for a festive Friday night."

I pick my phone up from the coffee table and see that I have three new text messages. One is Matty—finally, one is Lyla, who got out this afternoon, and the other is from Ben, who wants to take me out tonight.

"Listen, Sutton, are you going to pout all night? Because if you are, I've got better things to do."

He moves his arm so he can look me in the eyes, "Oh, is that right?" he says with a smirky challenge that only serves to piss me off. He shouldn't assume that he is my only lifeline. I've been fighting people's assumptions my whole life, so my hackles are pretty much permanently up.

"Yeah."

"Okay, hotstuff, don't let me hold you back," he says with a chuckle that seals the deal. I'm going to go out with Ben. That should really give Sutton something to pout about.

I text Ben, and then get up to go turn off the stove. Sutton can make his own dinner tonight, I've got to get dressed for my date.

I'm fairly confident Sutton thinks I'm bluffing the whole time I'm getting dressed and finishing my hair, but when Ben knocks on the door, all that changes. I rush out of the bedroom to try and intercept any problems.

"Hi, Travis," Ben says.

"Hey, Ben, what's up?" Sutton asks, probably expecting Ben to ask for a cup of sugar or something. I squeeze past my pouty doctor, who seems to be taking up the entire doorway.

"See you later, *Travis*. Don't wait up," I say over my shoulder as I try to make a hasty exit.

"**Wait**. *What*?" Sutton calls out down the hall, but I grab Ben's arm and tug him onto the elevator before this gets any worse for me.

***

When I come home from the date that I explained to Ben needs to be purely a friendship kind of thing, Sutton is in bed reading. Fuming, but reading. I get ready for bed and change into my new PJs in the bathroom.

When I walk out of the bathroom, and round the bed to my side, he tries to ignore me, but he can't ignore the lace and satin, super short, and *super* sexy 'nightgown.'

"Night, Roomie," I say as I snuggle in, facing him, but still playing coy.

"Is that how this is going to be?" he asks—I think, referencing my attire and not the date.

"I love these sheets, what are they? Flannel?" I ask, completely ignoring his question.

"Yeah. Flannel." And that is the last thing he says to me before pretending to read for the next hour while I try to fall asleep while looking sexy.

***

My heart is pounding so hard, it is trying to suffocate me. They have me pinned down while the box is opened, and the Prophet retrieves a snake. It's big. Mama says it's the little ones I need to worry about because the young can't control their venom and will release much more than they need to. But this one terrifies me just the same as it's laid heavily on my young body.

I can taste the scream in my mouth, and it's rising still. It is only a matter of time before I feel the blistering pain because the screaming and chanting and singing are frightening the snake too. He hates the box, but he wants to go back. They starve the snakes so they are complacent, but a weakened snake can still strike—

"**Mercy!**"

"Wake up."

"Honey, it's me. You are safe, there are no snakes."

My lungs have seized and are burning with the need for oxygen. When Sutton's voice breaks through the cultish haze, I suck in a breath—my first in days.

"Open your eyes, that's right. I've got you," he says as he pulls my stiff body into his warmth. "Everything is fine, you were having a nightmare. Are you okay now?" he coos.

Instead of responding, I dissolve into tears. They soak his pillow while he caresses my back. My heart still races, but Sutton holds me and coaxes me away from the trauma that has branded itself to me. *It was just a nightmare* he soothes over and over, which would calm me—were it true.

A long time passes inside of his embrace, maybe even an hour or more. His caress is gentle and slow and continues as though he knows I'm still awake. When he moves his palm tenderly to my cheek, he speaks softly.

"Mercy, what can I do?"

"Don't push me away."

"I'll hold you all night if that's what you want," he says, as if that's what I meant. I'm too shaken and too exhausted to correct him, though. So, I drift off to sleep in the only place that's ever felt unconditionally safe.

Chapter 34

When I blink my eyes open, Sutton is still here. It's Saturday morning, and the warmth from falling asleep in his arms is still with me. When I look up to his face, he is awake and looking at me as well.

"Did you have fun last night?" he asks, and at first, I think he's talking about my nightmare, so I furrow my brow.

"With Ben. On your date."

"Yes, I had fun, I guess."

"Was he a gentleman? Or do I need to kick his ass?" he asks, revealing his jealousy.

"It's too early for the third degree," I say, avoiding the question. I should tell Sutton that Ben started off in the friend zone and that nothing has changed, but not just yet.

"I guess I'll make coffee then. Oh, also, I filled new scripts for you. I figured they got left behind."

"Thank you," I yawn as I make my rumpled way into the bathroom. When I see my reflection, it makes me decide not to get dressed quite yet. I told Ben that I have a boyfriend, so I will need to provoke Sutton in other ways. Plus, I've never been able to lounge around in jammies on a Saturday—much less, ones that make me look like this.

I brush my teeth and then decide to put on a little mascara and lip gloss before I pad out to the kitchen in my skimpy outfit for some coffee. I've never worn so few clothes, and I can feel a breeze *everywhere*. I'm trying to follow Lyla's advice regarding men being visual creatures, and it's high-time I test the theory.

"Happy Saturday," Sutton says with his back to me while he dresses up his coffee. "I'd ask you how you slept, but I already know the ans—" he turns to face me and abruptly loses his train of thought.

"Ohhh, yum. Hazelnut creamer," I say as I retrieve a mug and pretend not to notice the ogling look on Sutton's face. "What are your plans for the day?" I ask innocently, as I lean back on the counter and bring the mug to my face to hide the smirk resting on my lips.

"I have no plans. You?"

I shake my head playfully slow. But, if I get my way, I'm going to get to know Sutton…Biblically.

"Do you like eggs? I'll make us some breakfast," he says, turning around quickly and rifling through the cabinet for a pan.

"Good. I'll help. I plan on ditching all my life skills classes next week," I say as I grab the bread to make toast, "So I'll need all the practice I can get."

"We actually have to talk about that, because pretty soon, I'm going to get a call that my patient has gone MIA. And I need to decide how I'm going to deal with that." He walks over to me and stands closer than is strictly polite. "How do *you* propose I deal with that?" The way he stands over me, with his bare chest an inch from making contact, dries out my mouth. Then he tips my chin up, so I'm looking in his eyes. *"Hmm, Mercy?"*

Trying to maintain my slipping composure, I suggest, "How about I call my social worker and tell her I moved out of the state?"

"Because then you can't exactly continue your treatment at the hospital, can you?"

"Sutton, you can't keep me under your thumb. I'll be twenty-one in a month and a half. Do you know how quickly the doors of the state hospital will slam shut once my stay is no longer paid for by government funds?" I challenge. "Even if you get your way, and continue to treat me at the hospital, it won't last. You might as well lose track of me right along with Hilary and Theresa."

He lowers his lips to mine and kisses me softly. "You might be right, but that's not how I planned it. It's too abrupt."

"Did you plan on treating me until my birthday and then just saying goodbye?"

"No. I never planned on saying goodbye to you," he says as he reaches around me and then hoists me to his hips. "I just hadn't worked out the details quite yet." Then he kisses me again, deeply. It's enough to abandon breakfast altogether.

Chapter 35

When I walk into Sutton's office for my state-mandated appointment, I step into an ambush. Hilary and her air of staticky chaos are perched on the couch, and both sets of eyes are hotly on mine. Each pair saying something different. Sutton's gaze is imploring me not to screw this up, and Hilary's speaks to her eroded spirit and lack of time to contend with such foolishness as this.

I'm already demoralized from my weekend of mixed signals from Sutton, and I have no idea how this next hour will play out. One thing I do know, is that tripwires are all around me, and I have to be *very* careful how I handle myself.

"Sit down, Mercy," Hilary begins, with a prick of irritation in her voice. "It has come to my attention that you no longer reside at the step-down facility." She glances down at her notes, "Not since last Thursday. Is that correct?"

"Well, you see…I feel in my heart that there are more deserving people, who would be better suited in a pla—"

"Mercy, the state requires us to follow a certain protocol. You running away and skipping classes and employment interviews, makes our job rather difficult, don't you think?" Sutton interrupts with a haughty challenge. Pretty rich for someone who implemented my whole disappearance, if you ask me.

"Yes, I know, but—"

"Independent living requires compliance. You need to obtain gainful employment, complete your life skills classes, learn to manage your medications and finances on your own, and perhaps, more importantly, you need to follow the rules laid out before you," Hilary says.

"Or what?" I ask. It's an innocent enough question, but it still makes Sutton suck in a sharp breath.

"Or you will no longer be supported by the state," she says with a hand on her chest and shock blooming across her face from the strength of her astonishment.

"I'm fine with that. What's next?" I ask as I risk a look at Sutton.

"You may be fine with that, Mercy, but you need to understand the regulations that dictate this process," he says, almost begging me to shut up with the look in his eyes.

"Listen, I know you both mean well, but the fact is that I am an adult. I will not be told where to live and how to conduct myself during the day."

"Lack of compliance disavows you of the federal scaffolding that's been put in place to help people like you," Hilary says. The way she says *people like you* makes me wish she would choke on her tongue.

"Actually, Hilary, *people like me* do not need federal scaffolding because we've learned resilience—in fact, it's been shoved down our throats. *We* are the survivors that keep getting up even though we've been knocked down all our lives. *We* are the fighters that eek through life, never giving up on ourselves even when everyone else has. *We* are the Gladiators that face impossible odds and then overcome them. Why? **Because we have to!** Do you think a six-hour life-skills class can teach me that? Do you think bagging groceries at the corner store is all I aspire to? Do you think clipping my wings will keep me from flying? Because if you do, you're the crazy ones! I've trained my whole life for this, so with all due respect, you two can step right outside and go fuck yourselves."

After I finish my tirade, I'm panting, and the fire in my chest has worked its way up to my indignant glare. Neither of them says a word as they digest what's just been spat before them. I think Hilary expected a delicate, fractured soul. Never realizing that fractures calcify and heal stronger than before. My fractures have been fortified by life, and I haven't been delicate for a very long time.

Sutton is looking down at his hands, it's possible he is even smiling. Hilary, on the other hand, looks at me like I just peed down her leg. She smoothes her skirt and then evidently changes her attitude because, following a small cough, she softens her gaze.

"In that case, I'll need you to fill out some paperwork. Dr. Sutton, I'll email you the forms and keep you both abreast of any legal technicalities that may arise. It is my belief that any hearing on the matter would take place after Ms. Kavanaugh reaches the age of majority, and would, therefore, be a waste of federal and state resources."

"Hold on, now. Ms. Kavanaugh has not yet completed her treatment goals and is currently under both Dr. Gingham's and my care," Sutton says rather directly.

"I'm sorry, Dr. Sutton. We can't have it both ways—"

"Then file the paperwork for a ward of the court termination hearing."

"I told you, that will take months. Ms. Kavanaugh will be twenty-one by then."

"Yes, but her treatment will still be covered until that time. As far as the residential and employment conditions, you'll have to take it up with the judge. I'm her doctor, not her caseworker. My concern is her mental health, not the legislation behind her status as a ward of the court."

The stare down that ensues between them has my eyes bouncing back and forth between the two. It's evident that my social worker is not sure how to proceed. All three of us know I will age out of the system in less than two months. Sutton wants to remain my doctor, and Hilary wants to wash her hands of me. And any deciding vote from the courts would happen months after it's no longer relevant.

"I have other cases to tend to. I'll be in touch, Dr. Sutton. Mercy, good luck, I wish you all the happiness in the world," Hilary says as she rises to her feet and then makes a rather unglamorous exit. She leaves the air of defeat in her wake but seems happy enough to put me in her past.

"The part she directed at me sounded kind of final, don't you think?" I ask Sutton. It's not really a question, it's more of a gleeful triple backflip.

"Mercy, what am I going to do with you?" he laughs as he drops his head.

"*So* many things."

"We…uhh… we still have a lot of work to do before you age out." He coughs. "We left off last time with you speaking cryptically about tarnish. I'd like you to expand on that."

"Tarnish?"

"Yes, we were discussing your foster home placements, and how you have carried rejection around with you your whole life. I'd like to really dig into that sense of rejection."

"When you look at me and pretend to work, do you picture how I looked in my skimpy nightgown?"

"Mercy."

"I mean, it *is* a pretty sexy nightgown...if you can even call it a nightgown," I press.

"Mercy, we are talking about tarnish. Not how hot you looked in that nightgown. You are beautiful, striking even, but discussing that fact will not get us very far."

"That's just it, Sutton. Everyone wants the beautiful, the striking. Wars were waged over beautiful things. Gods and Kings fought to possess the striking. But everything is so damn fleeting. Beauty and promise lose their luster, and when the tarnish begins to show through, it's the ugliness that gets thrown back. The raw. The real. People turn their backs on us. The tarnished and the misunderstood lose their glow, and consequently, any appeal we may have started with."

"You're wrong, Mercy."

"I'm not wrong. When the spit and the shine have lost their luster, when the cracks begin to show—that's when things start to fall apart."

"No, Mercy. It's the spit and the shine that are fleeting. The polish and the pretense that people present to the world. The tarnish and the cracks are what's beautiful. The raw and the real—that's where true beauty lies."

"People can't handle the raw and the real. It shines too bright of a light on the world's suffering. A blind eye is easier than empathy. It's too easy to judge someone instead of trying to understand them."

"We are all beautiful. And we are all tarnished. Mercy, that's what makes us human. We are not molded into who we become based on a certain body type or hair color. We are molded into who we *are* by our experiences and by overcoming the obstacles on our path. *Beauty doesn't define our character, the tarnish does.*"

"So, you are saying I should embrace the tarnish that got me abandoned by my parents and rejected from every foster home?"

"I'm saying you would be a different person today if you hadn't experienced everything you have."

"Wouldn't that be a good thing?"

"No, it wouldn't be a good thing. You could be a pretentious asshole or a spoiled brat, or an entitled narcissist...you could be anything. But you wouldn't be you. And I kinda like you just as you are."

"Are you trying to get me to change my perception about myself?"

"Perception is everything, Mercy."

"You still don't perceive me as broken or messed up?"

"You aren't broken or messed up."

"What about when I was diagnosed as a schizophrenic?"

"Still not broken or messed up. Just you."

Chapter 36

Matty, Lyla, and Veronica haven't changed a bit. The only difference in our friendship cluster is the setting and the intoxicating aroma of coffee that seduces people into the café like a horde of crusaders.

When I look around at three of the most important people in the world to me, Sutton's words rise to the surface of my thoughts. *Beauty doesn't define our character, the tarnish does.* All of a sudden, his prophetic words make sense. Sutton is right. The weight of our hardships may be heavier at this table than others, but each of us is who we are because of our unique experiences.

If we were stripped to generic beings who all fit in the same standardized mold, never struggled, and never had to overcome those struggles, who would be sitting at this table right now?

The thought tightens my throat. I want my friends to be happy more than I want that for myself, but I also love them no matter what struggles they bring to the table. They are beautiful. And they are tarnished.

"Mercy, are you always this sappy on the outside?" Veronica asks with a laugh, as she dabs a tear from my cheek.

"I'm just so happy to have found my family after all this time," I say as my heart overflows with emotion.

"Oo, oo," Matty says as he raises his hand excitedly in the air, "Can I be the big sister?"

We all fall apart laughing, but I put my hand on his and squeeze because if God himself asked me to choose a big sister, I would absolutely choose Matty.

Lyla garners everyone's attention by clearing her throat and announcing, "Okay, settle down, it's time to be serious," then she giggle-snorts, letting us know that being serious is not really on the agenda this afternoon.

She opens her purse and takes out a box wrapped in red wrapping paper and a gold foil ribbon. "We all splurged and got you a gift for busting out of the state hospital early."

I look around at each of them. Their smiles are genuine even though I fully suspect the gift will challenge my virgin sensibilities and most likely bring the flush of embarrassment to my cheeks.

"It's actually two gifts. Their usefulness depends on your ability to snare Sutton," V adds, bringing another round of laughter to the table as I tear open the wrapping paper.

They got me condoms and a pale-pink vibrator.

I love my friends.

Chapter 37

"How was your afternoon with your friends?" Sutton asks as he pours two glasses of wine, then hands one to me.

"It was amazing. We had lunch at Mirabelle's, then had coffee at that cute little corner café. Have you ever been there? The one with a cobblestone floor and those insanely good pumpkin scones? Anyway, Lyla and V are going to some swanky art exhibit tonight, so they left early to go get ready, and Matty took me computer shopping."

"I see that," he says as he looks towards the stack of electronics boxes in the living room. "Did you tell them where you are living?"

"Of course," I say casually before I take a tentative sip of wine.

"Mercy, you shouldn't have done that."

"Why not? They are my people. They've seen the devil through my eyes and stuck around."

"Why not? Do I even need to answer that?" he asks as he crosses his arms over his chest and leans back on the kitchen counter." The posture is relaxed, his face is not.

"Plus, they think I should ditch the rest of my appointments with you anyway," I say as I go back for another sip of wine. It tastes heavy, yet smooth in my mouth, but I'm not yet convinced why everyone likes wine so much.

"Why are they encouraging you to ditch your appointments with me? That isn't very responsible of them. Don't they want what's best for you?"

"Of course they do. They just happen to disagree with you about what that is," I say before setting my wineglass down and hopping up on the counter to watch the chef at work.

He doesn't budge, let alone tend to the sauté pan that's currently crackling with the sound of mushrooms and onions about to burn.

"And what have your unlicensed medical expert friends decided is best for you?"

"I can't tell you...I'd rather show you," I giggle into my wine glass. Damn, my cheeks are getting hot. Apparently, wine turns me into a flighty, giggly, teenager.

He stares me down, probably trying to decide if he is a doctor or a man tonight. Then, without comment, he turns around, gives the sauté pan an expert shake, and sets it down on an unlit burner.

"I'm going to throw the steaks on the grill. Why don't you get started on a salad," he says over his shoulder as he walks to the patio door. He really needs to seek therapy for his issues with avoidance. He doles out advice all day long about facing things head-on, but he should preface each time with a, *do as I say, not as I do* disclaimer.

What I didn't share with him is that my friends want me to find a new doctor pronto, so Sutton and I can put all these evasive games and tactics behind us. I agree with them, and as the head-rush I get when I hop off the counter can attest to, I'm feeling a little tipsy and ready for him to forget all about that stuffy doctor routine.

***

Dinner was business as usual even though I tried my level best not to talk about mundane things and re-hash the entire day with a blow by blow retelling.

I tried multiple times to steer the conversation in a sexier direction, but each time, Sutton batted my attempts away like they were badminton birdies flying at his head.

It is becoming crystal clear that Sutton intends to treat me as his patient until the bell rings, announcing the turn of my twenty-first year, and the official stoppage of the state's responsibility to me.

Well, as Lyla and Veronica concluded, there is nothing he can do if I start seeing another doctor. I feel like my therapeutic days with Sutton have already ended anyway. So, in honor of that, it's time to kick things into high gear.

I've already shampooed and conditioned my hair, shaved everything reasonable, and loofa-scrubbed myself to a soft shine when I call out to him.

"SUT-TON."

"**SUUUUT-TON**."

"**SUTTON!**"

"What the hell? Is your hair on fire—OH FUCK! Jesus Christ! I didn't know you were still in the shower. I'm sor—" he is backing out of the bathroom, stammering an apology, but I know he's had an eyeful. Still, it's not enough.

"Sutton, I called you in here so you could do me a favor. Stop acting like you've never seen a naked woman before." The glass is steamed up, so I swipe my hand down the shower glass, so I can see him better, and of course, so he can see me better. He is trying not to look, but he can't rip his eyes away.

"Anyway, can you please hand me my wine?" I ask innocently. "It's right over there on the bathroom counter."

There is a short pause of waring conscience before he looks at the wine glass and then back at me. Just when I think he is about to reject me altogether, he strides forward and takes the wine glass from the counter.

He opens the shower door and leans on the threshold. Now, he is the bold one, because he's not even trying to hand me the wine.

"Are you sure you want more to drink? You're already a little buzzed, and let's not forget, you are underage," he smiles wickedly as he takes a challenging sip of my wine. Then he rakes his eyes over my body, and I feel his gaze every bit as much as the cool air he is letting in.

"Yes, give it to me," I state as I tip my head back to rinse my hair again, and to release my eyes from his heavy stare.

"I'm not sure you can be trusted if you have any more to drink, Mercy," he says as he tips it back and finishes the glass. "In fact, I'm not sure you can be trusted at all," he continues as he sets the glass down and then pulls his shirt over his head in one smooth motion. Besides being mostly hairless, his chest is the most masculine thing I have ever seen. His muscles flex with the movement of removing his pants, and all of a sudden, I feel like I'm being hunted.

I back up against the cold tile wall as he stalks me, naked, and as hard as a steel post. Despite the predatory glint in his eye, we melt together in a very naked, entirely raw embrace under the spray of the shower.

His kiss is immediate but gentle. It's almost like he is giving me time to adjust to the feel of his bare skin against mine, not to mention, the predominance of the erection between us.

"Fuuuck, Mercy. You feel so good," he mumbles against my mouth as his hands slide from my shoulder blade and ass, to my breast and jaw. I'm completely dizzy from the electricity of his touch, and when my hand wraps around his pulsing erection, I know he feels the same.

Long after the bathroom air grows heavy with steam, the kissing and touching continue. The feel of his wet skin beneath my touch has my body shivering with need. And when he kisses his way down my neck and then sucks a nipple into his warm mouth, I moan out loud, unable to stop the vocalization. The sensual sound is echoed back to me, and then repeated by Sutton.

He cups my face and murmurs, "Mercy, baby—I want you so bad, but I won't take your virginity while you're still my patient."

The sexual haze dissipates in an instant. We have literally spent hours upon hours discussing the ritualistic sexual abuse that my hypnosis sessions have brought to the surface. Sutton knows I'm not a virgin.

"Sutton, a sick old man took my virginity under the guise of healing me with love. Why would you sa—"

"No, Mercy. That ruthless predator may have torn through your hymen, but sweetheart, *I'm* the one who is going to take your virginity." His lips crush mine and leave no room for argument.

Not that I would argue. The idea of the Prophet taking something so special from me is a nauseating thought. I prefer Sutton's revolutionary perspective that his dirty claim to me is nothing more than a thin membrane and is of no consequence.

Sutton gave my virginity back to me. He gave it back, so *he* can take it—this time, with love. The Prophet's hold on me is slipping away. The best part about that is that I can let it go. I can put down that horrific burden and direct my energy toward the future.

Seemingly of the same thought, when I wrap my arms around Sutton's neck, he lifts me to his hips. The bare nakedness of my core pressed against his sexy body makes my heart pound loudly in my ears. It's so simple, yet so terribly erotic at the same time.

He turns off the water and then carries me out of the shower. The cool air that hits my dripping wet skin is a welcome relief and helps mitigate the light-headedness that I feel from the long, hot shower.

He doesn't break our kiss as he gives our clamped bodies a cursory once-over with a thick gray towel and then carries me straight to his bed. The need in the base of my belly has started to blossom, but nothing prepares me for what he does next.

Sutton places his hands on my calves and then pulls me to the edge of the bed. Then he kneels on the floor and spreads my legs. The shock I feel from being displayed before him like this, naked and vulnerable—completely open and exposed—vanishes the moment I feel his mouth make contact.

My gasp freezes in mid-air, then shatters, and rains down on me in the form of contented moans. The act is completely lewd—his face between my legs—it's invasive and shocking, but the sensation is intensely pleasurable.

The flicker and press of his masterful tongue are disrupted intermittently by the long swipe of his intimate kiss, and a suckling pressure from his lips. His skilled focus makes my back arch off the bed, but at the same time, it makes me grip the sheets in tight fists to keep from floating away.

"Do you like what I'm doing to you?" he asks in a sexy, raspy voice.

"Unggh," I groan completely unintelligibly.

"I want you to know how it feels to be adored, Mercy. Can you feel how much I adore you?"

"*Yes.*"

"I want to taste your orgasm, baby."

"*Oh, God.*"

"I want to feel your release against my tongue."

"*You're so filthy…so good*," I pant, trying to address everything at once, but hardly able to string two thoughts together.

"I want to hear you call out my name when you come," he says right before he presses his warm tongue firmly against my clit and wiggles it back and forth.

"*Oh, God. Oh, God. I'm gonna—Sutton, Oh, God. Sut….t….o…n…*" I cry out as I wrench my head back.

"Yes. *Just like that*," he groans as he coaxes every last spasm from my sparking body.

After, while I lie limply stuck to the sheets, he moves my thighs off his shoulders and stands. Then he crawls up my body, hauling me deeper into the expanse of the bed, and kissing a ticklish trail all the way to the hollow of my throat.

"That's just the beginning, Mercy. There is so much more for me to show you," he whispers against the fluttering pulse in my neck.

"Show me everything," I whisper as I find his lips with mine. "Absolutely everything."

Just having his naked body next to me feels like it's enough to make me happy forever, but the press of his erection reminds me that our bodies are starving for one another.

As I start to trickle kisses down his chest, he stops me. "No, Mercy, tonight, I just want to hold you and kiss you like you're mine."

"But—"

"And, one day soon, I *will* make you mine.

Chapter 38

I've decided that today is the day I fire Sutton and Dr. Gingham. I'm not saying I'm cured, because I never will be, but I think I'm ready for regular-people therapy. You know? Like once a week, or twice a month. Something more manageable than five days a week. Plus, with Sutton as my doctor, I can't focus on my mental health anyway. And *now* I've seen him naked and felt what his tongue can do to me, so there is no hope for any kind of focus in the future.

I left a message for Dr. Gingham this morning. I lied and told him I was moving away, and to take me off his books. I thanked him too, and even got a little choked up when I did it. He was an integral part of my mental health evolution, and I will be forever grateful for the months he devoted to me.

I also arrived early for my appointment with Sutton because I wanted to see Colleen and make sure we had each other's phone numbers. She was a good nurse, but she was so much more than that to me. Even though I feel strongly that today will be the last time I come here, I wouldn't be able to do it if I couldn't take her with me.

Now, it's time to fire my doctor. I don't know how he will take it, but I'm nervous as hell as I sit down on the couch in his office. His smile fills the room and makes me wonder what lecherous thoughts he is having.

"So, what's on the agenda after you leave here today?" he asks. "Are you going to tackle your computer setup, or do you want to wait until I can help? Maybe we can go look for a desk this weekend," he offers.

"I wasn't going to set it up until I got settled in my new place. So it's easier to leave everything in the boxes for now."

The smile dissolves from his face, and his mouth pops open like he wants to say something, but he doesn't.

"I can move it all to a closet if you want it out of the way," I suggest.

"I was hoping you would want to stay," he says softly.

"You want me to stay?" I ask, stunned. I thought his place was only temporary until I could get settled. When he brought me there, it was a last resort, not my future residence.

"I will help with whatever you decide. I don't want to hold you back—I was just... I just really want you to stay."

I think about what he said for a long minute. Besides a few instances of weakness, he has been mostly unreadable about my presence in his place. *He wants me to stay with him.* Sutton wants to keep me.

He must know what I'm thinking. He's spent countless hours deconstructing my issues with not feeling wanted. I've been abandoned and tossed back my whole life, him wanting me to stay with him is so much bigger than just a place to live. It's a place to belong. Finally.

"Say you will stay. At least for now," he says. His eyes are sincere, almost pleading.

"*I'll stay,*" I whisper. After another lengthy pause, I speak again.

"You're fired."

"Is that right?" he asks, almost laughing.

"Yes. I'm going to find a psychologist that specializes in PTSD. A woman this time, for sure. I've already looked into it. I'll have to pay out of pocket, but I figure I've received free therapy for over a decade, so if you amortize the out of pocket cost over my lifetime, it's pretty reasonable."

"Hold it. You are serious right now?"

"Yes. You're fired."

"In that case, will there be anything else?" He looks offended, as if I fired him for not being a good doctor. The truth is, he gave me a life. A life that's free from the grip of my past. A life I can move forward with. And I love him for that…but not in a *transference* kind of way. Don't get it twisted.

"Actually, there is something else," I say as I stand up, grab my purse, and walk around his desk.

"This ought to be good," he smirks and then slides his chair back from the desk to make room for me to squeeze between them. I ease onto the desk and then primly cross my legs in front of him.

"So, my friends bought me something, and I'm afraid I have no idea how to use it," I say coyly. "Maybe you could help me figure it out? It would be a show of good faith, and it would let me know that you harbor no hard feelings about being shit-canned by a patient."

"Why don't you tell me a little more about this gift from your friends?" he says, equally as coy. But he goes from leaning back leisurely in his office chair, to sitting forward with interest. He places both hands on the back of my bare leg and slowly begins to run his palms up and down.

"How about I just show you?" I say as I pull the vibrator from my purse.

"Ahh, yes. I recognize this particular device." He smiles the way an apex predator would smile at a lonely, bleating lamb. Then he twists the bottom of it, releasing an insistent hummmm.

"Spread your legs," he says as he glances over to make sure his in-session light is on. I do, but the fabric of my skirt falls between my thighs.

He slips his hand up my skirt, probably to investigate exactly how bold I actually am. He lets out a groaning breath when he finds me pantiless and bare.

His fingers toy with the silkiness of my body, teasing me while indulging himself. Our eyes are locked together as the vibrator hums persistently from his lap.

"Lift your skirt, Mercy."

I hold my breath, and slowly raise the front of my skirt. My nakedness is on full display now—as I sit on the edge of my doctor's desk in full view of his intent stare.

He runs a finger leisurely up my crease and then fiddles with my clit until I'm breathing heavily and starting to squirm. I almost cry out when he swipes the vibrator through my wetness and then uses the tip of it to circle around, and rock against my sensitive parts.

I can't sit up anymore, I have to lean back on my elbows and drop my head because I don't have the strength to support it any longer. As raunchy as this position is, I feel like I can't wrench my legs open wide enough.

As the insistence of my climax ratchets up, I feel a new sensation as Sutton slides a finger into me. I whimper as he begins to ease it in and out.

"Ooooo, that feels so good," I whine.

He turns off the vibrator and lays it on the desk next to me. Then I feel his mouth on my body as his finger continues to pump in and out. He slips in another finger, amplifying the snugness of the fit.

"Baby, squeeze my fingers and focus on what I'm doing with them," he says before once again lowering his lips to my writhing core. I can feel him rubbing against the inside of my vagina as he continues the rhythmic pumping motion.

When I squeeze around his fingers, he lets out a sexy groan that vibrates against me and pushes me over the edge.

My elbows dissolve, and I fall back onto the desk, grinding my teeth closed and trying to stay quiet while my orgasm suffocates me and pins me down.

When the violence of my release calms to a gentle pulse, I open my eyes. Sutton is standing between my spread legs and leaning over me with supporting hands against the desk on both sides of my body. He lowers a kiss to my lips, then says simply, "That was incredibly sexy."

I laugh, but when I wrap my arms around his neck, it pulls him closer, and his stony erection brushes against my overly-sensitive wetness, causing me to gasp.

"Slide it in," I whisper. He is still wearing pants, but I want to feel his hardness.

Now *he* laughs, "I'm not going to fuck you on my desk. I'm not a barbarian."

"I want to feel it, Sutton. Please."

He doesn't answer me, but he does unzip his pants. When he glides the head of his penis through my slit, I shiver. It's hot and silky as it slides back and forth, bumping against my swollen clit and then pressing between my lips as if he were about to enter me.

"I have to stop before it's not possible to stop," he murmurs, but repeats the slick sequence again, in defiance of his words.

"Put it in a little," I coax. "I want to feel you inside me."

"I don't have enough self-control to do that. I want to, but I can't. Not here," he says quietly as he rests his forehead against mine.

"Just a tiny bit. I'll go crazy if I can't feel it inside me right now."

He kisses me sweetly to pacify my need for him, but after a minute or so, I feel the smooth head of his dick part my lips and press in. My eyes fling open as I feel the press and stretch of the intrusion.

He only enters me for a few seconds, and only about an inch, but it scares him enough that he quickly backs away from me. He scrubs his hands over his face and then runs his fingers through his hair before dropping into his chair.

"*Jesus*," he exclaims in a whisper.

I sit up and attempt to make myself presentable. I smile at him wickedly as he strokes his deprived cock, eyes locked on mine. I slide off the desk and get on my knees between his legs.

I swipe his drop of wetness around with my tongue, tasting the saltiness as he combs his fingers through my hair along the scalp. The motion tugs at the roots and brings a chill up the back of my neck.

We both freeze when there is a knock at the door. Then we fly into action and do our best to neutralize the last hour in the space of thirty seconds.

When I exit his office, it's with a handful of tissues held to my face as if I'd been crying. I mumble a quick, "Sorry about that. Today was a rough one," to Sutton's next patient as I breeze past.

When I leave the hospital, I feel none of the sadness or anxiety that I expected to feel. It's been home to me for a long time, but there is no longing ache. No swollen lump in my throat.

I'm taking the good parts with me. My friends, Sutton, my education, and career. I'm taking the happiness and life skills with me.

Anything of value is a part of me now. The rest is just the garbage I get to leave behind.

Wait.

Didn't Sutton say something like that to me once?

Chapter 39

I've spent the last four hours on my phone watching computer set up videos on YouTube and trying to get everything set up and installed before Sutton gets home. He's right, I need to get a desk this weekend. The kitchen island is not an ideal place for a home office.

In defense of my computer splurge and the extravagant setup, I've always wanted dual monitors. On top of that, my old laptop was a fossil. It was given to me by one of my graphic design professors as a donation from the university, and only *after* it lived a full life on campus and eventually became obsolete for anything more than use as a paperweight or a door stopper.

Speaking of paperweights and door stoppers, I now have a shiny new, three-inch-thick Photoshop manual that I will never read because that's what YouTube is for.

"Hi, beautiful."

"Oh shit!" I yell as I spin around to see Sutton is home. "You scared me!" I say as fight or flight endorphins dump into my system. "I mean,...*Ta-Daa!*" I say as I theatrically throw my arms out to the sides. "I got everything set up!" I say excitedly.

"I didn't know you worked for NASA. Tell me, will you be launching rockets straight from the kitchen, or do you require a more sophisticated network, like the Kennedy Space Center, perhaps?" he teases. I know he is proud of me though, his eyes twinkle with it. He is also holding flowers behind his back. Roses. Big ones. Big, red ones.

"Are those for me, or did you get them for, Ben?"

"Ben already got your first date, he's not getting flowers too," he says as he produces them from behind his back. My heart is already so full with Sutton, there's almost no room for the roses.

I walk up to him, but instead of taking the offered bundle, I slip into the space between his chest and the sweet-smelling flowers. When I pull his head down to mine, he meets me for a passionate kiss, one that is full of gratitude—but not for the roses.

"Let's go out. I want to take you somewhere special," he says against my lips.

"I'm a little sweaty and gross, I need to take a shower." His eyes widen at my mention of a shower, but then I have a better idea.

"No, let's take a bath!" I have always wanted to take a bubble bath, and although we had tubs on the unit, the stoppers were removed, so the most you could hope for was a hair clog and slowly draining shower water.

"If we take a bath together, the date is getting sidelined."

"Dates are all about getting to know someone. We could do that in a crowded restaurant...or we could do it here—in your Olympic sized tub."

"It's hard to argue with your logic," he says as he finds a spot on the counter for the roses. "What about food? I'm starving."

"I'll make us some snacks while the tub fills!" I say, way more excited for a bath than a person should be. He chuckles at my enthusiasm, but my guess is that he would rather stay in, too.

***

When I walk into the bathroom with a tray of misfit food, Sutton is shirtless and brushing his teeth. He winks at me in the mirror, probably after catching me gawking at the muscles in his back.

"I struggled a little bit with snacks, but we won't starve," I announce as I present the tray of toast and RedBull. In truth, I didn't try all that hard. Sutton introduced me to Nutella toast last weekend, and since then, I've consumed enough Nutella to sink a ship. I put it on everything, waffles, bananas, strawberries…a spoon.

"It's okay, I had to improvise too," he says as he points to the bottle of dish soap on the edge of the tub. The water is still running, but there is no telling how deep it is because of the crazy amount of bubbles. I'm sure Sutton wants to take a bath with a grown woman, but I'm not too sure I won't act like a kid when I get in there.

I move the rolled-up, purely for decoration, towels from the back ledge of the tub, and set the tray there, so it's within easy reach. Then I remember my roses and decide to go get them as well. Maybe they will add some sophistication to the grown woman splashing around in the tub.

When I came back, Sutton had dimmed the lights and lit some candles, adding yet another layer of sophistication to the mountain of bubbles forming a stadium dome over the tub.

"Oooo, so romantic," I say, as I reach for my new electric toothbrush.

"Yes, apparently we've frog-leaped over the first date and headed straight for a sensual bubble bath," he says as he comes up behind me, brushes my hair back from my neck with his fingers, and then kisses me right beneath my ear. It's hot enough to make me brush my teeth faster.

As I'm rinsing my mouth and spitting into the sink, Sutton slides his palms down my hips and thighs, effectively pushing the skirt down my legs. I turn around into his kiss, but when I try to slide his pants down, he moves my hands to his chest and whispers, "Slow down, baby."

I want to tell him twenty-one years *is* slow, but I'm distracted by his sculpted chest and his illustrious mouth.

When he lifts my naked butt to the bathroom counter and peels off my shirt in almost the same motion, he demonstrates his authority, as well as successfully accelerating the pace. He looks appreciatively at my pretty, lace bra for all of a second, then that's gone too.

His hands go immediately to my breasts, where he thumbs my nipples back and forth and effectively drives me crazy. The sensation creates a lit path to every erogenous zone on my body.

"I love it when you do that," I say as I lean back on my hands and totally submit to his skilled touch.

"Do you like it rough?" he asks, as he leans down and sucks a nipple aggressively into his mouth while he twists and boldly flicks the other one.

My answer is a throaty moan and a gentle dampening between my legs. He has yet to relent, so my head rolls back in erotic bliss.

Next, he pulls a rose out of the vase next to me and grazes the soft petals lightly across my humming nipples. "Or gentle?" he asks.

"Both," I whisper. And after the ticklish touch brings me to the edge of lunacy, he casually drags the rose down my cleavage, over my abdomen, and between my legs.

"Do you have any idea how sexy you are?" he asks as he rolls the petals back and forth over my body. Then he pulls me forward, where he places his hand on the side of my neck in a possessive way and then kisses me—also, in a very possessive way.

While we kiss, he toes off his shoes and undoes his pants, shoving them down his legs in one smooth motion. My shoes are next, but he has to unbuckle them, so he breaks our kiss. It also gives me a chance to take in his engorged penis. It's hard as stone and swaying in a taunting manner.

I don't remember anything about the evil appendage that ripped through my innocence when I was a kid, only the searing, burning pain it caused. I'm a woman now, but I can vividly remember the agony. I would be lying if I said I was excited to be penetrated by the huge, veiny mast in front of me.

"*Hey*, is everything okay?" Sutton asks as he cups my jaw in his hands. It's clear he reads something on my face, something that I can't hide from.

"I'm feeling a little triggered right now," I say. It's the catch-all preamble that I've learned to use when I've identified a spike in my anxiety.

"Okay, let's talk about it," he says as he pulls his pants back up his legs. He doesn't fasten them, so they hang open, and I can still see the root of his penis. Covered like that, with just a peek showing, it's back to looking sexy, and I feel a little silly for saying anything. He covers me with a towel and then sits on the edge of the tub.

"Just because you fired me doesn't mean we aren't going to work through this the same as everything else."

I hop off the counter and wrap the towel around me before I take a seat next to him on the edge of the tub. "I suddenly was afraid that sex with you would hurt, that's all," I explain as I place my palm against his cheek. I know he can't turn off the doctor instinct, but I want to kiss him just the same.

"Mercy, I would never hurt you."

"Not on purpose, but that thing will hurt."

"Did it hurt earlier today in my office?"

"No," then a smile curls my lips, "In fact, I seem to remember begging for it."

"Did my fingers hurt you?" he asks, just as serious as ever.

"They didn't *hurt*, it was more like a *stretch*."

"Mercy, I can promise you this, we will not take that step until you are ready. *You mean everything to me.* The last thing I want to do is hurt you."

His words are the tenderest words I've ever heard spoken. My response to them gets stuck in my throat, but I straddle his lap and bring my lips down on his poetic mouth anyway.

After a few minutes, he pulls back and says, "How about you take your bubble bath, and I will go make dinner—I mean, something besides Nutella and toast."

"NO," I say emphatically, "I want us to get in together…and I want to kiss you all over," I throw in for good measure as I drop my towel. Reluctantly, he follows.

When we get in, the bubbles have already receded by half, and we need to add more hot water. The tub is big enough that we can sit facing each other with my legs draped over his thighs.

"This is luxurious," I say as I lean my head back and feel all my muscles relax at once. Sutton takes one of my feet and begins to massage it. "Now, it's even better."

A few quiet, reflective minutes pass, but then I get bored relaxing and say, "Tell me about your family…and your childhood…no, tell me what made you want to be a psychiatrist."

"Actually, I can tell you about all of that because it's all intertwined," he says as he sits up a little more, showcasing his lickable chest. I want to know everything about him, and I'm excited to be the one listening for once.

"I grew up in Alaska because my great-grandfather inherited over fifty acres from a family friend who died with no heirs. It's a lot of land, but it's pretty remote, so we needed a seaplane to get anywhere."

"That is the coolest thing I've ever heard. Go on," I press. It's hard not to ask him a hundred questions, but I resist.

"We lived off the land, had an out-house, chopped wood—the whole nine yards. My brother, Dominic and I were really close in age. And besides our parents, there wasn't another soul for miles, so we did everything together."

"That's really sweet. Who's older? You or Dominic?"

"Dominic, but I was always bigger than him," he smiles, but the ghost of something passes over his face. "Anyway, when Dominic was about fifteen, he started talking about seeing demons."

I mouth a silent, "No."

"Yeah. Our mom homeschooled us, but that didn't stop me from reading everything I could get my hands on about psychiatric disorders. I became obsessed with helping him. When I was eighteen, I moved to Anchorage for my undergrad, but I still wasn't convinced I was doing enough, so I pushed and pushed myself. Eventually, it paid off because Johns Hopkins accepted me for medical school."

"Do you even know how amazing you are?" I ask with stars in my eyes. He scoffs, and that's when I know this story doesn't have a happy ending. He stops rubbing my foot, and he has a faraway look in his eyes, the final two nails in the coffin for this story's outcome.

"Dominic hung himself during my first year of residency."

Oh, my God!

I scoot closer, so I'm sitting on Sutton's lap and clutching his body to mine. "*I'm so sorry,*" I say over and over as my heart bleeds out. I

I think about how much he helped Matty and Veronica—and me, everyone really. But none of it matters because he couldn't save his own brother.

I think of how he took me up the mountain to release balloons and a letter to my brother. What must he have been thinking? Surely about his own brother, right?

"What would you say to him if you could?" I ask. It's not balloons and a letter, but maybe he has some words left unsaid, too.

"I would say, *hang on, buddy, I've got you. I'll fix this, just hang on.*" Sutton tightens his arms around me, and I can feel his pain. Both of us were powerless to save our brothers, and we are both condemned to carry around that guilt forever.

"I feel him with me all the time," he says with tears in his eyes but a smile on his face. "I can hear his voice sometimes. It's in my head, but not my own thoughts," he chuckles, "Now I sound like a paranoid schizophrenic."

"I don't think so. You sound like someone who had an incredibly close bond with your brother." I lean in to kiss him, and I can feel his penis start to stir.

"Do you really hear him?" I ask, fascinated.

"Yeah, I do."

"What types of things do you hear him say?" I ask.

"Just random stuff, nothing profound. It's almost like my brain is filling in things that he would say…but that I'm not thinking about. Like when you sat down in my office the first time, he said, *take it easy with this one.*"

"He did? He talked about me? That's the coolest thing that's ever happened to me. Do you hear him all the time?"

"No, no. Not at all, only three times in total. It makes me feel better though, like he's letting me know he's okay."

"I love that one of those times was about me! What do you think he meant?"

"I think he knew you were special."

"Awwwww, and that you would help me," I say as I wiggle on his lap a little, drawing even more interest from below.

"Mercy, I've helped a lot of patients over the years, but I've never fallen in love with one of them before."

I sit back, processing. *Did he just…*

"Does that surprise you? That I'm in love with you?"

"I…it…," I attempt to speak, but my voice is restricted. I put my hand on my chest to slow my galloping heart. "It…it takes my breath away," I finally get out in a woosh of air.

"Okay, good. I'm fine with that reaction," he laughs, and then leans forward and bites down on my bottom lip, tugging me forward and sliding his body deeper under the water.

"Close your mouth, though, or you'll catch flies," he laughs. I don't think that's how he pictured proclaiming his love for me, but his teasing prevents me from making what he might see as an obligatory response. As if my heart wasn't completely bursting with love for him. He has no idea.

We kiss for a long time while I absolutely bask in the glow of his words. I don't want to voice that I love him too because he will think I'm only saying it because he did. But I *do* want to demonstrate how I feel.

"Sutton, I want to taste you. Show me how you like it. I don't want to do it wrong." I see his jaw tick before I realize I never mentioned oral sex. He must know what I'm talking about because he slides a finger into my mouth and gently moves it in and out while I suck. Then he pulls his finger out and swipes it around my lips before sliding it back in.

"*Mercy*," he says with an angsty crack in his voice, "You're not going to do it wrong." He drops his head back in woozy-headed anticipation as I slide off his lap. He rises to the edge of the tub while I sit back on my heels, biting my lip in nervous contemplation. My girlfriends walked me through this process more times than I'm entirely comfortable admitting. So, I know how to do it, but the fact that it is Sutton fills me with a little bit of awe.

I slide my mouth down his length, and it quickly becomes apparent why Lyla and V said to use my hand, too. A year ago, I would have rather choked on my own vomit than put a man's penis in my mouth, but now? Now I relish it, and his reaction to my sucking mouth is only fueling the fire.

"Yes, baby. Just like that. *Ohhh*." His panting groan gives me more confidence, and I take him deeper, pushing him to the back of my throat and then up again.

I employ some of V's advanced tactics around the crown of his head, eliciting a *fuck yeah*, and a *damn, Mercy*, before I go back to the basics of showing him how much I adore him too.

When he pulls out of my mouth and shoots pulse after pulse of warm ejaculate on my neck and chest, I'm a tiny bit disappointed he pulled away. Lyla absolutely never lets guys come in her mouth; Veronica always does. I was going to be the tiebreaker, and I still don't know if I like it or not.

"That was amazing," he says with an impish grin.

"Did I do it right?" I ask. It felt right, and his reaction was certainly right, but I ask the question anyway.

"You were perfect," he says, further boosting my confidence as he slides back in the tub, then wipes his cum off of me like a gentleman.

"Mercy, I want to take you out on a real date. Have you had enough of a bubble bath experience for one night?" I grin in response, but when he starts to get out of the tub, I stop him.

"Wait. What about the snacks?"

He eases back in and slides me forward onto his lap. While he kisses me, he slips his hand through the back of my hair and tugs my head back while he kisses and nibbles on my neck.

"I'm taking you out for real food. Not Nutella and RedBull," he says as he cups my jaw in his palm.

"But I worked really hard on that," I tease.

"You're right," he says, then he grabs a piece of Nutella toast and drags it across my chest, scraping the rough toast over both nipples and sending them to a scratchy Nutella party.

Then he proceeds to lick and suck the chocolate off in such a way that it infuses my giggle with a heady mix of rapturous need. With a few more playful flicks and a mischievous grin, he asks, "Still hungry?"

"Absolutely."

"Good, let's dry off and go eat."

"I'm also kind of thirsty."

"Is that so?" he asks as he cracks open a can of RedBull and pours a small sip into my mouth before dumping the icy drink all over my chest and diving in to quench his thirst. The fizzy liquid makes my nipples throb and tingle at the same time, but his follow-up performance makes them purr.

Chapter 40

Sutton took me out for Sushi, which I loved despite how I initially felt about eating raw fish. I wanted to try everything, which made him beam with a look I've come to recognize as one of sexy, rugged pride. However, Saki, I am not a fan of. That suits me just fine, though, because I didn't want to get all giggly like I did the other night anyway.

Now, it's late, and Sutton has to work tomorrow, so I'm starting to think all the flirting we did at dinner has led us to an unrequited, sleepy outcome. He kills the mood even more by making a doctor type of observation.

"It's been a few days since you've had a nightmare. I feel confident about the adjustment to your anti-anxiety medication. This dosage seems to take the edge off while still letting you process your feelings."

"Wow, this evening certainly has taken a clinical turn in vastly the wrong direction," I deadpan.

He scoops me up and carries me to the bedroom, "Quick, Mercy! Before I take your blood pressure or something else doctorly!" He tosses me on the bed and then straddles my body with his hands on the comforter by each of my shoulders. Then he pins me with a stare, which is entirely sexy because I like this dominant side.

"Seriously, though, don't let your new doctor make any changes without running it by me first, okay?"

"Ugh! Didn't I fire you?"

"As I keep saying, it's all about perception," he grins. I try to scowl back at him, but he is too perfect, so I grab his face and kiss him instead.

"I love you, Sutton," I say against his lips, making it part of our kiss.

He opens his eyes but keeps his lips frozen in place, still touching mine. Then he blinks and says, "What did you just say?" without removing his lips.

"I said, I love you."

"Yeah, that's what I thought," he says with a giant smile.

"Hold it, does that mean I have to start calling you, Travis now? It doesn't have the same ring to it that *Sutton* does."

"As long as you don't call me *doctor*—oh, wait...you've never called me doctor, so that's a non-issue, I guess. Now, take your clothes off."

"Oooo, is it time for you to tuck me into bed, *doctor*?"

"If you're into role-playing, I'd really prefer to be a firefighter," he says as he whips the dress over my head, leaving me in nothing but black lace panties.

I help him remove his shirt then he finishes undressing on the way to turn off the light. When he comes back to bed, he kisses me the way everyone dreams about being kissed—aaaand then he slips his hand into my panties.

He rubs until I'm moaning into our kiss and fisting his hair, then he presses his finger inside. Slowly at first, then not so slowly.

His thrusting finger is trying to lessen the building pressure I feel, but it's not enough, so I whimper the word *more*, and he pushes another finger inside. By this point, I'm dizzy with something that feels a lot like desperation.

He slides his fingers out of me and then brushes the wetness across my mouth before kissing me again. His patience for my panties runs out at the same time, so he works them down my legs with the same skilled fingers that just introduced me to my own taste.

"Tell me what you want," he whispers, his voice scratchy with restraint.

"I want everything."

"Do you want my tongue?"

"I want all of you, Sutton. *Please.*"

He hesitates like he is going to say I'm not ready, but then he reaches into the nightstand and retrieves a condom. I've fantasized about this with him for a long time, so much so that I'm trembling with need.

"Let me taste you before I put it on. I want to make sure you're ready," he says as he slowly strokes his hardness. He doesn't wait for a response before spreading my legs. Soon enough, they are shaking.

Before I've even come down from my orgasm, I feel him place the slick head of his cock at my entrance. He doesn't enter me, it's more like he is notching it in place. Then his fingers are brushing a few strands of hair from my cheek, and his sweet face is inches from mine.

"I love you, Mercy. I want to give you everything. Not just me, I want to give you the world."

"You already have."

His kiss is so tender, I feel like I could crack apart. It does feel like he has already given me the world. He took my past and made it manageable. He allowed me to own what happened so I could learn to leave it behind, and he never made me feel like something was wrong with me. He accepted me when my soul was broken, and then he showed me it was possible to heal.

He taught me to live.

He taught me to *love*.

Not just him, but he led me to love *myself*. Perhaps that was my biggest obstacle all along.

At some point during his tender kisses, he begins to slowly press inside me. My body welcomes his as though it belongs, and the stretching fullness feels more like rapture than an intrusion.

He works his way in with controlled movements, stopping periodically to let me adjust—all the while distracting me with the adoration of his lips. When he's all the way inside me, he whispers, *you're mine now, Mercy*, and then he begins to gently rock, back and forth.

***

After surrendering myself entirely to the man I love, I lie on his chest, listening to the rhythmic beat of his heart as he casually runs his fingers through my hair. Right at the point where I feel like I'm going to burst with happiness, I hear a young voice say,

I knew you could live again, Te-Te.

Epilogue

This is our second time around the loop of kennels. The first pass was a cursory one, but I underestimated the sheer quantity of longing glances and brown-eyed eagerness within these walls. The puppies all share a look of general optimism, whereas the older dog's sense of idealism has long since faded into the urine-soaked concrete beneath their paws.

Sutton has the patience of a saint, and though he has his favorites, I know he is leaving the decision up to me. One of the first times we talked, I told him I wanted a dog once I was free of the system. Not just any dog, though. I said I wanted a haggard one that nobody wants. A dog beat down by life and drained of hope. I said such a dog was my spirit animal.

"What about this one?" he asks as he squats down and tries to coax the petrified little bundle out of the back corner of her cell. I squat down next to him and give it some thought. There is little doubt she has suffered abuse, and though she isn't likely to trust easily, she will come around when shown kindness.

"She is only two years old…and doesn't have enough tarnish," I say as I chew on my thumbnail. "She will get adopted and live a happy life. I want to rescue one that is completely hopeless. A dog nobody has ever wanted. One that is resigned to the fate of the needle that will end his suffering."

Sutton doesn't respond right away, but he rises in solidarity. We walk in silence for a few more minutes, mentally calculating each animal's probability of adoption rate. Still gnawing on my thumbnail, I come to a tentative decision.

"I think I know the one. Follow me," I say as I head toward the back of the loop. I noticed the dog on our first pass but wanted to make sure there wasn't a more dire case.

As we approach the kennel, I wave over one of the volunteers. She looks surprised by our interest in the desolate soul, who hasn't so much as raised his head at our arrival.

"Duncan?" she asks, her eyebrows rising in question.

"Yes, Duncan. What can you tell us about him? Sutton asks firmly, putting an end to the volunteer's dismay.

"Well, he is roughly twelve years old. He's a mutt, but I see some terrier as well as some Aussie. He came in with a terrible case of mite infestation. That's why you see some bald spots. He only eats canned dog food—or at the very least soft, moistened kibble due to his teeth."

"Can he walk?" I ask.

"Yeah, he walks…but, just so you know, his limp is from an old injury that didn't heal correctly. It's not anything that we can treat now."

"Okay, we'll take him," I announce, hoping he can sense a change in his fortune.

"Great, let me go get an adoption coordinator, and they can help you with the next steps," the volunteer says before she turns and walks past the kennels of wagging tails and echoed whines.

"Mercy, are you sure? Duncan doesn't look like he has much time left, and I'm worried he will break your heart," Sutton says as he clasps my hand and then brings it to his lips for a kiss.

"Sutton, that poor animal has known nothing but heartache and struggle. I want him to experience kindness and love, even if it's just for a short time."

"You're right. Let's spoil him rotten and teach him that even in a world of darkness, there is also light," Sutton says. It sounds hopeful and full of promise. It also sounds like something every living thing should know.

His words touch my heart because sometimes, all we have is hope. Hope that our circumstances will change. Hope that our future will be brighter than our past. Hope that the next day—or our next breath will be better than the last. The hard part is learning to trust in that hope. To hang on with everything we have until finally, the light cautiously begins to encroach on the dark.

Duncan gets up from his spot in the back corner and walks over to the front of the kennel where we are. Then he plops down with his nose poking between two bars of the crate. The series of movements is undeniably trusting.

"We need to take it easy with this one, Sutton," I say, and it sounds familiar.

"Yes, my love, we do," he smiles with a nostalgic gleam as he allows Duncan to tentatively sniff his hand.

"Hey, buddy. Do you think you can learn to trust me?"

Also by KC Decker:

Standalone Books

Little Dove

My name is Etta Freeman.

There is something special about me.

Not special in a good way, though, more like special in a way that will get me killed one day.

It's not something I talk about with anyone, but that doesn't stop me from trying to snare my neighbor in my devious web.

He is angsty and brooding and completely sexy in a scrappy, bloody knuckle kind of way.

I should also mention that he's a scheming, felonious drug dealer and I'm drawn to him like flies on shit.

The problem is, he doesn't yet know his role in my narrative, but he will fall in line.

They always do.

Trigger Warning: Little Dove contains content that some readers may find distressing.

Of Ash and Angels

** Silver Medal Winner of the International Reader's Favorite Book Awards*

Justin:

I've never had a therapist I didn't want to punch in the face. As a collective group, they all say there is no way around grief, only through it, but for me, grief has become who I am. The idea of shedding it is as ludicrous as stepping outside of my own skin.

The fact is, some things can break you. I mean, shatter your soul and cast it into the wind in a billion tiny pieces. To think you might one day be able to find all those infinite pieces of yourself, patch everything back together, and move on with life—well, I don't even need to dignify that with a response.

Norah:

A few months ago, I shaved off a hundred and eighty-five-pound parasite. Then, once I was rid of him, I wondered why I didn't stick it out because the dating world is treacherous these days. Turns out, so is unemployment.

I suppose, to offset all the swiping left and streaming marathons in my life, I should take this job. There is a massive problem with the position, though.

The problem's name is Justin Abernathy.

Gradation

Friends. Ride or die, right?
Always have your back.
Know all your dirty little secrets.
Love the shiny parts of you, and embrace the crappy ones.
Yeah? Well, I don't know about all that nonsense because my friends are a bunch of assholes.
They're taking over.
They're commandeering my love life.
They're constructing a dating profile for me, and it's bad…
Because I don't even have the *password* for it,

and I have to do *exactly* what they say.

Mercy

INTERNATIONAL BOOK AWARDS FINALIST and KIRKUS FEATURED REVIEW RECIPIENT!

My parents abandoned me a decade ago to the walls of this institution. They believed my troubled childhood mind was something sinister instead of homegrown or explainable. The truth is that my condition is complicated. It's messy and often misunderstood.

I've worn all types of labels over the years: Non-believer, pariah, deranged, *orphan...* It's all in my file if you care to understand me better. However, the label that implanted the deepest and garnered the most attention is the one I wear, like a Scarlet Letter. It precedes me when I enter a room and gets whispered about like a schoolyard crush.

Paranoid Schizophrenic.

Dr. Sutton has some lofty ideas about my condition and claims mental illness is only one aspect of hundreds that make me who I am. Not one to shy away from a challenge, he thinks he can help me. His confidence is legendary, but I've carried this burden for a long time. Despite what he thinks, I can't be fixed.

He doesn't realize I'm falling for him or that I have some lofty ideas of my own. He should know better because people like me deserve a hero, too.

The Jessie Hayes 4 Book Series

(Must be Read in Order)

1462 South Broadway (Book 1)
**Winner of the National Excellence*
in Romance Fiction Award)

It's said that a bird never has to doubt the stability of her branch because her trust is in her own wings.

I myself, am trying to grow some wings of my own, but I'm kind of mired in place right now.

My roommate fondly calls my situation *a rut* and seems to think he knows how I can climb out of it.

The problem with his solution is that he's stone-cold crazy.

There is no way in hell I'm going to a *sex club*.

A scorching, witty, and unexpectedly tender story about finding courage in the unlikeliest places—and discovering the kind of freedom that doesn't come from a stable branch, but from daring to fly.

720 Linden Street (Book 2)

My kinky introduction to BDSM has been less about dipping my toe and more about being tossed into the deep end…bound.

That simple fact has required me to make some pretty hefty leaps outside of my comfort zone.

Turns out, there is a whole lot more to the BDSM scene than I initially thought.
There's a staggering array of possibilities, all wide open for me to see and experience.

You see, my boyfriend owns a sex club.

And I have a lot to learn.

Trigger Warning: 720 Linden Street contains content that some readers may find distressing.

1700 Grant Street (Book 3)

Have you ever found yourself at a crossroads on your journey, with your entire future depending on tiny little decisions here and there?

Do you resist temptation and stick with your current choice? Or will you always wonder how life *could have been*?

When you get to this branching of your life's path, it's not enough to merely choose one direction. You must distance yourself from the rejected road. Because dancing between the two will slowly unravel you.

And it will start with your fickle heart.

945 Cedar Avenue (Book 4, Salinger's Story)

A wedding engagement is a joyous occasion, right?

Well, I suppose that depends on your perspective.

If you happen to be on the side of the path that branches to the left, when the love of your life chooses to go right, you may have a different opinion.

So, what do you do when someone else's choice annihilates the future you counted on?

The answer to that may depend on your membership status at a certain sex club.

Namely, 1462 South Broadway.

COMING SOON!

The Space Between

Midnight Sun

JOIN KC DECKER:

Mailing List: www.KCDeckerBooks.com

Instagram: www.instagram.com/author_kc_decker

X: www.X.com/KCDeckerBooks

Facebook: www.facebook.com/kc.decker.79

Bookbub: www.bookbub.com/profile/kc-decker

www.KCDeckerBooks.com

Dedication:

This book is dedicated to anyone who has ever given a new author a shot. To believe in someone who hasn't yet risen to the ranks of having an agent, publicist, marketing strategist, or even a proper editor, is to place your trust in something much bigger than bestseller lists and giant publishing houses. Recognizing the unknown, the different—the fledgling authors and the crisp new voices, paves the way for dreamers like me. Thank you for that trust. I assure you, I do not take it lightly.

—KC